SPORTS FREAK

Shannon OCork

St. Martin's Press
New York

Copyright © 1980 by Shannon OCork
All rights reserved. For information, write:
St. Martin's Press, Inc., 175 Fifth Ave., New York, N.Y. 10010.
Manufactured in the United States of America

Library of Congress Cataloging in Publication Data

OCork, Shannon.
    Sports freak.

    I. Title.
PZ4.0223Sp   [PS3565.C66]   813'.5'4   79-22850
ISBN 0-312-75331-4

For Linty, whom I was loving at the time

.....1

When Lovable Lou LaMont, rookie quarterback of the High Mountain Climbers, was killed on the football field of the Colossus Complex, nobody realized what was happening. Except his murderer, of course.

I was getting his picture for the *New York Graphic*, and thinking Barkley would probably chew me out again, unjustly, for another ho-hum shot of a quarterback sacked by a slightly illegal head-butt.

But LaMont got dumped at a good angle for me. He dropped back to throw left, and Billy "The Badman" O'Leary of the Coastville Johnny Rebs came through the line like the little choo-choo that could. He slammed his helmet into Lou's adam's apple so deep he butted LaMont clean into the air. LaMont jack-knifed forward, holding onto the ball. Then, oddly, his body doubled back. He walked on air for awhile like Evel Knievel's motor bike and then fell flat on his back and head. He fell alone, no shadows on his face, and his body had a kind of wrong-way curl to it. He still held the ball, and under his face guard he was smiling.

Barkley, my editor at the *New York Graphic*, loves any kind of picture that shows real violence or injury. "The only way you'll make my front page, Baldwin, is if you get the punch from which the turkey never gets up." Forget page one. Barkley hadn't run a picture of mine on any of the 452 pages that made up the *Graphic* for the last fourteen working days.

Before Barkley hired me, I'd been a free-lancer, running the streets with a press card I'd sent away for from a body-building magazine. Amazing the doors it opened. One night I managed to smile my way into an illegal cockfight held in a high-toned Gramercy Park brownstone basement. I came away with a hot exclusive in luscious Kodachrome that was worth two, maybe three, nice weeks in St. Croix. Instead, I traded it to the *Graphic* for a week's salary of $212 and a job as back-up photographer in the sports department. Barkley said I would regret it. I didn't tell him I would have sold

... 1

my soul. He'd just say there wasn't any market for it.

The cockfight photo story ran six pages with two double-trucks in the *Graphic Sunday Magazine*.

Floyd Beesom has never mentioned it to me. Floyd is the *Graphic*'s regular sports beat photographer. He is short and tubby and bald and surly. He is also a master of the action shot. He is supposed to be showing me the ropes and teaching me the how-to, but he sabotages me every way he can. There's only work enough for one by-line sports photog on the *Graphic*, he says, and Beesom means for it to stay him, as it has for the last three hundred years, he's that old.

"When we need extra, we use AP. They got a hundred guys in the field," Floyd said when we were introduced.

"Used to be," I said back. "Now you use Associated Press and T.T. Baldwin."

"In that order," said Floyd. He's a real welcome wagon.

This time Beesom was busy making tomorrow's four-to-six picture center pages, playing big shot with his zoom, trying to catch Wanda, the glittering redheaded cheerleader, from underneath doing her air splits. So me, I focused in nice on Lovable Lou LaMont falling, and got the whole series of shots.

It was barely seven minutes into the opening game of a new season. This was the first game for both new NFL franchises, the High Mountain Climbers and the Coastville Johnny Rebs. We were in the Colossus, a brand new sports complex in the chi-chi town of High Mountain in upstate New York.

It was the professional debut of Lovable Lou LaMont, the National Football League's newest highest-paid contract player. He had a ten-year no-cut clause, too, in his contract with the High Mountain Climbers. Unheard of. And of course being a rook, nobody knew for sure whether he could really star in pro ball, even if he *had* had three years of 10-0 seasons at Penn State. It was an impossible record, but there it was, and that's what made Lou lovable. And that's why Mrs. Marcella Snowfield signed him up the way she did. Well, for the publicity value too, I guess.

And that's why I was there tagging Beesom, instead of looking for obscure polo matches in the High Mountain parks to offset Beesom's backpage specials. I was going to be buried on page thirty-seven with a sidebar pix showing how not everyone in High Mountain is interested in football. No foolin'. That had been my original assignment this Sunday. But at the last minute, the previous night at the press party to be exact, Barkley had called me on the telephone, paging me in the Colossus restaurant, and switched me to the game.

I thought he was going to fire me right then, with my hand in Mrs. Snowfield's caviar and my eye on the cracked lobster. But what he said was, "Forget the polo, Baldwin, and back up Floyd on the field."

"Right, Bar," I said, figuring he'd found out what I'd known all along, that there wasn't going to be any polo. I went back and ate up.

You see, I hadn't had the time to get confident about myself yet. I'd been with the *Graphic* less than three months. And so far Barkley had been bloody to me, and Floyd Beesom never got friendly until after about six scotches, which I could say was often enough. But Beesom wasn't friendly when it counted, which was on the job. Beesom was okay until I started slinging my Nikons over my shoulder, and then it was every man for himself. And I'm female, which makes it harder.

Lou LaMont didn't bounce back up. The Climbers' coach, Skyhook Reesenbach, called time. Reesenbach is a skinny, loose-string of a man, very tall. He walks slumped over with his head hanging down. That's why they call him Skyhook. He ran out onto the grass and over to the quiet curled body with its face smiling at the sun. Reesenbach's hands flopped from his wrists as he ran, like forgotten mittens.

Trotting out with the Coach was Dr. Jose "Call Me Joe" DeBianco. Dr. Joe was an upper-class Cuban who had come to this country when Castro took over his. He'd made a reputation as a muscle-and-ligament man. This season he'd been hired exclusively by Mrs. Snowfield, and if you pull something or tear something and go to Dr. Joe, he treats you as charity, and Mrs. Snowfield gets a tax deduction. That is if he treats you, which, unless you're in with the Climbers organization, he probably won't. He'll send you to one of his Park Avenue buddies.

Dr. Joe and Coach Reesenbach stood in a huddle over the body of Lou LaMont. Dr. Joe bent over and pushed LaMont a little and poked him, but he didn't get a response.

I started to get that prickly dancy feeling inside I get when I think I've scored a beat with some pictures. I could just see Barkley

... 3

smiling fondly at me as he fingered my proofsheets like they were deeds to precious ore mines. I could see him shaking my hand and giving me a raise. I could hear him telling Floyd to ease up on me, that I was the future of *Graphic*'s sports.

On the sidelines, the band began to play. Overcoat, the Tibetan mountain goat imported at a fancy dollar to be the Climbers' mascot, was leashed to the players' bench. He chewed a mouthful of something over and over.

David Livingston, who coordinates the sideline entertainment, tried to give Overcoat a walk for the crowd, but the goat planted its hooves and David had to drag the little feller.

Livingston had dolled himself up for today in a rainbow robe splattered all over with stars and half moons. He calls himself "The Astrologer." Other than his costume, his one sideline talent is twirling a baton. His baton is a three-foot, Fourth-of-July-type sparkler, the kind you light with a match, that was custom made in Moose County, Tennessee. It's supposed to represent his celestial scepter. He has sixty in a box which he says will last him through the Super Bowl.

Besides David Livingston and the mountain goat mascot, the High Mountain Climbers have five salaried cheerleaders. They are collectively called The Scenic View. While Livingston dragged Overcoat, the girls pumped their pom-poms, showed their panties, blew on dimestore bugles and screamed for the Climbers to cream the Coastville Johnny Rebs.

The Scenic View climbed each other to form a five person pyramid and led the fifty thousand fans in a cheer:

> Climb that mountain!
> Climb that moor!
> Get those Johnnies!
> SCORE! SCORE! SCORE!
> We *KNOOOO-OWWW* You Will! *YAY*, Climbers!

The crowd clapped and whooped and spilled beer on their neighbors and tossed popcorn like confetti and bit down into mustard-smothered hot dogs.

Out on the field they brought a stretcher.

By now Beesom was wise something important was happening. He found me hunkered down by the five-yard line using my 300

4 . . .

mm lens to get in close on Coach Reesenbach's face to catch the worry in the eyes.

"Okay, ace," he said, "you follow LaMont in, cover the whatever, and stay with him until you've got the injury report. I'll stay out here and cover the field."

Beesom planted his monopod where I'd had mine and gave me a jerk of his thumb as a so-long. In the newspaper business they call you "ace" and "scoop" and "star" as a kind of reverse putdown. When they stop telling you how good you are, you know you've passed initiation. If you're smart, you never let them know you notice.

I left Beesom with exclusive coverage of the play and did as I was told.

I took pictures of the white stretcher being carried over the grass out of the sun toward the dark mouth of the rampway. Dr. Joe followed it, somber, his black bag jumping disrespectfully about in the stretcher's shadow. Coach Reesenbach jogged in front, signaling with his loose-wristed hands for an assistant coach to take over.

They got LaMont onto the table in the locker room. The equipment and maintenance supervisor, Stanley Farmer, the guy who does everything for everybody, began taking off the helmet. Lou's long Italian curls tumbled free and bounced down on the training table and over his forehead. His hair looked alive. It was thick and shone like the black hood of a mayor's turtle-waxed Cadillac. Lou LaMont was vain about his hair. He was always fussing with it, playing with it like a girl.

Coach Reesenbach started on the shoes. Dr. Joe scissored through the jersey. Nobody said anything. The game was back in progress and the stadium shouts came through like crowd noises on video tape. The body on the table smiled up into the overhead arc light.

The light was just right over the training table. I stood on a chair and shot three-quarter portraits of the group, and then full-length shots down the table, my lens wide open, no depth of field, the working hands and exposed body bouncing out of a misted background of floor and locker doors shut tight. I got lost in my pictures: Dr. Joe massaging LaMont's chest, trying to get the heart to beat again. The carved muscles of the abdomen, stiff already. The tan skin going gray in my lens.

Dr. Joe looked up at me. "Get out," he said.

I went out and sat down outside on the hallway floor, hugging my cameras. I didn't know how Floyd Beesom was doing, but I'd got good shots.

Ssssss.... Ssssss.... Down the hall I heard the spaceage Rolls Royce that little Harv Potter calls a wheelchair. It glided toward me like a soundless UFO. Harv was all muffled in the beige and chocolate-brown colors of the Climbers: souvenir wool cap, Climbers' sweater, brown gloves, a cashmere chocolate blanket fringed in beige tassels with an almost lifesize mountain goat needle-pointed across his lap and knees. Only his too-blue eyes, which looked like they'd been dyed in Tintex, and his sharp little nose were unwrapped.

It wasn't really a cold day. It was late September, in the high forties. There was a brisk wind with snap in it, but I'd been comfortable outside in jeans with a heavy sweater over my shirt. Personally, I think little Harv bundled up to emphasize his fragility.

I confess I didn't like the kid. He'd had muscular dystrophy since he was five. He is sixteen now, and makes a career out of being a cripple. He whines sometimes and brags sometimes and usually smells of cod-liver oil. He reminded me of a warped alien from Klingon or somewhere. But he rated 1-A around the Colossus. He was Mrs. Marcella Snowfield's pet.

The chair rolled closer and little Harv geared it down and stopped it on a dime. Yep. Cod-liver oil. Close up, his face looked as gray as Lou LaMont's had.

"Hi there," he said. "Is L-Lou going to be able to play? It's nine them, six us now." He hadn't finished with the changes of puberty. His voice was squeaky on the *l*'s.

I shrugged. "I don't know. Dr. Joe threw me out of there."

"Oh. I didn't mean to bother you. We, L-Lou and me, we did a commercial this morning. For Perfect Body Vitamin E. On how he had a perfect body, and Vitamin E is helping me get perfect too."

"I bet you really take it too," I said.

"Yeah," he smiled. "They give it to me free."

"Yeah?" I said. "You get scale and a half for working Sunday? Double scale?"

I could tell he didn't know what he got, because before he'd been bragging and wearing his ain't-I-great face, and now he had on the poor-little-me look and wasn't saying a word.

"Instead of filling your knapsack with freebies maybe you should get your agent to jack up your hourly rate."

"I have the same agent as Walt-the-Talk," he said, bragging again. Walt-the-Talk Amos was the Climbers' play-by-play announcer. He also had a radio talk show on WZAP.

"Only agent in town," I said, knocking him down again.

"When I get well, I'm going to be just like you." He smiled. He was very pretty when he smiled, if you like pretty boys.

"I bet you tell that to everybody," I said.

He didn't answer that. He held out his game program. "Would you autograph this for me, please?"

I signed it, self-consciously. I had a feeling the kid had beaten me at something. "Now go on and get out of here. I'm on the beat, working."

He smiled again, blushing a little, and nodded his head vigorously. "Okay, sure, on the beat. I understand. See ya."

He pressed a button or two on the computerized braindeck under his fingers, and the chair seemed to pivot like a pony and *sssssss*'d away. The kid gave me the spooks.

I went on waiting in the hall. After what seemed like a long time later, Coach Reesenbach came out, flopping his hands, snapping his fingers the way he does when he's nervous.

"It's almost the half," I said.

"He's dead," he said. "Lou's dead."

"Dead, why?" I said. "He got knocked too hard?"

He snapped his fingers. "Dr. Joe says he can't tell. He doesn't know. Maybe a brain concussion. Maybe an embolism." His head was hanging so low his chin almost bumped his chest. "Ambulance is on its way. The police." He paused again and looked out toward the playing field. "Dr. Joe's in there talking crazy. Says it might even be murder."

"Murder?" There was wonder in my voice.

"Murder. Yeah." There was wonder in his voice too. There was also acceptance. Maybe not conviction, but acceptance.

Coach Reesenbach looked out to where the Climbers were moving, third down and two to go on the Johnny Reb thirty. He had beautiful, graceful hands. Unconsciously, he snapped away with his fingers, softly, like an old familiar habit. Like me, unconsciously reaching for a cigarette in times of stress.

"We were gonna take this team all the way. We were going to the Bowl with that boy. Now all I've got is Black Jack. I don't know if he can do it. I just don't know. Asked me yesterday, I would have said no."

We could hear the crowd stomping and cheering as Racehorse Maddox got to a long pass and put the Climbers at first down on the twelve.

"Well, Jack is black," I said. "First you got to convince yourself. Then you got to convince him you got the faith. Then you got to convince the team that Black Jack can take the Climbers as high as Everest is. Me personally, I think he can do it."

Coach Reesenbach remembered what I was. He looked down at me still sitting crosslegged on the cement floor. From my angle of vision, he looked more like a question mark than a skyhook. He also looked angry.

"Anything you heard just now was off the record. Don't take advantage. We're not going to announce the death of Lou LaMont until this game is in the record book and the people gone home. And what I said just now about Black Jack Flowers I'll deny and call you a liar if you put it in print. I'll also call you a troublemaker, a muckraker, and anything else that comes to me at the time, and I'll call the *Graphic* and get you transferred off this assignment. Got that, sister?"

I've learned you have to respect a source's anger and take it seriously. If you don't they never forgive you.

"My name is T. T. Baldwin," I said, "and I'm an only child. And the last time I got bullied he was twice as big as you."

"I don't approve of women like you," he said.

I nodded. I'd heard that before.

"Always pushing back. Always pushing," he said. "Always hinting you know how to jerk off a guy." Oh, wow.

He stepped back into the locker room, softly, absent-mindedly, snapping his fingers. I was really glad I'd made another friend in High Mountain.

The Climbers scored. Happiness roared up from the stadium. For the moment, Lovable Lou LaMont had been forgotten. Black Jack Flowers carried the ball himself up over the middle two feet to the goal line. Sinister Sam Zambrowsky, the left-footed place kicker, made the point after.

The bell went off, signaling the half. A violin scratched a solo *A*, a tuba two octaves lower matched it, and some kid in the high school band with a new stick tried to find *A* on his drum.

Coach Reesenbach stepped back out into the hall. "I'm sorry," he said, "forget what I said."

I nodded. "Climbers, thirteen-nine, Coach."

"We got a chance," he said. He tried to smile at me, but he was rusty at it. "I never had a boy die on me before."

The Climbers were pounding down the ramp now, heading our way.

"Into the schoolroom, boys. Nobody in the locker room for now." He blocked the door and herded his team into the big room opposite.

He followed them in, rubbing his hands together. I heard their voices, loud and boisterous, asking about Lou, happy, scuffling with each other, high on their four point lead. They complained about not being able to get into the locker room, and I heard Coach Reesenbach say soon.

I stayed at my post in the hallway. The police came. An ambulance backed up to the ramp's mouth and white-suited men moved past me into the room where the body was.

What used to be Lou LaMont was taken away in a body bag. I got down on one knee, slowed the film because the light wasn't good, screwed on my fastest telephoto, the 85 mm, opened her all the way, and shot down the hall into the back of the ambulance as they loaded the body bag, slammed the door, and screeched off. These weren't my best shots of the day, but I'd completed the story photographically, and that's what I'm paid to do.

Stanley Farmer, the jockey-sized janitor with the grand title of Equipment and Maintenance Supervisor, went to the schoolroom and opened the door. Five tons of team poured out across the hall and into their locker room. Almost right away the toilets began to flush.

I leaned against the wall, alone again. Murder, I said to myself. How could it be murder? I shivered a little in the cool hallway. I felt all prickly and dancy inside. What if it was? God forgive me, the thought made me happy. Me, and only me, I'd got the shots. It was worth at least a Pulitzer.

..... II

Floyd Beesom came chugging down the ramp like a man in search of a drink. If you didn't know him, you'd think he had a kindly face. Two tufts of anyhow-brown hair sprout luxuriously over his ears and give his bald head a kewpie-doll quality. And he has an easy smile when he's headed for a bar that can trick you too.

Beside him, matching him stride for stride, was Gilbert Ott, or more informally, only not to his face, Gilly Fats, senior sports writer for the *Graphic*. Gilly Fats can write the best copy with the thinnest material of anybody on the sports desk. And he frequently does. The first time you meet him, Gilly Fats is intimidating. He stands taller than 6'2", and he's built like a Las Vegas bill collector. He has thin greasy black hair and shrewd little pig eyes. But Gilly Fats is as gentle as a sugar jelly donut, which is his favorite food.

Gilly Fats smokes large, wet-ended cigars from start to finish whenever he has a chance to relax. It takes him twelve minutes to finish the job, and he only knocks the ash off once. The cigars are so big and smelly, I thought they'd cost about a dollar apiece. But Gilly Fats says that just proves I don't know cigars, and that he gets them down on Ninth Avenue for thirty cents each and he overpays. He buys them loose, two or three dozen at a time, and carries them back to his *Graphic* desk in a brown grocery bag. Wherever Gilly Fats is going to be for awhile, he brings a bagful of cigars along to keep him company. There's one right now in the back of the *Graphic* Chevie.

A couple of steps behind Floyd and Gilly Fats jogged Toby the messenger boy. He was there to pick up the film and drive it back to New York City. This way, pictures of the game's first half would make the 6 P.M. deadline for the bulldog edition of Monday morning's *Graphic*. Gilly Fats has a later deadline. He can phone in his copy. Up in the press box there is a telephone with a direct line to Barkley, and all of us carry about twenty dimes in our pockets for emergencies.

10 . . .

I turned my film over to the messenger. I'd tagged it and identified it. He dumped it in a bag stamped *Graphic Sports* and dropped that bag into the larger one he wore over his shoulder. He waved and loped off. It was about 3 P.M. now, and he ought to have the film to Barkley by 5:30 max.

I told Floyd and Gilly Fats as much as I'd learned about LaMont's death. Floyd snapped at me. "Well, don't hang around, Baldwin. Take the Chevie and get your butt down to the morgue. We'll be here when you get back."

I switched my camera bag to the other shoulder and got going.

"Jee-sus!" I heard Floyd behind my back. "Baldwin drives me to drink." Gilly Fats rumbled a laugh.

Outside in the parking area reserved for the press stood the sturdy, grimy-yellow *Graphic* Chevie. Leaning up against it was one of the Colossus cheerleaders, Patty Cambron. She was writing on a paper flattened against the windshield. Patty was the only cheerleader of the five who had short hair. It was medium brown and curly and today she had lots of little light and dark brown bows tied into the curls.

The cheerleader costume is supposed to suggest mountain climbing: kneehigh brown boots with flat serrated soles, dark brown walking shorts and a light brown T-shirt with a painted picture of the mountain goat on it. Patty's nipples stuck out where Overcoat's eyes were.

"You're not leaving?" she greeted me as I walked up.

She was very excited, and I could tell by the way her slanty gray eyes kept shifting from me to the empty space behind me that she was looking to see if any other member of the press was coming out here. She probably thought a man would be more trustworthy.

Patty Cambron had a monkey-cute kind of face. Not beautiful, but the winsome kind Mr. and Mrs. Apple Pie would want Sonny Boy to bring home from college for the weekend, pinned. I knew she choreographed the cheers for The Scenic View, and was the cheerleader captain, so I figured she had to be more intelligent than she looked.

"I'm coming back," I answered her evasively. "Can I help you at all?"

She seemed to be trying to make up her mind if I were more intelligent than I looked. She pursed her lips and chewed the lower one for awhile.

Then, "I heard Lou's dead," she said.
I nodded. "I'm going after the autopsy report."
"Did Dr. Joe really say he didn't know how come?"
"That's right," I said. "Do you?"
She chewed on her lower lip. "I don't know, I'm sure. I mean, I shouldn't know, should I? I mean, I don't even know who I'm talking to, do I?"

I reached in my camera bag for my card and gave one to her. I didn't say anything. I rarely know what to say to people, which is one reason why I take pictures. I opened the door of the Chevie and tossed my monopod on the seat in the back and dumped my camera bag on the passenger seat in front. After all, I thought, I only take the pictures. I'm not responsible for print pieces. But if I can get some information for Gilly Fats to use, or the *Graphic* generally, I will.

"T.T. Baldwin," she read out loud.
"It's Theresa Tracy," I said, "but I've been T.T. ever since I was little."

She seemed to decide something. She scrunched up the paper in her hand. "Listen, ask Dr. Joe about the needles. But please don't tell him who asked you to. Just ask him if it could have anything to do with the needles. He'll understand. I've got to be getting back inside."

"What kind of needles?"
"Listen," she said, almost whispering, "you don't think it was natural, do you? His dying, I mean?"
"Well, Dr. Joe didn't seem to think so. I guess a heart attack is possible—"
"I hope so," she cut me off. "I mean, I hope he died naturally." Then she started whispering again. *"But I don't think so!"*

I studied the squared-off toes of my Frye boots but they didn't give me any idea of what to say. So I said the first thing I thought of.

"Right now there's no reason to think anything except Lou LaMont died from an act of nature. . . . Do you have any reason to think differently?"

"Yes," she said, nodding her head and making the little bows in her hair dance. "Yes, I do! *And I hate myself for it*," she whispered again. She kept shifting her eyes, looking beyond me, looking around the nobody-there-but-us parking lot.

"But I'm going to wait. I'm not going to gossip about my friends. Sometimes you can misinterpret something, and hurt people. . . . Intermission's almost over. I've got to get back."

"I'll look for you later," I said.

"Yes, I want to know. And remember, don't tell Dr. Joe who told you. Just ask him to look for the needles."

She ran back toward the Colossus. As she ran she stuck the balled-up paper she'd been writing on in the pocket of her shorts along with my business card.

She'd almost reached the players' gate when she slipped on the loose gravel, slid sideways, and scraped her knee. She looked back at me and laughed and shouted "damn" pointing to the blood starting to ooze out around the kneecap. Even from where I was I could see she'd scuffed the knee pretty badly. Little bits of fine rock stuck in the cuts where the skin had been broken. Blood and dirt trickled down her calf.

Patty got up, dusted off her bottom, and ran on, limping now, toward the Colossus complex. Drops of bright blood flecked from her knee to the gravel, staining a little trail.

Back in the shadows of the entrance, David Livingston, the fruity baton-twirler, gestured for her to hurry. At least I think it was David Livingston. He was standing just inside the portal and the sun was too low to reach his face, but I could see the gown with the stars and the half-moons all over it.

I got into the Chevie and rolled down the window to get out the smell of Gilly Fats' cigar smoke. I could hear the crowd shouts starting up as the second half got under way. I pointed the Chevie toward the highway, gunned it a little, and headed for the morgue.

Down the High Mountain Highway, maybe five miles in toward the town, was the one police station. It looked like a well-kept realtor's office, with its pruned shrubs, its Sur-Gro vitaminized grass, and its window boxes filled with ivy. It had a brick facade and a cherry red door with old fashioned black hinges.

Almost directly across the highway from the police station was High Mountain General. A small extension of the building, virtually independent but connected to the hospital by a walkway, was the city morgue.

I left my cameras in the Chevie, locked it, and went through a white door into a white room with a white-uniformed male nurse sitting at a black desk. The male nurse ignored me.

. . . 13

Two uniformed policemen I'd seen earlier when the ambulance had come to take LaMont's body were slouched against the white wall on the far side of the reception room.

I went up and introduced myself. They introduced themselves, maybe over-politely, but I never know how the police are going to react and I don't worry about it. I accept the police like I do the weather. I take 'em as they come.

Lieutenant Jason Weatherwax of the High Mountain Police was big-boned but gaunt. He had a full head of gray hair and a face like a Sioux Indian who's just been driven off his land for good by the palefaces. His face looked as though everything he'd ever seen had been a cause for sorrow.

His eyes were fungus green and his eyelashes and brows were colorless. They made his eyes look rimmed in ice. He had the saddest smile I've ever seen except for the basset hound that advertises Liv-A-Snaps.

His subordinate, Detective John Xavier, on the other hand, was a hunk of grade-A protein. His uniform clung to his muscles like a $300 custom job, and his belt looked Dunhill and his shoes Peal & Company. His sandy hair waved sensually over his forehead and he smiled slowly and deliberately and watched its effect on you. His eyes were dark and glowy like a log-cabin fire.

"I'm here to get the autopsy report from Dr. Joe," I said, "and to ask him a few questions."

"Have a seat then," Lieutenant Weatherwax indicated a bench. "That's what we're waiting for too."

I decided to make some conversation. "Is Dr. DeBianco the regular medical examiner for this county?"

Lieutenant Weatherwax shook his head. "No, there isn't any permanent one. Doctors here share the duty. Dr. Joe asked to be the M.E. on this, and it's okay by us."

"But isn't he an interested party, being the team doctor? He's the one responsible for the players' health check before they play."

"Well, maybe," Lieutenant Weatherwax eased his hat back on his head. "But until a question of propriety comes up, there's no reason to object to Dr. Joe doing the work. You raising such a question?" He might have been smiling, but his expression was so forlorn, I wasn't sure.

"No, just routine," I said, throwing back at him the excuse the police use when they don't want to tell you why they're asking something.

As if on cue, they both nodded.

I decided to try again. "Did Dr. Joe tell you what he thought was the probable cause of death?"

Detective Xavier answered this time. "Heart failure," he said, and snickered. Lieutenant Weatherwax grunted and they threw each other wise-guy grins. Maybe they thought they could shut me up that way.

I kept trying. "How many murders have there been in High Mountain so far this year, Lieutenant?" I kept my tone formal and my grammar correct. Even the police fall for this gambit sometimes, and will tell you things they wouldn't ordinarily if you ask the questions like a computer print-out instead of like a person.

Detective Xavier answered again. "Not a one, honey. Not last year, either. In fact, I've been on the force going on eight years now, and the only murder I remember was three-four years back, I reckon, when Salty Ferregamo got good and mad at his wife running round while he baked the bread all night. Blew her head off with that old possum gun he kept to keep the rats away. 'Member that, Jason?"

Lieutenant Weatherwax smiled like a man walking the last mile. "Poor ole Salty. Got four years for that, didn't he?"

"Yeah," broke in Detective Xavier. "But he got out this January. Paroled for good time."

"Yeah, yeah, that's right, John X. He up and married Tom Atkinson's girl, didn't he?"

"Yeah. Beatrice." They were really trying to stunt me.

"Yeah, doing fine now. Best biscuit in town, Salty's. Married the right girl this time." Detective Xavier gave me one of his nine-hundred-watt smiles and waited for me to roll over dead.

Instead I went right on, acting dumber than Phyllis Diller. "I guess ole Salty confessed right away?"

They were starting to enjoy it. "Yeah. Yeah." Both heads bobbed.

"Came right in to headquarters and laid that big rifle down on the desk. I was desk sergeant that night. 'Member, John X.? I sent you to get a sloppy joe for the poor guy. He was shook so bad."

Detective Xavier *ha-ha*'d and shook his head. "And a strawberry malt," he said.

We all chuckled at that.

"Then I guess you're really not prepared to investigate a murder case here in High Mountain, being so inexperienced. That right,

Lieutenant?" I kept my tone light. After all, if LaMont's death were murder, I'd need to be friends with these guys.

Lieutenant Weatherwax took it well. "Let's hope we don't have to," he said. That ended the fun.

From a door in the rear wall, Dr. Joe DeBianco came out. He was wearing a white jacket, open, over his black business suit.

"We've got a problem," he said.

Both cops drew themselves away from the wall they'd been slouched against, and stood up straight.

"Major arterial collapse. Suffocation. Damned if I know why. I'm ordering toxicological tests."

I butted in. "Needles, Dr. Joe. Did you find any needles?"

He turned his patrician head toward me and looked down his nose. He didn't seem to know who I was.

"I beg your pardon?"

"That's the message I have for you. Look for a needle, or needles. You're supposed to know what kind."

He raised a hand as though to protest, then turned, and went back through the door and away again.

This time we just sat and waited. Weatherwax and Xavier looked halfway amused at my needle suggestion. They didn't ask me about it. Maybe they wanted to see from Dr. Joe if I was on target before they pounced.

I went through three cigarettes and a terrible cup of machine-brewed coffee. Lieutenant Weatherwax, Detective Xavier and the male nurse, whom they called Huey, played liar's poker with the serial numbers on dollar bills. Huey came up winners.

Dr. Joe entered briskly, looking very much the doctor-in-charge this time. He was wearing a stethoscope, for God knows what reason, and carrying several sheets of some official forms. He huddled with the policemen and I looked at my toes and shut my eyes and tried to eavesdrop. I didn't catch much.

They broke off the huddle and Lieutenant Weatherwax gestured toward me. "Give it to the press, doc."

Dr. Joe frowned, but he gave it to me. "I've found the needle you asked me about. In his skull. It was hidden by his hair." He cleared his throat, and I knew we'd be getting back to why I'd asked.

"Trying not to be too technical, what happened was this. A needle, the kind usually used only in acupuncture, was imbedded into the middle portion of the brain stem, right where the *pons Varolii* and the *medulla oblongata* meet. These organs are relatively small parts of our brain, but they're necessary in keeping us alive. Our nerves follow the brain cavity along this *pons Varolii* and through the *medulla oblongata* to join up into nerve trunks that run through our spinal cord. At a certain point, just under the skull cap and down inside the *medulla*, are the vital centers which control our breathing and the circulation of our blood. Following me so far?"

I nodded as though it were old stuff to me.

"Good. Now what happened to Lou LaMont was that this long needle punctured the *medulla* and the *pons*, destroyed the vital cell centers that keep the body breathing and the blood flowing. LaMont was temporarily spastic, then paralyzed, then in coma, and then deceased." He waited for me to get that.

"And," Dr. Joe gave a deep sigh, "in my opinion, this can't have been a tragic accident. The odds against any such event being accidental are negligible. First of all, the exact place of insertion must be probed to be found. Second, it must be recognized when found. And third, it's deep under a shelf of bone. Very unusual for a needle to be able to penetrate the distance and the bone density. The skull protects it. The hair protects it. And Lou LaMont was wearing his helmet which protects it. . . ." His voice trailed away, remembering something, or maybe just distracted. Then he continued. "And it couldn't have been self-inflicted for the same reasons. Ridiculous even to consider."

"How could it happen, doctor?" Lieutenant Weatherwax asked.

The papers Dr. Joe was holding in his hands shook ever so slightly, and his swarthy complexion paled almost to the color of mine.

"I'm not sure, Lieutenant. It would be difficult to do without the victim's being aware of it, I should think."

Personally, I thought he might have an idea or two.

Detective Xavier had been busy making neat shorthand strokes in a notebook. He looked up at the doctor.

"And so this needle pushed into the brain is what killed him?"

Dr. Joe shook his head. "Oh no. Not the initial insertion—it wouldn't go deep enough. No, what was needed, the *coup de grace*, so to speak, was a great pressure to push the needle home, all the way to the point of damage and death. It's my opinion that many physical blows such as are sustained in the game of football would have been sufficient to drive the needle deep enough.

"And when Billy O'Leary tackled Lou LaMont, that tackle—however unmeaning on the part of Mr. O'Leary, and however unfortunate—that tackle was the force that drove the needle through the cranial mass and caused death. The tackle, that is, along with the fall Lou LaMont took because of it, when his back and head hit the ground...."

I could see it again as the doctor said it. The picture sequence reran through my mind like the film ran through my camera.

Lieutenant Weatherwax broke my reverie. "Okay, Baldwin, let's have it."

I knew what he meant. "I'm sorry, Lieutenant. I promised I wouldn't. Confidentiality of source."

That really made him mad. "WHAT!" he boomed at me.

I swallowed hard and said it again. "Confidentiality of source."

Detective Xavier tried to charm me out of it. "Aw, come on, honey. This isn't a celebrity interview. This is a murder investigation."

"Murder," repeated Dr. Joe abstractedly. "Yes, it is murder, isn't it? Has to be."

"Look, Baldwin," Lieutenant Weatherwax took a giant step toward me, smiling like a bloodhound on the stalk.

I stood up. "Hey, wait a minute, Lieutenant. I'm willing to cooperate. But if it's not necessary for me to tell you, then I don't want to. You're going to question the Colossus personnel, aren't you? Well, if who told me doesn't tell you, then I will. But I'd like to give the person a chance to do it on his own. That's all. Why should I blow a source if I don't have to. I gave my word."

"Blow a source," Lieutenant Weatherwax snorted. "You sound worse than a C.I.A. operative." But he smiled sadly at me and left me alone.

"Let's get going," he said to Dr. Joe. "We've got some questioning to do."

Dr. Joe looked bewildered. "Back to the Colossus?" he asked. I wondered where his mind had been these last few minutes.

Lieutenant Weatherwax nodded. "Back to the Colossus, doc. We've got to find our own sources, it seems."

"Thanks, Lieutenant," I said. "I'll follow you back."

"Oh, sure," he said. "I expected that."

It was six P.M. now and quickly growing dark. I trailed Lieutenant Weatherwax and Detective Xavier into the Colossus restaurant. Dr. Joe poked along behind me, mumbling to himself about the odontoid peg, whatever that is, and cervical vertebrae, which I think are the bones of the spinal column in the neck.

Everyone concerned with the Colossus sports complex and the Climbers was gathered in the restaurant for what the press kit billed as the Climbers' victory party. What it was was a police interrogation. I didn't even know yet who'd won the game.

And to tell the truth, I was very disappointed in the eats. All this past pregame week Floyd and Gilly Fats and I had been out here for the press promotion along with other press people. We'd been feted and feasted like astronauts plunked out of the Pacific after a successful splashdown. This was the final free feed, supposed to send us off stuffed and contented to write our raves and spread our pictures over the sport pages.

A long time ago my mother taught me never to go to a dinner party hungry. She said it wasn't ladylike. Well, Mums never wanted me to be a sports photog, either. And tonight I wasn't merely hungry, I was ravenous, and what we were getting were hot dogs.

Spaced around the main diningroom were three hot dog wagons. Manning the wagons were the five cheerleaders and the baton-twirler David Livingston. They stood two to a wagon, wearing starched-stiff chef hats, red aprons, oversize red kitchen mitts, and holding large two-pronged forks. Steaming away in the wagons were hot dogs, potato knishes, and weiner buns. Oh joy.

On the tables were shelled peanuts and the condiments in little brown jars with "Climbers" written on them. There were two kinds of pickle relish, a smelly red sauerkraut, a spicy french mustard, chopped raw onions, and Climber-brown cooked onions in a candle-heated brazier. They smelled worse than the sauerkraut.

The condiment jars circled a small galvanized tub centered on each table. The tub was filled with crushed ice, bottles of beer, and beer glasses dunked upside down to frost them. No soda. No scotch.

Me as a nondrinker, and Floyd as a hard one, had to go into the small room over to the left which held the bar and a few private tables to get our drinks. That is, I had to go for the two of us. Floyd plunked his surly self down at our table and laid his drink order on me. Gilly Fats drank the beer, glad to have the tub to himself.

I didn't really mind fetching for Floyd since it suited my purpose just fine. Weatherwax and Xavier were using the privacy of the bar tables to question the Colossus personnel, one by one. If I timed it right, I'd have an excuse to saunter in to the bar at least three times to hang my ear out before the police got finished. And by doubling up on Floyd's drinks, I could pretty much decide when I wanted to hit the bar to listen in and when I didn't.

While everybody was getting settled and greeting each other and gossiping in low tones about Lou LaMont and Badman O'Leary, the lineman who had sacked him, I looked around at the hot dog wagons to see which one Patty Cambron was at.

Wagon number one was manned by David and Babs Livingston. They'd met when both took jobs with the Climbers, she as a cheerleader, he as their publicity and promotion man.

For all David Livingston's swishing and flamboyant dress, which he said was just attention-grabbing and good Climber-publicity, Livingston was considered very good at his job. Abe Hirshaw, Climbers' general manager, told Gilly Fats that Livingston was a genius. Of course, that was for press release. When he wasn't on the sidelines doing his act, Livingston seemed a happily-married, hart-hitting career man on his way up.

The Livingstons had only been married three-four months. I think he made a good choice in Babs. Babs was low key and friendly, with a private school shine on her. Handsome rather than pretty, she wore her long, blonde-streaked hair straight down to her shoulder blades and then curled it under at the ends. She had a lean body and a longish face that would wear well in later years. And she was very proud of her David.

At hot dog wagon number two giggled Amy Bland, High Mountain's Marilyn Monroe look-alike—all platinum waves, false lashes, red lips and wiggles—and the olive-skinned Rachel Hirshaw who hated to be called Ratch and therefore usually was.

Rachel was the only child of Abe Hirshaw, Climbers' G. M. Her mother had died when she was very small and an aunt had raised her. Earlier in the week, Ratch told me the aunt had been obsessed with the violin and rarely left the house. The aunt had died when Rachel was fifteen, and after that Ratch ran the house and looked after herself.

Abe Hirshaw was inordinately fond of his daughter, and she too thought a good deal of herself. She also told me she was having what she called a tempestuous love affair with Dr. Joe right under the nose of her father who didn't know a thing about it. She said Abe didn't approve of Dr. Joe because he was a Cuban and a necrophiliac which, she said, just shows how prejudicial some people can be.

Rachel Hirshaw was probably the most beautiful of the five cheerleaders who made up The Scenic View. But she lacked fire. There was an almost archaic perfection about her. She was like a Hepplewhite highboy smug in a museum behind ropes and stanchions which kept you from reaching out and smudging its hand-rubbed gloss. You sighed at the lovely thing and then walked past and forgot about it. Ratch and Amy Bland were the best of friends.

The real star of The Scenic View, if there was one, was the redheaded Wanda Pettigo. She's the one who tied up Floyd's zoom while I was out-scooping him on the Lou LaMont shots. Wanda and Patty Cambron were serving up the hot dogs at wagon number three.

Circling around tables to get to wagon number three I almost collided with Detective Xavier. He moved me out of his way with a bump of his hips. He didn't apologize. He was escorting Mrs. Marcella Snowfield, sole owner of the Climbers and the Colossus, into the bar. Lieutenant Weatherwax was ready to take her statement. I wanted to hear part of it, but I had to talk to Patty Cambron first.

I got to the hot dog wagon and had to wait my turn behind Walt-the-Talk Amos, the play-by-play announcer. He was making a date with Patty for Monday night after cheerleader practice. While I waited I ate a naked frankfurter on a bun that Wanda handed me.

Walt-the-Talk finally got out of there and I inched up alongside Patty.

"Tell me," she whispered, shifting her eyes past me to make sure no one was listening in. "Soft, in my ear."

I swallowed the last of my hot dog. "I told him," I said. "He couldn't find anything wrong before I did. Then he went back. He was gone a long time, looking for the needles, I guess. Then he found one."

She pulled her head away from me and said, "How many, Stanley?" to the runty janitor with the wrinkled face.

Stanley jerked his head happily. "Think I'll start with two, Miz Patty. How ya doin'?"

"I feel just awful about it, Stanley. Don't you?"

"Yas'm. Thankee." He jerked his head again, and headed for a table near the rear of the room, a weiner and bun in each hand.

Patty stepped close to me again, looked at me with her gray eyes wide and whispered. "Dr. Joe *found* one? Just *one?*" Then she shifted her eyes around the crowd.

I talked to her ear. "Just one is what he said. Stuck deep into the brain. All it took was a good smack to push the needle in far enough, he said. And that head-butt Lou got from The Badman did it."

She gasped. Wanda looked over at her. "What're you doing, Patty? You're just making it worse for me." Wanda's eyes were red as though she'd been crying. Maybe she had liked the guy.

"Oh, Wanda," Patty sighed. "You just don't understand. I'll tell you later. But there's something I've got to do first. Then I'll tell you everything, I promise."

"What can you tell me?" Wanda sounded more disgusted than distraught. She flung her head saucily and the auburn waves fell back into place, precisely. "Nobody's ever going to tell me anything again. . . . How many, Lil Harv?"

I hadn't heard him and I didn't smell the cod-liver oil this time, either. He sat in his wheelchair smiling his pretty smile, all tow-haired and baby-blue-eye'd, linen napkin over his lap robe and another tucked under his chin.

"Two, Wanda. With all the fixin's. Hi, Patty. Hi, Miss Photographer. Great game, huh?"

I still didn't know the score. "I missed the last half, Harv," I said. "How'd it end?"

"Oh, it was great," he said. "We finally won with a touchdown on a long bomber pass by Black Jack right to Racehorse on the seventeen—"

"Here's your dogs, Harv," said Wanda. "You put the fixin's on yourself, at one of the tables. Want a potato knish?"

"French fries."

"No french fries, Harv. Want a potato knish?"

"Okay," he said. "So anyway, then Racehorse stumbled and almost dropped the ball—"

22 . . .

Patty interrupted. "But he recovered and ran it in, and Sinister got the last point. Go on away now, Harv. We're talking."

"What was the final score?" I really wanted to know.

Little Harvey pounded the arms of his wheelchair. "Climbers twenty-three, Johnny Rebs nineteen!" He shouted it out and there was a smatter of applause around the room. But then I guess every one remembered there'd been a death in the family and the room got quiet again.

"See you later," Harv plopped his potato knish between his two hot dogs and rolled soundlessly away.

Again Patty got close to me and focused her eyes into lookout position.

"That's all I can tell you," I said. "One needle, purposely pushed into Lou's brain, so that when he fell he'd be a dead man. Dr. Joe doesn't know who. But he tried to get me to tell him how I knew anything about it. The police want to know too. I didn't tell them. I told them to ask around." I stopped talking.

"Oh, Jesus God. What am I going to do?" Her shoulders slumped and she hung her head.

"Look, Patty, if you know something, you ought to tell."

She still wasn't looking at me. She nodded. "Yes, thanks, T.T., you've been a friend. Thanks for not telling."

"Anytime," I said. "I guess I'll have another hot dog now. No, better make it two."

Listlessly, she handed one over to me. The bun was steamed almost to tatters. Wanda gave me the other one. Its bun wasn't even hot. I thanked them and headed back to my table.

I wanted to talk to Patty some more, but this wasn't the place and I didn't have the time. I wanted to hear what Mrs. Snowfield was telling Lieutenant Weatherwax.

At the table Floyd was working himself into a snit. "Come on, T.T., I'm dehydrating. You trying to kill me?"

I put my hot dogs down on the plate they'd saved for me. "That's not funny, Floyd."

"You're telling me. I'm in pain."

"Did anybody ever tell you you have a drinking problem?" I walked away to the bar. I could do with a Dr. Ray's Celery Tonic myself.

Abe Hirshaw didn't like it, but he was doing it. He stood behind the bar at parade rest, back straight, nose in the air, looking very

... 23

much the high-priced legal counsel he is in his blue mohair suit and clubby tie. He was trying not to dirty himself while he handled ice cubes and the cocktail shaker and salted glasses for margaritas.

Every bartender has a bar mop, a damp towel to keep the hands dry and the bar surface sponged off. Abe had a stack of team towels straight from Stanley's linen closet piled on a stool.

He was standing now at scornful attention with a Climber towel draped over his forearm, like I guess he imagined Jeeves would do it if Jeeves were downtrodden enough to hire out as a barkeep.

I made for him, not looking at Lieutenant Weatherwax talking *sotto voce* with Mrs. Snowfield, nor at Detective Xavier sloping his neat shorthand into his notebook. They noticed me all the same.

"Hiya, Abe," I chirped in my friendliest voice.

Abe lowered his eyelids and then raised them back to half-mast. "*Yuuss?*" he murmured.

"... has to do with it, my dear," I heard Mrs. Snowfield behind my back.

"Gee, you look great back there. Look like you were born to it," I teased.

The eyelids drooped again and stayed shut while the nose sniffed. Then the lids came up halfway again. I could tell he was not amused.

"*Yuuss?*"

So okay. "Do you have any celery tonic, Abe?" I asked, half wanting him to say no so I could take my time hemming and hawing over a substitute, and half wanting him to say yes because it's my favorite soda and it's hard to come by outside of New York City.

This time his eyelids opened up all the way while he thought about it.

"... zoo's (or *zoose* or something close to it) the only one who would know, Inspector." Mrs. Snowfield's voice was audible. I just didn't know what a zoo's was.

"... don't know, Miss Baldwin," Abe Hirshaw was saying to me. "No one's asked for it. Shall I take a look in the fridgie?"

"Thanks very much," I said.

Abe Hirshaw nodded and stepped mincingly down the wooden grid that covered the bar floor, vaingloriously attempting to keep the shine on his bench-made Italian lace-ups.

"... could I, since I wasn't in the players' wing before the game? Really, Inspector, dear are you trying to trap me?"

"Hey, Baldwin!" I heard the smart-ass tenor of Detective John

Xavier. "What you hanging around here for?"

Abe Hirshaw had his nose into the refrigerator, but he lifted it and peered disapprovingly at the two policemen.

"Dreadfully sorry if I'm slow, gentlemen, but I am *rah-ther* new at this." Eyelids at definite midpoint.

"You said this was to be private, dear Inspector. We sent the catered help home." Mrs. Snowfield had an edge on her voice. "Had to pay them all, of course."

I wanted to turn around and smirk but I didn't. I just shrugged my shoulders to signify it wasn't my fault.

"No, ma'am," Lieutenant Weatherwax continued his conversation with Mrs. Snowfield. "No, ma'am, I'm not trying to trap you. Just trying to keep these things as straight as I can. . . ."

Abe Hirshaw was back in the bar cooler. He whooped a mild victory cry. "Ha! I see them. Way in the back here. Just a minute, Miss Baldwin."

"Take your time, Abe." I almost smiled, but I thought Detective Xavier might catch it in the bar mirror. I didn't look into it. I watched Abe Hirshaw push around soda bottles trying to reach the celery tonic and keep his cuffs dry.

". . . suppose I was more friendly with Lou than with some of the other players, Captain. After all, he was a valuable investment on the Climbers' part. He was spoiled, you know, dear, and we all went out of our way to keep him happy."

". . . insurance," I heard the dropped voice of Lieutenant Weatherwax.

Abe Hirshaw placed two bottles of the celery tonic on the bar. His knees cracked as he straightened up.

"I never realized this was such demanding work," he said. "Think I'll have a Dr. Ray myself, Miss Baldwin."

"Here, Abe, let me open them for you," I offered. "It's tricky sometimes. You might get sprayed."

"Why, that's awfully nice. Get you anything else while you're here?" He was readjusting his tie.

"Yes, for the guys." Meaning Floyd and Floyd. "Two double scotches on the rocks in tall glasses."

"Coming right up," he said, almost cheerily. He was loosening up a little.

". . . ask Abe here. He's my business arm."

". . . enemies you know of."

. . . 25

"Not really, dear man, not really. You know, just the normal friction and competition of a new team with money in it making its debut. I think your aspersions about Wanda are a bit silly. No one tried to murder Lou LaMont, for goodness sakes. I don't care what Dr. Joe says. He's just being melodramatic. It's his Latin blood. It's all a terrible accident, an act of God. I suggest you go talk to Zoo and let nice people alone."

"We intend to, ma'am," Lieutenant Weatherwax went inexorably on, "and you're sure you didn't see or talk with Lou LaMont before today's game?"

"Really, Inspector. I think I've accounted for every minute."

"You were seen, Mrs. Snowfield. . . ."

Abe Hirshaw handed me a cork-lined cocktail tray. "There you are, Miss Baldwin."

"*Who* says so?"

Even I jumped at the quick freeze dripping from Mrs. Snowfield's voice now.

Lieutenant Weatherwax didn't answer. I glanced into the bar mirror and saw both policemen and the elegant white head of Mrs. Snowfield. They were all looking at me.

"Thanks, Abe." I got out of there and no one said a word until I did. I looked back once and Mrs. Snowfield still looked frozen for posterity and Abe Hirshaw was cleaning his fingers with wetnaps.

Wending my way back to our table I noticed that the cheerleaders had abandoned their stations behind the hot dog wagons and taken seats for themselves. From now on, if you wanted a frankfurter, you were supposed to help yourself. Over at wagon number one I saw Coach Skyhook Reesenbach spearing himself a good one.

Rather than pass out from *delirium tremens*, Floyd was sipping at a beer. He looked as disgruntled as I've ever seen him. No kewpie-doll face now. He must really need his hootch.

Gilly Fats was sitting back expansively, blowing his ring-within-a-smokering up into the air. He looked like the exhaust pipes on Mario Andretti's Porsche.

On the plate where I'd left the two weiners lay one hot dog smothered under a layer of congealed cooked onions and red sauerkraut. The juice from the onions and kraut and the mustard slopped all over had wet the bread so much the bun was falling apart as it lay on the plate. Somebody had been playing games. Well, what can you expect?

Floyd greeted me. "I knew you hated me, T.T., but I didn't know you hated me this much."

"Slow bar," I said. "And I brought you two to make up." I set down the two glasses, about a quarter pint of scotch between them. "Cheers."

"I don't feel so good," said Floyd, wrapping his hand around the glass closest to him. He did look a little sweaty. He drank off most of a double scotch with one long quaff.

"You're something," I said. "I don't see how you keep focus in your action shots when you're pie-eyed all the time."

"Practice," he grunted, wiping his mouth with the back of his hand. "Don't forget, ace, I'm the pro. I know the tricks."

I guess he did at that. There was a lot I could learn from Floyd. The trouble was getting it out of him.

"What happened to my dogs?" I said.

"There's your dog." Floyd jerked his thumb at the little heap of trash on my plate.

"I think I'll start fresh."

Floyd shrugged. Gilly Fats still sat like a Buddha, in the rapt contentment of cigar heaven.

Wagon number two was nearest so I headed for it, longing for the cracked lobster we'd eaten Saturday night.

I got myself a dog and a nice warm bun. Bent over the wagon, I looked toward the bar. They were questioning David Livingston now. I looked over at Floyd and Gilly Fats. Floyd was eating my rejected weiner and seemed to be enjoying it. His second double scotch already looked dangerously low.

The closest table was a back one, a corner booth. I went over and decorated the hot dog with some mustard and pickle relish. Curled up on the booth was Lil Harv, fast asleep under his lap robe. I smiled down at him. I guess it wasn't easy being crippled the way he was, hanging around jocks all the time. I remembered reading somewhere you didn't live too long with muscular dystrophy, and they can't cure it.

I looked around for Harv's spaceship. It was parked against the back wall, and Stanley Farmer was asleep in it, his mouth a little open, snoring evenly. Stanley fit the wheelchair as well as Lil Harv did. They were just about the same size, although Stanley probably weighed about ten-twelve pounds more.

I stood at the table, eating the hot dog. I glanced toward the bar. They were talking to Patty Cambron. I didn't want to go in while she was there. It might tip something to Weatherwax and Xavier. I munched away. It's not bad if you're hungry enough, but it's not Fettucine Alfredo. I finished and wiped my hands with a napkin and dusted off my face.

Patty Cambron left and went over to Coach Reesenbach and spoke to him. He went into the bar, sat down beside the cops, and started mouthing away.

I headed for the bar to get Floyd some refills. I almost got there. Abe Hirshaw saw me coming, actually gave me a wave, and started filling my order before I could ask him.

Three loud wet belches stopped me; stopped everything in the room. I looked around and saw Floyd trying to get up out of his seat. He fell back. He tried again, staggered, turned away from our table, got two steps and fell against a table where David and Babs Livingston were sitting holding hands.

Straddle-legged, Floyd propped himself against their table, while David and Babs held it on their side to keep it from tipping. They didn't look very surprised. Maybe they're used to things like this happening.

Sweat was popping out all over Floyd's face. His facial muscles had gone slack. His nose was running and he was working his jaw but it was going sideways instead of up and down, and belches were still coming out of him. Saliva formed on both sides of his mouth and dribbled over his hands clutching spastically at the table.

I knew Floyd wasn't drunk. Floyd has a place he gets to when he drinks and he stays there. I don't know what it's called, but regular drinkers know what it is. I can recognize it when I see it. And what was wrong with Floyd now had nothing to do with alcohol.

I made for him, cutting around the tables as fast as I could, but by the time I got there, Gilly Fats had Floyd stretched out on the floor on his belly, and Floyd was trying to vomit into a red apron Babs had handed over. He was breathing funny in short high gasps, and the whole room seemed permeated with a smell of cooked onions turned sour.

Where Dr. Joe came from I don't know, but he was there, massaging Floyd's chest, and giving orders. Tables were being pushed back to make space. Stanley was not only awake now and on the spot but scurrying off somewhere. Gilly Fats was rubbing Floyd's arms, and Babs Livingston was sponging off Floyd's face with a napkin dipped in water from a beer tub.

"You," Dr. Joe said to me. "The kitchen. Find a new bottle of mustard that's never been opened. Make sure of that. And a long handled spoon."

The kitchen was easy to find. There was a huge five-pound bottle of mustard maybe a third empty lined up with other big condiment jars on an aluminum table. I left it alone. Off in a storage area, very high up, I saw other large bottles just like it. It took me awhile to find the ladder, but I did, and took the most inaccessible five-pound jar I could reach. Down from the ladder, I couldn't get the top off. It was too large and screwed down too tight. I banged the top of the jar against the edge of the butcher-block counter, and finally the top loosened.

Then I started opening drawers looking for a long spoon. Just as I found one, I heard someone in the kitchen behind me. I whirled around. Rachel Hirshaw was scooping up the opened mustard jar.

"Put that back!" I snarled at her, ready to knock her down if I had to. She looked as scared as I felt, but she put the jar down.

"Hurry then," she said. She sounded just like my third grade school teacher, Terrible Two-Ton Tinnemar. I hurried.

As I half ran across the dining room to where Floyd was, I noticed Lil Harv still curled up under his lap robe in the corner booth, still asleep. I thought that seemed a little odd and then forgot all about it.

Everything was a hub-bub in the cleared space around Floyd. I pushed through and set the mustard bottle down on the floor. Floyd was on his back now, his arms and legs relaxed, looking all rubbery, with no muscle control. His eyes were open but the pupils were small condensed dots and a hard gleam shone out. His mouth was pulled back like a Doberman's growl. The stink in the air was atrocious.

Dr. Joe was just drawing a needle out of Floyd's arm. He handed the needle to Stanley Farmer who seemed to know what to do with it. Between Stanley's legs, Dr. Joe's black medicine bag was open, and Stanley reached into it and disassembled the hypodermic needle.

Dr. Joe forcibly worked Floyd's jaw open and began force-feeding the mustard down Floyd's throat. At a signal from the doc, Gilly Fats turned Floyd's body half-over and thumped on his back, trying to get him to vomit.

"What else can I do?" I asked Dr. Joe.

"Just stay out of the way," he said.

... 29

Floyd started to retch then, and I moved back out of the circle, feeling sick myself. I decided to take a little walk.

Lieutenant Weatherwax and Detective Xavier were wall-slouching again, this time against the wall where the entrance to the bar area was. Just in front of them, at an unused table, Mrs. Snowfield sat by herself, twisting a lace handkerchief in her fingers and sipping what looked like sherry.

I asked the policemen if I could get a breath of fresh air.

"Why not?" cracked Detective Xavier.

"An almost successful job of poison," said Lieutenant Weatherwax.

"I'll be back soon," I said.

"No hurry," said Detective Xavier.

Lieutenant Weatherwax gave me his Pagliaccio smile. "No hurry," he agreed.

I nodded and went out into the long hall. Doors and windows must be open all over the Colossus, I thought, because it was chilly in the hall, and the air smelled wonderfully fresh. I leaned against the wall for a few moments with my eyes closed and just breathed autumn air with no stink in it.

..... IV

Then I walked down the hall, down the flight of steps, and down another hall toward the wing where the locker rooms, training room, and offices were. From habit, I'd slung my camera bag over my shoulder as I'd come out. I didn't want to think about Floyd then so I looked for pictures to take. That's the way I relax. I look for pictures.

I wandered along until I came to the door to Dr. Joe's office. It was closed and I half expected it to be locked, but it wasn't. I went in.

It looked like any old doctor's office that charges you $50 just to sit down. And that was unusual for a doctor's office in a sports stadium. It was roomy, though narrow, and there was a great big desk I wish I had, with loose papers stacked neatly and held down by *millefiore* paper weights. Dr. Joe seemed to be a collector of nice things.

The medicine cabinet had tall glass doors, and these doors were locked. I looked in at the shiny picks and scissors and doctor's tools, and at the dark bottles, formally labeled. I looked closely at the labels to see if there were any skull and crossbones printed on them, but I didn't see any.

On one shelf there were some longish needles spread out on a towel and some cans that looked like hair spray with "Novocain" printed on their fronts. Novocain is a local anesthetic dentists use when they work on your teeth. It is an unfortunate fact but true that you don't play football long and keep your teeth. I've never met a football player yet who doesn't put most of his mouth in a glass of polident after he says good night. Or should.

I wondered if Dr. Joe were licensed to pull teeth.

I took a few wide-angles of the office, then snapped off a few close-ups of the medicine cabinet because it was there.

I left Dr. Joe's office and went through the connecting door into the schoolroom where the players learn what a Blue 42 Blitz is and a Reverse 39 Trap. There were chairs scattered around and the blackboard had a play diagrammed out. I ignored that and stepped back out into the main hallway.

I went into the Climbers' locker room where earlier I'd shot the last portraits of Lovable Lou LaMont. It was so clean it didn't even look like a locker room. Stanley Farmer must be one of those spit-and-polish guys, I thought. The place had even been sprayed with a room freshener. Some kind of artificial magnolia. A few hours earlier, a dead man had lain in here. A game had been won and players had celebrated, dressed, and dispersed. Now the room looked like the inside of a sardine can before the factory puts the fish in.

Most players' lockers don't have doors on them, they're just open three-sided cubicles. But the Climbers' lockers did. The lockers looked like miniature wood armoires, with two doors to a cabinet which opened from the middle out. The doors had carved curlicues on them and a name plate with each player's name and number hand-lettered in some kind of calligraphic script. *Ve-ry* nice.

I scanned the name plates looking for Lou LaMont's name. Somewhere outside, close by, I heard a door shut. I hoped whoever it was wouldn't find me before I'd finished snooping.

Lou LaMont's locker was at the far end, last in a row of six. I opened it. The inside of his locker doors was wall-papered with pictures in color of pretty girls doing nasty things to themselves and to some physically privileged guys. I looked over the photographic quality. First rate.

One of LaMont's jerseys, number 1, was hanging from a hook. Next to it were some brown uniform pants. Three pairs of football shoes were neatly lined up on the bottom. On the locker's high shelf were some shaving stuff and men's colognes, a bottle of hairsetting lotion and a plastic bag of pink hair curlers. I should have known Lou curled his hair to get his waves that way. Just goes to show you. I smiled a little remembering how alive his hair had looked on the training table. "It looked beautiful, Lou," I said out loud.

Pushed behind his toiletries some red satin showed. I reached up and pulled out a bright red heart-shaped pillow with "You and Me Forever Wanda" stitched across it in rhinestones like an arrow. Uh-huh.

I pushed the toilet articles to the back of the upper shelf and plumped the pillow up full front. Then I adjusted the locker doors so that the dirty pictures showed. I took about six frames from different angles. Then I shut the doors and put the pillow on the floor in front of his closed-forever locker. I took several shots of that. If Barkley didn't want such shots, I figured I could sell them to one of those European magazines that specialize in scandal. They pay well when they buy.

I put the pillow back and closed the locker doors. Then I looked into the little side room that opened off the left wall. It was a small but professionally appointed hair salon with mirrors and basins and hair dryers. Some *Sports Illustrated*'s and some old *Playboy*'s were tossed randomly around on the salon chairs, with some *Today's Hair-Do*'s, *Coiffure*'s and a couple of *Vogue*'s. I figured the players must share their beauty parlor with the cheerleaders.

I shook my head in admiration. Mrs. Marcella Snowfield really goes first class, I thought. She thinks of everything to keep her boys in style.

I didn't take any pictures. No reader interest here. I started back.

Passing the training room where the gymnastic equipment and the weights are, I heard the almost famous voice of Walt-the-Talk Amos. He sounded as though he were auditioning for another commercial. Naturally I stopped.

The voice rolled sonorously forth. Urgent. Professional. Very nice to listen to, really. I leaned up against the door and eavesdropped.

"I think we're close to a score now," he was saying in his intense baritone. "I think we're going to score. . . . Just a few more yards, baby. . . . It's a touchdown!" A few soft grunts. "We've made a TD, lovvy, a TD! Spike it! Oh, lovvy, lovvy, lovvy, spike it!"

I had to look in, so I did. There he sat, wearing his shoes and socks and nothing else, perched like a plucked parakeet on the vaulting horse. Sitting on his lap, face-to-face, wearing nylons, a peach-ribboned garter belt, knee-high boots, three strands of dainty pearls and nothing else sat Mrs. Caroline Potter, the mother of Lil Harv. I don't have to tell you what they were doing.

I couldn't resist it. I snapped the picture. Then I just stared. I thought Walt-the-Talk was cozy with Patty Cambron. So did she.

They saw me. Mrs. Potter covered her face with her hands. Walt-the-Talk swore, but didn't turn her loose.

"Excuse me," I said, and shut the door and walked away as fast as my dignity would let me.

It didn't seem the best of taste, I thought as I beat it away from there, such shenanigans on Walt-the-Talk's part. I'm no prude, but Lou LaMont had died, Dr. Joe said been murdered, for God's sakes, and Floyd was upstairs coughing his guts up, and Walt's steady girl Patty Cambron needed someone to talk to, and the police were in the building, probably watching over Caroline Potter's crippled son who was waiting to be picked up by his mother. It could have been Lil Harv floating down here in his UFO who'd caught them instead of me.

And then I wondered why they hadn't done the obvious thing and locked the door. Maybe they wanted to get caught. Maybe Caroline Potter wanted Lil Harv to see.

Whole damn bunch of freaks!

When I got back outside the main door of the Colossus restaurant, I saw Gilly Fats using a public telephone. The phone was one of three hung on the wall and separated by metal shields about neck to ears, so I stood behind him and listened to him talk, patting his rump to let him know I was there.

He turned half around and waggled a finger at me in greeting. "That's right, Bar," Gilly Fats was saying, "the doc here says some kind of nerve poisoning, he thinks."

The phone buzzed like a bee behind glass.

"Yeah, he's on his way to the hospital now. Get his stomach pumped out. . . . Sure, we can stay here. T.T.'s still healthy. I can use her for any pictures I need. . . . Yeah, the lady-owner, Mrs. Snowfield, says we can bunk in at her place. Says Floyd can convalesce there if he wants. . . ."

More buzzing. The bee sounded angrier than ever.

"Whatya mean, no film?"

My heart stopped. They'd lost my film on Lou LaMont?

"Saw it, Bar. I saw Floyd put his film in early, right after the kid LaMont went down. . . . Well, the bag was on the sidelines. Maybe Toby wasn't tied to his bag the whole time. . . . Yeah, well, I'll tell her. Get back to you." Gilly Fats hung up.

I'd been through quite a bit today, but I was really white-faced now. "They lost my film?" I croaked.

Gilly Fats patted my head. "Not yours, T.T. Floyd's. Not a roll. And that's strange because I saw Floyd put three cans in Toby's sack before Floyd relieved you on the field after LaMont went down. Toby's sack was tucked under the players' bench. I saw Floyd put his film in there."

I had color back in my face now. "Where was Toby?"

Gilly Fats smiled. "Who knows? Takin' a breather. He got your film in okay. Bar said he liked it."

I smiled like a fool.

We went back into the restaurant. "How is Floyd?" I asked.

"See for yourself."

I looked over where Floyd had been spread out on the floor. He was up now. I saw him weaving between chairs like a cockroach that's been zapped with Black Flag. His legs wouldn't follow his body, and he was pulling his legs along with the help of Lieutenant Weatherwax on one side and Detective Xavier on the other. Behind the two policemen and Floyd walked two ambulance corpsmen, one holding a stretcher rolled under his arm.

Gilly Fats grinned. "Look at that. Too tough to use the stretcher."

"Somebody said poison," I said.

"What the doctor said too. Said it was probably in the sauerkraut or the cooked onions or that french mustard. Something spicy to hide the smell. Seems to think it was on the two hot dogs Floyd ate off your plate."

"*My* plate? What makes him think that?"

"Only two hot dogs Floyd ate," said Gilly Fats.

Floyd and the policemen reached us. Floyd looked wrung out, not like the Floyd I knew at all. Some one had given him a fresh white shirt and dressed him in it without buttoning the sleeves. He stopped and tried to point a finger at me, but it was somewhat wide of center.

I thought he was going to be mad, but what he said was "Take care of yourself, T.T.—Meant for you."

"We'll tell her, Mr. Beesom, we'll tell her all about it," crooned Detective Xavier. "You just keep coming with us."

Floyd's head lolled on his neck, and he tried to keep talking. "Wait," he said, but they trundled him off out the door, his legs going every which way, and finally got him onto the stretcher and into the ambulance.

Detective Xavier didn't tell me anything. "Catch you tomorrow," was all he said.

I wasn't really worried. What Floyd said didn't hit home. Why should anyone want to poison me?

In the restaurant, most of the people had gone. I was ready to wind it up and call it a day. We'd already signed out of the motel we'd stayed at during the week, and our suitcases were packed and snug in the trunk of the *Graphic* Chevie. Gilly Fats said we were staying over in High Mountain at Mrs. Snowfield's place. That was fine with me. All I wanted was to go to sleep. Before I hit the

. . . 35

pillow, I'd say a prayer for Floyd and then I could drop off with a clear conscience.

But Gilly Fats seemed as genial as ever and in no hurry to pack it in. Gilly Fats never hurries.

Detective Xavier was back at the bar collating his notes. Lieutenant Weatherwax was talking to Lil Harv's father who'd just arrived.

Harvey Potter Sr (he signed himself Potter Sr no comma no dot) was well known for his handmade furniture. He was considered to be an artist. Barkley, editor of the *New York Graphic*, had a Potter desk and he was proud of it. Barkley said when Potter Sr died all his pieces would become instant antiques and quadruple in value.

But Harvey Potter Sr sure didn't look like the English gentleman his name made him out to be. He looked more gutter-Irish. He was bald with a long white scar across the top of his pate which he usually covered with a grease-stained and rumpled French beret which had once been green but was now mottled from too much clorox so that it looked like army camouflage issue. The beret was a bit too large. It hung on his ears which stuck out at right angles to his head like handles on a crock pot. He had a basketball belly which rode unashamedly upon a rope belt which more or less held up his greasy chino slacks. He was tanned beer-bottle-brown. His forearms bulged with muscles. He had thin lips that didn't say much and quiet eyes. His eyes reminded me of a guru I used to study meditation with. I was supposed to meditate until my eyes got as quiet as that, but I never managed it.

His red sport shirt had lost two of its buttons and his chest was thick with curly brown hair tinged with gray which popped out in the opening of the shirt.

I sat in a kind of semi-alertness watching Lieutenant Weatherwax talk with Potter Sr. Lil Harv was still snoozing like a champ in the corner booth. I guess a person does get tired and have to sleep alot with his kind of disease.

Gilly Fats was sitting beside Detective Xavier being chatty and making friends. Gilly Fats seemed to be getting along just fine with the investigative staff. But then Gilly Fats has a way of getting along with everybody.

Walt-the-Talk Amos came in. He was dressed as though he were about to go on mike to do his show. He was all buttoned up in his double-breasted Climbers blazer. His kinky brown hair was shining and almost flat with water combed through it. He carried two books

36 . . .

on sports and a manila folder filled with loose papers. He went over to Lieutenant Weatherwax.

"Just been in contact with Jeremy at ZAP. He wants me to do the eleven o'clock sports news and give a recap on this situation. Got to get down there right away. Do I have permission to give your summary over the air at this time?"

Lieutenant Weatherwax shoved a sheet of paper toward him. "Here you are, Walt. All ready for you. If you're in a hurry, I'll get your statement tomorrow. How's noon?"

Walt-the-Talk laughed. "A little early, Lieutenant, but okay. Appreciate it. Hello, Potter. Awful this thing, just awful, isn't it? Could ruin our season. And I thought for sure we had a winner. Just saw your wife outside. Real upset. Well, why not, we all are. Hope Lil Harv doesn't take it too much to heart. Lovable Lou was his number one hero." Walt-the-Talk looked over at Lil Harv snuggled up in the lap robe. "Guess I'm number one now," he said. "Your son just amazes me, Potter. What a competitor. He's sure number one with me. Love that little boy."

Most of the time Walt-the-Talk's sentences sounded like he was describing play-by-play. I guess he didn't know how to talk any other way.

Potter Sr didn't react much. Just stood there with his eyes quiet and didn't say anything. He shook hands with Walt-the-Talk, and the sports announcer strode importantly toward the exit. As he passed my table he winked at me and I gave him the peace sign. He blew me a kiss and was gone. I had the feeling he was proud of himself for some reason.

Caroline Potter came in then. She was wearing a long mink coat and a mink hat. Potter Sr might not dress himself, but his wife seemed to do okay. Her face was paler than it might have been, but she was composed. She was very pretty. She had a nice head of dark glossy hair which she wore twisted neat at the nape of her neck. She was tall for a woman and slender without being obviously thin. And her perfume was expensive even if she did use too much of it. She looked like a woman who knew how to get what she wanted even if the means she used weren't all that original. Or thought she did.

She went immediately into the arms of her husband. "Dr. Joe gave me a sedative, I think, darling, about an hour ago. Please let's go home. I'm so tired."

Lieutenant Weatherwax greeted her. "No need to take your state-

... 37

ment now, Caroline. If it's all right, I'll drop by your place tomorrow. Won't take long."

"Statement?" She sounded surprised. "What statement can I give, Jason?"

Lieutenant Weatherwax smiled as though the world were about to end within the minute. "I'll drop by tomorrow, Caroline."

"Yes, I see. Thank you, Jason." She sat down while Potter Sr picked up his son, carried him to the wheelchair, and pushed a button for manual operation. Lil Harv woke up, saw his father, smiled, and then went back to sleep. Caroline Potter avoided my eyes as Potter Sr took his wife and son away.

Finally Gilly Fats came and said we could go. I shouldered my camera bag and trudged out to the parking lot with him.

The Colossus stood eerily luminescent under the winter stars. I looked for the little dipper and found it. It was tipping starspace right over the parapets of the Colossus onto the playing field.

I figured ten minutes' exposure by starlight.

"Do you mind, Gilly?"

He leaned against a fender of the Chevie and lit up one of his Ninth Avenue specials. That gave me twelve minutes. I set up my tripod, loaded the Nikon with hi-speed Ektachrome, and used a cable release.

Gilly Fats' cigar was my timing device. We stood there, tired together, and watched the world tilt and the Colossus not budge a millimeter.

Gilly Fats drove, and I fell asleep and dreamed of taking pictures in a world where the playing field was glass, and I had exclusive rights to shoot straight up from underneath and catch all the great plays from a brand new angle.

I didn't even wonder how a poisoned hot dog got on my plate. Or why.

..... V

I woke up in a huge four-poster bed canopied over in rosebuds and ruffles to the clanging noise of the bedside telephone. To make it stop, I picked up the receiver and said hello.

"The Badman's skipped, and I can't locate Gilly Fats," said Barkley.

"I'll find him and tell him," I said.

"Yeah. Tell him Billy O'Leary didn't make the team flight back to Coastville. Never got home at all last night. Have him call me."

"Right," I said.

"And keep taking pictures, T.T."

"Right." He rang off. And thanks for the how-are-you.

According to my Timex, it was 7:22 Monday morning.

The room I was in was a large bedroom with varnished hardwood floors, tall ceilings, a fireplace that looked like it might work, and windows that were really doors covered by gossamer curtains, giving me a gauzy view of the postcard landscape of the east lawn of Snowfield's.

Out on the lawn, under an ancient weeping willow, at a glass-topped table with pink curlycue legs, sat great big Gilly Fats, sipping coffee, blowing smoke rings, and staring at a copy of the *New York Graphic*.

I got dressed.

The Monday *New York Graphic* ran my picture of Lovable Lou LaMont being tackled by Billy Badman O'Leary four columns wide and six inches deep. On the front page. Under the picture in small black type was my credit line: *Graphic* photo by T.T. Baldwin.

Gilly Fats' story ran on page three with my picture of Lovable Lou being carried off the field on the stretcher trailed by Dr. Joe. "Good go," said Gilly Fats.

There were no pictures by Floyd.

I told Gilly Fats what Barkley said and Gilly Fats told me I had twenty minutes to eat whatever I was going to. "We'll hit the hospital together and see Floyd. Then we'll split up. I'll stick with the police, you shake down your own story. Get pictures of the

... 39

suspects, maybe. Poke around the Colossus."

"Why can't we work together?"

Gilly Fats smiled at me, holding smoke in his lungs, looking like a trout that has just swallowed a fly with a hook in it. Then he swooshed out a twelve inch smoke ring.

"Weatherwax says one of us ought to be enough."

Oh.

"And we'll cover more distance this way, T.T. Don't take it personal." Oh sure.

He went away to call Barkley, and I looked at the box of Special K that was sitting there and the overripe banana and the empty bowl, and sighed, and had breakfast. At least the coffee was in a big silver pot.

Hospitals make me jumpy. Floyd was in 213 North, which means somewhere on the second floor in the north wing. I went up ahead of Gilly Fats because Gilly had bought a dozen gooey donuts, stuffed with an assortment of custard creams and fruit jellies and dusted with confectioners' sugar, as a get-well offering. He stopped off at the gift shop to try and buy a bow and the latest *Penthouse* to perk up Floyd's morale.

As hospitals usually do, High Mountain General smelled faintly of chlorox and medicines. Everyone not wearing white and carrying a chart or pushing a trolley looks out of place, and you can't stop your heels from clicking on the linoleum-tiled floor. Unless you wear sneakers. And then you squeak.

At the nurses' desk on the second floor, the corridor runs both right and left. I paused to see which way the numbers ran. Down the left hall I saw David Livingston, looking very much the single-breasted business man, softly closing a door. Or opening it up. He was glancing both ways with his hand on the knob, and I don't know if he saw me or not, but he saw something that spooked him because he zipped away from me toward a red exit sign and shouldered himself through the door without looking my way again.

I switched my camera bag to my left side, the way I do to keep myself from getting lop-shouldered, and headed after him. I pushed the door open, leaned over the railing and looked down the stairwell. He must have been flat-out traveling, because I just caught the final slip-slap as he hit the last two steps of the staircase. I saw one neatly shod foot disappear as the door two flights below me, like a slow film dissolve, swung silently shut.

Of course the door he'd been fiddling with was 213.

I went in and said hello to Floyd. He was looking good. He'd either put some kind of bronzer on his face or they'd kept him under a sun lamp all night. His two tufts of hair were combed jauntily over his ears, and his surly face was kewpie-doll cute with a smile on it. Except for the pint jar of glucose inverted on a stand, and a colorless tube needled into his left arm, he looked like he was on vacation. I told him so.

"Not too tough," I said. "Bet you're gonna live."

"You'd know about tough, wouldn't ya, Baldwin? Bring me any scotch?"

I had. I opened my camera bag and passed him a quart of Thousand Pipers. "Top of the line," I said.

He smiled at the cheap scotch. "I'm smiling," he said.

"How you feel?"

"Don't think I'll ever eat weiners again. Your weiners, anyway." He spun off the top of the scotch bottle and swigged deep.

"Those hot dogs I brought over had nothing on them, Floyd. Just frankfurter and bun. I set them down and then went to get you your double scotches."

Gilly Fats boomed through the door. "Sweets to the sweet," and sailed the donut box across to Floyd. The box landed on Floyd's knees. "Hell-*o*, Beesom-baby."

"A little short. Hits the rim but tips in. Oh no, Gilly, not donuts!"

"Donuts," said Gilly Fats. "Custard cream donuts. Open it up and I'll have one. And the *Graphic* with T.T.'s pix smeared all over. And *Penthouse*. And a few other lusty readables." Gilly Fats dropped the magazines and newspaper on Floyd's shins. "Go on, open it up. There's a new kind. Marshmallow lime."

"Hoo, boy," said Floyd. "And for a man who's just been poisoned."

"Naw," said Gilly Fats. "Yesterday's news. Today, you're 'recovering nicely, thanks very much,' according to Miss Starchskirts at the desk."

"Glad to know it," said Floyd. He lipped at the bottle of scotch, then passed it around. I turned the offer down, but Gilly Fats played he-man and drank some.

"Hide this soldier, pally, if a nurse comes in."

"I'm leaving after lunch."

"Hell you are."

Floyd was cradling the bottle like a baby. "Know what happened, Gilly?"

Gilly Fats sat his bulk down on the foot of the hospital bed and it creaked. He lit a cigar with his cheap throw-away lighter.

"Somebody tried to snuff you, boy. And your film got lost too."

Floyd gave me a nasty smile. "So that's how Baldwin scooped the old man. You play quick-fingers with my film, ace?"

"It never even occurred to me," I said solemnly. "Don't joke about things like that."

"Who's joking," said Floyd.

"Open the donuts," said Gilly Fats.

Floyd tucked the scotch bottle behind his pillows, and punched the pillows up to sit a little higher.

"Feel a little weak in the pins. Other than that, I'm ready for the Boston marathon."

"Who put the condiments on my hot dogs?" I said.

"I've been going over that in my mind," Floyd said. "A lot of people came and went, you know. Gilly and I'll try to piece it together best we can."

Gilly Fats blew a ring within a smoke ring. "Coach Skyhook talked to us first," he said.

"That's right," said Floyd. "He kept babbling about how Black Jack Flowers used to be the glory boy of the L.A. Rams. Backup glory boy, he kept saying."

"Yeah," said Gilly Fats. "Said it wasn't him that didn't have faith in Black Jack. It was Black Jack who didn't have faith. Talked about climbing Everest. How it's tougher in the dead of winter."

I remembered my short conversation with Coach Reesenbach. "Poetic," I said.

"I'm gonna do something with it," said Gilly Fats. "Make a nice think piece. You gonna open that donut box?"

Floyd bumped his knees under the cardboard box, making it rock back and forth. It had a lurid purple bow pasted to its top.

"Nice bow, Gilly," I said.

"Cost me fifty cents. It's self-adhering. Sticks to anything."

"They got everything nowadays," said Floyd. "Hell of a bow."

"I like it," said Gilly Fats. "But don't let it stop you. Open the box."

"Okay, Gilly. I'm opening the box." Floyd used his forefinger to break the scotch tape. He swung open the top. Inside all the

plump, white-faced donuts quivered at him. Floyd made a face. He passed the box around.
"Don't mind if I do," said Gilly Fats.
I said no thanks.
Floyd said he'd suck on a little scotch instead. He found his scotch bottle under his pillows and Gilly Fats enjoyed his donut. I wanted to bring the conversation back to the hot dogs and who could have fooled around with them. But I didn't want to get Floyd upset or testy, which is very easy to do. I let him get a little more scotch in him.
I watched them, taking pictures in my mind. Floyd softly blowing, like kisses, into the top of the scotch bottle, then lifting it to take a gentle sip, patting its bottom like a best girl. And Gilly Fats, who looks like Ken Norton's sparring partner, devouring a coconut custard donut with the sensual pleasure Henry VIII must have once taken in Anne Boleyn. In his left hand, like a grenade waiting to go bang, the cigar leaked a line of smoke.
"Got your pad, Gilly?" I finally said.
Gilly Fats was licking his fingers. He nodded and patted his breast pocket.
"Let's get a sequence of who approached the table when."
Floyd leaned his head back against the pillows, tucking the scotch bottle somewhere between his hospital gown and the summer sheet.
"Okay, ace," he said. "Before you brought over the hot dogs, we were standing around the table, you know, talking to people as they walked by. I been thinking this over ever since I woke up this morning. I remember a funny smell. Before Baldwin even got near us with the hot dogs. Remember I mentioned it, Gilly?"
Gilly Fats blew a perfect figure eight, which is hard to do. "Yeah," he said, "yeah. Now let's see. I think I'd just cracked a beer. And you said, what the hell's that, or something, right? And I said what, 'cause I didn't smell anything. And you said smells like somebody's spraying for roaches."
Floyd nodded vigorously. "Right, Gilly. That was it. Only lasted a moment or two. Thought it was your beer, maybe."
"Yeah. We smelled the beer. Just smelled like beer."
Floyd shook his head. "Yeah. Then the smell was gone."
"Well, who was around your table then?" I prodded.
"That's what I'm not too sure on. . . . Walt-the-Talk was pushing the crippled kid. They were close by."

Gilly Fats stubbed his cigar out in the bed pan. "The kid wanted our autographs."

The little darling.

"But that was just before, I think, Floyd. I know I didn't open the beer until after I signed the kid's program." Gilly Fats flashed me a smile. "Right under your signature, T.T."

"Fame," I said, and shrugged.

Floyd shrugged too. "Then the redheaded cutie brought plates around. I asked her out and she turned me down. Told her I'd make her a star."

"Well, hell," said Gilly Fats. "I'd have turned you down too, Floyd. You were leering like Dracula."

"Yeah, well," said Floyd.

"Then Billy O'Leary came over for a minute," continued Gilly Fats. "Boy, was he scared! Said he'd tried to talk to the police and they wouldn't talk to him. Said they'd be in touch. Must have scared him to death. He never made the team flight. Ain't got home yet."

"Oh boy. The poor bastard," said Floyd.

"Yeah, nice boy too. He's gonna be a good tackle if this thing don't mess him. I told him I'd do a column on him, how this tragedy's affecting him. He was real grateful. Thought he'd never let loose of my hand."

"Anybody with hot dogs at this point?" I persisted.

"Walt-the-Talk ate peanuts," said Floyd. "That Lil Harv kid was jumping around in his chair, seemed very excited. The win and all, I guess. He did come over later with his lap full of dogs. But I'm trying to keep everything in sequence."

"Yeah, let's keep it in sequence," said Gilly Fats. He was writing it down. I've inserted Gilly's list at the end of this chapter.

Floyd put his hands behind his head and stared up at the ceiling. "That's it, I think. Working back from the smell: Walt-the-Talk and the crippled kid. Then the redhead. Then The Badman."

Gilly Fats joined in. "Then T.T. came over with the hot dogs—no, wait, Floyd, I had a hot dog at this point."

"Yeah, that gorgeous creature with the black hair. That Rachel. She gave you half hers."

"Yeah, and Marilyn Monroe gave you half hers."

"All of hers," leered Floyd.

"Well, you only ate half and then gave it back, right?"

"Right," said Floyd.

44 . . .

"And then T.T. brought over two plain, bare frankfurters in buns. Put them down on her plate, which was to the right of me, and proceeded to the bar to get a drink for herself and you."

"Correct," said Floyd.

"Let's get this straight," I said. "Between the time Rachel Hirshaw and Amy Bland ate hot dogs with you guys and the time I came over, nobody was around your table?"

They both thought about it.

"Dr. Joe?" said Gilly Fats.

"Dr. Joe," said Floyd. "That's right, Gilly. He did come over. Didn't talk to me, though. Just talked to you."

"Yeah," said Gilly Fats. And he had a hot dog. Almost doctored it up there at our table. Kept fussing with the spoons in the condiment jars, but didn't use any. Was checking on you, T.T. Wanted to know if you were *bona fide*." Gilly Fats laughed his low laugh. "I told him you were good as gold."

"What'd he say to that?"

"Said Lou LaMont was murdered. No doubt about it. Asked me if I'd attended the acupuncture lecture they had earlier in the week. I said I had, sure. Hadn't paid too much attention, though. First night I was here, Tuesday. You all didn't come in 'til Wednesday. I sat in on it, took Lou LaMont out after for a coupla beers. Got an interview. Likeable fellow. Very anxious to justify expectations."

"Lecture?" I whispered.

"Yeah. Mrs. Snowfield called in some medical expert. A Dr. Zu. Z-U. Chinese guy. Acupuncture. Gave a pep talk on acupuncture to the players. Almost everybody from the Colossus showed up. The cheerleaders. Mrs. Snowfield. You know, it was kind of a social thing, and kinda educational. I tuned out for most of it. Relieving pain. Psychosomatics. That kind of thing."

"And Dr. Joe asked you about it, Gilly?"

"Yeah. Wanted to know if I'd heard the lecture. Why, T.T.?"

"Because Dr. Joe told me and the cops that's how Lou LaMont died. A needle in his brain. An *acupuncture* needle."

Gilly Fats shifted his position on the bed. "Yeah, I heard. Maybe that's what he was trying to explain to me. Tell the truth, I didn't follow him too well. He was acting crackers. Mumbling in his beard. Said he wanted to talk to me after, and I said okay, sure. He said to keep it under my hat. Something about him missing needles out of his office, I think. Then he sort of drifted away. Still muttering. And because of ole Floydie here, I plumb forgot all about the doc, and he probably forgot all about me."

"Then I came over?" I said.

Gilly Fats nodded. "Then you came over, dropped your dogs, and went to the bar."

Floyd said, "And that's when Skyhook came by."

"And Floyd stole one of your hot dogs, T.T."

Floyd punched the air. "Nope, not then, Gilly. Later. Skyhook put stuff on his hot dog from our table. Didn't he?"

"I don't think so, Floyd. No, wait, I think *I* dressed up his weiner. Lemme think—I know I started to. He asked me—now let's see. He said something like 'put some mustard and kraut on this, willya.' Not exactly like an order, but not real polite either. He was standing, see, and blabbing about Black Jack Flowers' lack of faith in himself. He was blocking David and Babs Livingston. They were sitting behind us. And then Livingston said something like 'Hey, sportswriter, guess who's beneficiary on LaMont's insurance policy?' So I turned around and said who. And Livingston smirks like he's got the answer to the universe and says 'You know, doncha, Babsie?' and his wife nods, looking embarrassed, and then Livingston puts his elbow on the table, gives a limp wrist, and says 'You're holdin' the hot dog's hot dog.' And then ole Skyhook grabs his weiner out of my hands, gives Livingston the dirty gesture with it, tells Livingston he's going to lose his job for what he just said and stalks off."

"Holy smokes, Gilly! How'd I miss that?" said Floyd.

Gilly Fats shrugged his shoulders and took another donut. "Don't mind if I do."

Floyd was screwing up his eyes, thinking back. "Ha!" he yelped, bouncing in the bed and almost upsetting the donut box.

"I remember. That cute one with the bows in her hair, Patty. I was watching her arguing with the crippled kid. I thought she was going to hit him. They were over toward the rear, back where the kitchen is. She was leaning over the wheelchair barking at Lil Harv, and he was shaking his head no and trying to talk but she wouldn't give him a chance."

He grinned sheepishly. "I was lookin' at her panties. They were brown with rows and rows of little white ruffles up 'em. Gussie Moran's."

"You're all class, Floyd," I said.
"Bet on it, ace."
"Well, did you overhear anything?" I asked.
"Nope. They were too far away. But Patty kept pointing at a gym bag the kid had in the chair's side rack. Some chariot. That chair's got everything but air conditioning. Well, anyway, she pulls it out and opens it up, and starts riffling through it. And the kid just sits looking bug-eyed, you know. And she's yelling at him all the while. I don't think she found what she was looking for because then she stuffed it all back, and she's still motor-mouth, mile a minute. And the kid not saying a word."

"And all this happened while I was in the bar getting drinks. Wow."

"Can't catch it all, scoop," said Floyd with satisfaction.

"Yeah," I said.

"Chocolate," said Gilly Fats, his cheeks bursting with donut.

I looked at both of them. "Floyd's a slosher, and you're a sugar-freak."

"Yeah, and you're a clean liver," Gilly Fats said with his mouth full.

"I have to be," I said. "It's the only chance I've got."

Gilly Fats pulled a lock of my hair. "You've got a good chance, T.T."

"Okay," I said, embarrassed, "so what happened then? After Skyhook huffed off."

Both men settled back to thinking again.

"Then I ate one of your hot dogs," said Floyd. "And they were both dressed up to the nines by then. Mustard, sauerkraut, cooked onions. All the slop on it. I thought it tasted fine."

"And I talked with David Livingston and Babs," continued Gilly Fats. "They had a stack of hot dogs on a plate, and I ate one of theirs. Livingston is the Climbers' whole public relations department, you know. So he knows the background on Lou LaMont. Knows about the insurance policy. One million dollars, he said. Sole beneficiary: Coach Clifford Reesenbach, known as The Skyhook. For services rendered."

I shivered. "No parents?"

"Dead now," said Gilly Fats. "His mother died last year. Cancer. His father died five years ago. Bad ticker. Was a prison guard. State prison in Pennsylvania. Altoona, Livingston said. And Lou was an only child. Maybe he didn't like his relatives. Anyway, when it came time to sign the insurance papers, he wrote down Skyhook."

"So go on," I said.

"So then," said Floyd, "Lil Harv came by. Rolled up by himself. Talked about the game. He had a lap full of hot dogs but I'd already eaten one of yours by then. I asked him what Patty was yelling at him about, and he said she thought he had taken something he hadn't."

"And then you turned up with the drinks," said Gilly Fats.

"That's right. Lil Harv rolled off toward a back booth. Stanley Farmer was over there. Helped the kid into the booth, and pushed the wheelchair back against the wall. I watched that, and then you came back with my sauce."

"So either the hotdog or dogs were switched by then, or had been doctored at the table."

"Looks like it," said Gilly Fats.

"Yeah," said Floyd. "You said you didn't want the second dog, Baldwin, so I ate it. Only got half of it down before I got sick."

"Too fast," I said. "Maybe only the first frankfurter had been tampered with."

"Mebbe," said Floyd, looking weary now.

Gilly Fats patted Floyd's ankle under the hospital sheet. "Baby's tuckered," he said.

"Before you get some more beauty sleep, Floyd, I've got another question," I said.

"Shoot, scoop," Floyd said, leaning back, and closing his eyes.

"Did you have any visitors this morning before us?"

"Yeah. Doc Joe came by with the two dicks."

"David Livingston didn't drop in?"

"The fruit?" Floyd snorted. "What the hell would he drop by for?"

"That's what I'd like to know," I said.

Floyd was asleep before Gilly Fats and I left the room. I guess he forgot again to congratulate me on my front-page scooper.

Gilly's List:

  1. Walt-the-Talk nibbling peanuts. Peanuts in line with other condiments around beer tub.

2. Pushing Lil Harv who got autographs.
THE SMELL
3. Wanda, the redhead, put down plates.
4. Rachel with the black hair gave me half her hot dog in company with
5. Amy (Marilyn Monroe) who shared her weiner with Floyd.
6. Dr. Joe with hot dog fussed with condiment spoons.
    T.T. puts two hot dogs on plate 3:
        Plate 1—Floyd
        Plate 2—Gilly
        Plate 3—T.T.
7. Skyhook with hot dog asked me to dress it. Left in a hurry.
8. David and Babs Livingston sat behind us with a stack of dogs.
9. Lil Harv again, two hot dogs with everything.

.....VI

Going down in the elevator, I asked Gilly Fats if he thought the poisoned hot dog had been meant for me instead of Floyd.

He paused before he answered, and then he said very carefully, "I don't know, T.T., and until we do know, it wouldn't hurt to keep your left up, and not let the other guy box you inside."

"Do the Ali shuffle if I have to?"

"Yes, ma'am," he said, and we left it at that.

I drove Gilly Fats across the highway to the High Mountain Police house.

"Pretty little place," said Gilly Fats, getting out.

"No place like home," I said.

"Speaking of home, I'll catch up with you back at Snowfields."

"Good hunting," I said.

"You too."

I pulled away and in the rear view mirror watched him bang on the bright red door with the black hinges and go inside.

I nosed the Chevie out into the traffic heading back toward town. I figured I'd drop in on Wanda Pettigo and see what she could tell me about that satin heart-shaped pillow with its rhinestone message. For some reason, I was dreading it.

Tooling down the highway, I looked over the upper-middle-class town. Instead of the usual fast-food franchises and gas stations and the motels with their suggestive winking signs and the hard-sell billboards, High Mountain Highway was shaded with old elms like a boulevard.

It cut through what seemed a perpetual shopping mall. The shops and large stores were set back behind parking lots, and the parking lots were softened with trees and flower beds set at random to break up the monotony of white-lined concrete.

I think it was the Climbers' colors that first caught my eye, but I'm not sure. I shoot mostly black and white for the newspaper, but once the eye starts translating color into composition and light values, it always shoots the color. You have to, to get your exposure right. And in sports, colors and patterns are used all the time for identification. The race announcer identifies the horse by the jockey silks, for instance.

So maybe what I saw first was the chocolate brown Cadillac with the light brown top, and the hood emblazoned in mocha paint with a mug shot of Overcoat, the mountain goat. But before I pulled past it to notice the hood, and then turned off the highway to park beside it, I noticed the signboard scripted in neat Caladonia Italic:

> *High Mountain Monument and Marble Company*
> *Personalized Memorials*
> *All Stones Hand Cut and Lettered*
> *"He Maketh Me To Lie Down In Green Pastures"*

I took the time to check over my cameras, make sure I was loaded and that I liked the lens' lengths, and then got out of the Chevie and went to find out who was such a fast worker that he was ordering a tombstone before the funeral service.

They were walking among the rows of sample stones like lovers, holding hands and with their heads together. I took the picture from behind, and they never even knew I was there.

That was the second compromising picture I had on this roll of film. The first one was the candid grab shot of Mrs. Caroline Potter in action with Walt-the-Talk Ames. Good enough to give her husband a divorce and custody of the kid in all fifty states. The second was this one. I didn't know yet what it might be good for.

She was wearing a hat with a veil. He was wearing Sulka.

"Morning, Mrs. Snowfield. Hiya, Abe."

Abe Hirshaw must have learned his manners after he had grown up, because right then he forgot them. He just stared at me, dropped Mrs. Snowfield's hand, and smoothed the lapels of his suit jacket over and over.

Mrs. Marcella Snowfield lost maybe half a beat, but that was all. "You're Miss Baldwin, aren't you?" she said. "One of my press guests. You *do* stay on the job, don't you? Did you sleep well?"

"Like a log," I said. "I noticed the Climbers' car from the highway."

"I see," she said, with no expression in it.

"Depressing business, all this, Miss Baldwin," said Abe Hirshaw.

I nodded. "I just came from the hospital."

. . . 51

Mrs. Snowfield appeared interested. "And how is he?"

"Much better now, thanks."

"Do you think it was intoxication? It was so confusing last night."

"Dr. Joe says poison," I said. "Lieutenant Weatherwax seemed to think so too."

"I certainly hope they're wrong. Of course, somebody might be out to destroy me."

"Destroy you, Mrs. Snowfield?" I said.

"Me. Or my team. What else?" she said.

"Now, Marcella," cooed Abe Hirshaw. He had a groomed head of salt-and-pepper hair, and he took both his hands and smoothed them over his new dry look. He must have got hair spray on his palms, because he immediately went to a trouser pocket for a handkerchief and wiped his hands.

"Well why else, Abe, would someone want to injure Lou LaMont? Kill him? Immobilize my team, that's all."

Maybe she believed it.

"You're picking out a tombstone now?" I asked.

Abe Hirshaw dropped his eyelids to half-mast and stiffened his spine. "Obviously," he intoned.

"This is where we came to pick out our last home. Mine and Lemuel's. My late husband, Miss Baldwin." She sighed. "Being here brings it all back so vividly."

"My dear," murmured Abe Hirshaw, taking Mrs. Snowfield's left hand, and holding it between both of his. "Shall we get on with it?"

He turned me a shoulder, his nose, and his hooded eyes. "Sooner done, sooner forgotten. Would you excuse us, Miss Baldwin?"

I took a step back and had a sudden thought. I bet he hates it when I call him Abe.

"Let's take a look at that Italian striate-rose again, Marcie." They turned their backs to me and crunched down the gravel path. Abe Hirshaw was holding her elbow with one hand as though it were rare lapis lazuli, and picking lint off his shoulder with the other.

They didn't look back. I heard her say to him, "Abe, do you think that girl followed us? Do you think we're being precipitate?"

"No, my dear, to both your questions."

I followed slowly along behind them on tiptoe, trying to match my steps to theirs.

"Do you think she could possibly know about me?"

"She knows you're a handsome widow, very rich, who's bought herself an expensive toy to keep from being bored to death."

That about pegged it.

I'd gone as far as I could. The path sloped to the right and curved back. I stood there and watched them pick their way around the granite and the marble and the sandstone. I lost them among the mausoleums.

Wanda Pettigo and Patty Cambron roomed together in an apartment on the corner of Precipice and Clearview Drive. They lived on the second floor of a brick four-story house with eight apartments. By using a street map, I found it easily. It was just after 11:00 when I got there.

I rang the bell of 2-B for a long time before anyone answered. "I'm asleep," Wanda's voice came through the speaker. "Who is it?"

"T.T. Baldwin. *New York Graphic.*"

"Go away," she said.

"No," I said. "I want to know about the pillow."

"What pillow?" she said. Then silence. "He didn't throw that away a long time ago?" Her voice sounded wistful coming through the electronic mouthpiece.

" 'Fraid not," I said. "He kept it next to his Aqua Velva."

"He never used Aqua Velva," she said.

"Habit Rouge then."

"That either," she said, sounding safer now. "You're lying."

"No, I'm not," I said. "Cork tops."

She seemed perfectly content to converse this way, talking to each other through the speaker. "What about the pillow?"

"Let me in," I said.

"Why should I?" she said.

"If you tell me, maybe you won't have to tell the police."

"Oh, I'll have to tell the cops all right. I know that."

"Look, I'm here to help you. I'm not your enemy," I said.

"I'll bet you're a pest, though." And she laughed at that.

"Let me in," I said.

"Oh, gee whiz." She buzzed the door open. It wasn't a piece of cake, but I've had harder times getting in to see somebody.

She was waiting for me at her door, ballet-thin, with her auburn hair tumbling in natural waves down to the middle of her back. She was wearing a multicolored silk wrap. Her only makeup seemed to be the heavy coating of mascara on her eyelashes. Her eyes were a very dark brown with a yellow light somewhere deep inside. Maybe Maureen O'Hara had been this beautiful when she was in her twenties.

"I do need a friend," she greeted me.

I gave her a wide smile. "I bet you have lots of friends," I said.

"You'd be surprised," she said. "Come on in."

The apartment looked like a college girls' dormitory room. High Mountain Climber pennants hung on the wall. Cheerleader pom-poms were piled up in a corner like strange flowers, the furniture was cheap but functional, and clothes lay draped about waiting to be put away. It was a casual, cheerful place.

I sat down on a black beanbag chair. "Is Patty here?"

"Patty didn't come home last night," she said, tossing her hair. "I've got to have some coffee first. Want some?"

"Sure."

She went into the kitchen, and I waited for her. While I waited I wondered why Patty didn't come home. Was she afraid of Wanda? She hadn't seemed to be.

There was no door to the kitchen. I could see Wanda making the Maxwell House Instant. I called in to her. "Know where she went?"

"Milk? Sugar?" she said.

"Just milk," I said. "Do you know where Patty went? Where she is?"

She didn't answer. She came back with the two cups of coffee and sat down opposite me.

"I do need a friend," she said again.

I took a tentative sip of the coffee and the idea of poison popped into my mind. I started to sip again, but instead just smelled. It smelled like coffee.

She noticed. She seemed happy about it. "You see? You see? It's got you too. You were thinking I might be poisoning you, weren't you?"

I was embarrassed. I looked at her with a foolish smile on my face. I gave a deep sigh and nodded.

"Want to switch cups?" she said sarcastically. Her coffee had milk in it too.

"No," I said, "I'm sorry. I fantasize too much sometimes."

She seemed much friendlier now that she had scored a point off me. "I feel the same way," she said. "You might have come over here to murder me."

We both purposefully drank our coffee.

"Someone tried to poison my partner last night," I said. "Only maybe the poison was meant for me. It was on a hot dog that I'd put on my plate, and Floyd ate it instead."

"Which hot dog?" she said. "The one I gave you, or the one Patty did?"

I hadn't thought of that. Immediately I remembered the two frankfurters. The one with its bun in tatters, the other with a bun not even warmed in the steamer yet.

"I don't know," I said, surprised. "But maybe we can find out. Floyd only ate half the second one. Dr. Joe must have taken what was left and analyzed it. If only the first one was tampered with, I could tell which one, I think."

"And what if it was mine?" she said. "Would you trust me then?"

I thought about it. "You'd be right where you are now. In the maybe pile. Sure, I'd trust you. I don't think the poison had anything to do with the hot dog. It was in the spices. The mustard, maybe, or the cooked onions. Something with odor to it that drowned out the smell. But I couldn't count you out."

"I know," she said, nodding her head slowly, her voice wistful. "That's why I need a friend. I'm the one who's most suspicious. I'm the one who wanted Lou dead."

"He was your boyfriend," I said. "Wasn't he?"

"*Was* is right," she said, tears starting to form in her eyes. To stop them, she flung her head back and firmed up her chin. Her Irish setter hair floated around her shoulders like the fairy tale tresses of Rapunzel.

"You've got a great face," I said.

"Best face since Vivian Leigh," she said unselfconsciously. And then, with a pout, "A lot of good it's doing me."

"I found the pillow in Lou's locker," I said.

"I'll tell you," she said. "I need to tell somebody. Just give me a minute. I don't know where Patty's gone. I'm afraid."

I got the prickles and the dancy feeling down my back.

"You're worried about Patty."

Wanda scrutinized the pink pearl polish on her naked toes. On the coffee table was a bottle of nail polish, and she set her coffee

. . . 55

cup down on the floor and picked up the nail polish and began to shake it. The little ball inside that emulsifies the color clicked like a mexican jumping bean.

"Patty never stays out all night," she said.

She twisted off the top and began very deliberately painting a fresh coat of polish onto her big toe.

Bent over, her hair spilling down and touching the floor, she said, "I had the baby out five days ago." I couldn't see her eyes.

I didn't say anything. She went on stroking the little brush, dipping it into the bottle, carefully drawing it out again, removing the excess, and then stroking on the polish, coat after coat, toe after toe.

"He wouldn't marry me. Not even when I got pregnant. I thought he would, you see." She went on painting her toes. A tear splashed down on her thumb, and she brushed it away on her ankle.

"I'm sorry," I said.

She straightened up, twirled the cap on the nail polish and blew her nose on a Kleenex. "That's why he should have thrown away that pillow," she said.

"Yes," I said. "But he didn't."

"Wanted to brag, the dumb jock. Show it off to his buddies."

"No," I said. "He probably wanted to keep it."

"I know why he wouldn't marry me." Her voice was flat. "I'm so gorgeous, I thought for sure I'd win. But being beautiful wasn't enough for Lovable old Lou. He wanted money more. He wanted Mrs. Snowfield." She was looking straight at me, her eyes misty with tears she was trying to hold back.

"Mrs. Snowfield?" I gulped. Hoo, boy.

"Yeah. Mrs. Fifty Million Dollar Snowfield."

"She's old enough to be his grandmother," I said.

"So what? Maybe he figured he'd outlive her."

Odds wouldn't be long on that bet, I thought.

Wanda looked at me contemptuously. "Why else does a twenty-two year old weightlifter marry a sixty-three year old super-rich widow? Don't be dumb."

"Marry?" I gave a weak little laugh. "But she wouldn't care about him."

"Oh no? The hell she didn't. He was all night at her place more than he was at mine. Everybody knows about it."

"Even Abe Hirshaw?" I asked.

Wanda laughed a knowing little giggle. "Especially Abe. He's very smart. I'm sure he kept Mrs. S. up to date on Lou's motives."

"Well, then," I said.

"Well then what? Maybe Mrs. S. didn't care what Lou's motives were. Maybe she only cared about what she was getting. She was awfully infatuated. Maybe she didn't mind paying for the pleasure of his company. Maybe she didn't mind letting him have her money when she died. She doesn't have any children of her own. Wouldn't be the first time a rich lady married a poor boy."

No, I thought, it wouldn't. And he already had a million dollar contract from the Climbers. Spread over ten years, of course.

"Do you think he was in love with you?"

Wanda smirked. "Lou loved Lovable Lou. He liked me, liked me a lot. I found out he didn't like me enough." Her eyes started to mist over again. "I forced his hand. I let myself get pregnant. I really thought I'd win." She giggled a nasty little giggle. "I even went to Mrs. Snowfield for advice. What a hoot that was. She told me to follow my conscience, and wished Lou and me the best of luck. She was very ladylike about it. You'd never have known she was sleeping with him too."

"I don't see how he had time to practice football," I said.

"Oh, Lou had a lot of energy," she said offhandedly.

I drank the last of my coffee. "So you did have a motive," I said. "Revenge."

"Rejection," she said. "I've never been rejected before. I couldn't believe he'd turn me down. I'd have been such a credit to him. He couldn't have found anyone prettier. And we liked each other, we really did. And I'd have been true to him. It would've been great."

"Just like in the movies?" I said.

"Yeah," she said. "Like that."

"Well," I said, "did you murder him?"

She smiled at me maliciously. "If I did, I couldn't tell, could I? Maybe I'd get away with it." Then she stopped smiling. "Maybe I did kill him in a way. I killed our baby. I wanted him dead. On the operating table, while they were taking the baby out, I was wishing him dead. Every second. Maybe I put a curse on him." She was crying freely now, but she still looked like a *Town & Country* cover.

"Who performed the operation?"

"That's none of your business. It's legal now, you know. And it doesn't matter, anyway."

. . . 57

"It might," I said.

"Believe me, it doesn't."

"Dr. Joe," I said.

She changed the subject. "I wonder where Patty is," she said, blowing her nose again, and dabbing at her eyes. "Now Patty's missing. I hope she's all right. We've got cheerleader practice tonight at six. Where could she be?"

I was wondering about Patty too. "The last time I saw her was at the hot dog wagon," I said.

"Me, too," she said. "She said she had to go do something, and she'd see me later back here." She shrugged her shoulders. "I don't know where she went. After the photographer got sick, I left. Amy and Rachel said they'd clean up. I went home with David and Babs. I mean they dropped me off."

"She'll turn up," I said.

"Yeah," she said.

"Let me take your picture crying like this," I said, as though I'd just thought of it. "It'll be good for you. Give you public sympathy."

She wasn't dismayed at the idea. "Lou said I was beautiful even when I cried," she said. She dipped a long white hand into a soft pouch that sat on the floor by her chair. She looked into the little mirror she pulled out of it. "It's a lot better face than Rita Hayworth ever had," she said.

"It's a fantastic face," I agreed.

I took about fifteen pictures of her. She liked to be photographed. She could relax in front of the camera's eye, and she had that instinctive model's way of looking straight into the lens with affection on her face. She turned her face from side to side, as I asked her to, and moved her hair around.

"I take great pictures," she said. "You can't find a bad angle."

"You really are a knock-out," I said.

"I know," she said. "And take it from me, money counts for more than looks."

"Aw, I don't know," I said. "If he'd hung around, you'd have got him in the end."

Her eyes sparkled at that, and I snapped the shutter. "Yeah," she said. "Maybe I would of at that."

I packed my gear, getting ready to leave. "By the way," I said, "did you attend that lecture Tuesday night? That Dr. Zu?"

"What of it?" she said suspiciously.

"I don't know," I said. "But he was supposedly talking about acupuncture. And that's how Lou LaMont was killed. An acupuncture needle in his brain."

She sat down with a thump on a two-seater sofa. "Oh, no," she said.

"Didn't you know?"

She shook her head. "No. Nobody told me anything except Lou was dead. Murdered, according to Dr. Joe. I guess it's in the papers today. I haven't been out yet to pick one up. Dr. Harley Yong Zu his name is. He's from Hong Kong. He's going around the United States on some tour, explaining what acupuncture is and what it isn't. He's one of the top specialists in China. So that's what killed Louie?"

"What Dr. Joe says."

"The fatal positions, Dr. Zu called them. I think there's five of them. We all joked about it after." She got that wistful note into her voice again. "Even that night. We were supposed to go out, Lou and I. But Lou said we couldn't because Mrs. S. was there, and he didn't want her to see him leave with me. That was poppycock. The next day I was scheduled for my operation, and he didn't want to talk about it any more. He wanted to go out with a reporter and get his name in the newspaper again. A real publicity hound, Lou was. I told him then I was going to push a needle in his brain. You know, just for fun. We'd just heard about it. The fatal positions. . . ." Her voice trailed away.

"Anybody hear you?"

"I don't know." Her voice was very small. She got up and went over to the fireplace and stared into the mirror that hung there.

"I've got to go now," I said. "Thanks very much. I'll try to help you any way I can."

She lifted a lipstick that was sitting on the mantle and started putting color on her cheeks with it, staring at how the light hit her cheekbones and where the shadows fell.

"I'm in big trouble," she said to her reflection and went on looking at herself, tipping her chin, stroking an eyebrow with a long milk-white finger. She'd forgotten me.

I left her there, talking to herself, staring at herself in the mirror over the fireplace.

If she's a murderer, I thought, we're all in trouble. Just try and bring in a conviction against a face like that.

. . . 59

..... VII

It was coming up to 1 P.M. now, and I was hungry and I had to get my film mailed off to the *Graphic*. I drove over to High Mountain's main street and parked the Chevie by the post office, and then walked down about a block and a half to a coffee shop I'd noticed called Maggie's-at-Mid-Day.

Inside I took a booth toward the rear by the window overlooking the street. The waitress, a long-legged, fresh-faced girl with a yellow uniform short enough to be a tennis dress, frowned at me as she approached with a menu. I understood. I was one in a space for four at prime time.

I took two dollars out of my jacket pocket and pinned them under the salt shaker. "Now you won't be short-changed," I said to her. She still looked like she didn't trust me, but she smiled as she brought me a glass of water.

I ordered baked eggs and spinach and lots of coffee, and got a mailing envelope out of my camera bag. I filed a short report identifying the pictures of Mrs. Snowfield and Abe Hirshaw and included a warning to Barkley that the pornographic action shot would not be identified or explained until I spoke to him in person. Then I idly watched the street until my eggs florentine came round.

I noticed Lil Harv's father, Potter Sr, go by in a wrinkled black trench coat hanging unconcernedly open over some loose brown trousers and a white ski sweater. He went into a hardware store almost directly opposite Maggie's and came out a few minutes later holding a brown bag with something in it that sagged. Probably a can of Min-Wax or a box of nails. He held the bag by the top in his fist, letting the weight droop instead of holding it from underneath. Passers-by seemed to recognize him, and they smiled or lifted a hand, but none stopped to talk with him, and he didn't seem to respond to anyone's greeting. He walked like a man weighed down by some invisible burden that hurt, and the townspeople seemed to know what it was and to respect it. I wondered which sadness hurt him more, his crippled son or his profligate wife.

He was almost out of my line of vision when he paused beside a woman's dress boutique. Two girls were standing there, staring intently at the shopwindow, both wearing dark blazers. The blonde one swung a black attaché case from her right hand, bumping it against her legs as though it were an unfamiliar accessory she didn't quite know how to handle. I knew who they were: Rachel Hirshaw and Amy Bland, the odd couple.

It was Amy who stopped him. She impulsively reached out and caught hold of his arm as he was going by. He said a word or two and then walked on, his head bent, the brown bag looking about to burst its bottom swaying below his hand.

Rachel leaned close to Amy and whispered something to her, and Amy looked up and down the street, nodded vigorously, and set the attaché case down behind her. Then both girls turned their backs and stared with apparent concentration at a very ordinary paisley shirtwaist.

My eggs came just as I spied David Livingston coming from the direction Potter Sr. had gone. He was walking unnaturally slowly, and he had on the same business suit he'd been wearing this morning when he ran away from me at the hospital. Over his left arm draped a tweed topcoat, too heavy for the weather, and he was holding a black attaché case firmly in his left hand.

Maybe it wouldn't have seemed so obvious if I hadn't seen Amy deliberately set her attaché case out on the sidewalk and turn her back to it; but even so, it wasn't top-drawer espionage. I let my lunch get cold watching Livingston approach, act surprised at catching sight of Amy and Rachel, and set down his attaché case and switch his top coat to the other arm.

The three of them closed in a huddle with Amy's attaché case inside. The one David had brought sat beside the shop window. They buzzed to each other with seemingly friendly chatter. I kept my eye on Amy's case and almost laughed out loud when I saw David reach down to take it, awkwardly, with the same hand that was holding his topcoat. Then, with a lot of bad acting at spontaneous see-you-soons and waving, the huddle broke apart. David Livingston walked on, closer and closer to me staring out the wide window across the street, and then farther and farther out of sight. All the way he had a wide smirk on his face.

I considered leaving my lunch and following him, but I didn't. I wanted to get my film into the post office before two o'clock because I knew the mail plane left High Mountain at three, and I didn't think I'd find out what he was carrying by following him on the sneak.

I ate at my eggs and spinach, still keeping an eye on Amy and Rachel. They were heading my way too, natural now, easy and loose. Amy was being silly, and Rachel, in her own composed way, was laughing along with her.

They crossed the street arm-in-arm and headed toward the revolving door of Maggie's. The coffee shop had been gradually filling up. It wasn't full, but close to it. I bent my head over the creamed spinach. I was in a back booth, and hoped they'd take the first open spot they saw instead of scanning the restaurant for the best table.

They sat down in a booth close to the front. I'd eaten as much as I wanted, but I smoked a cigarette and had another cup of coffee to give them time to get their orders in and to make it inconvenient for them to decide to up and walk out.

My tab came close to four dollars, and the waitress told me I was supposed to pay the cashier on my way out. I gave her a five dollar bill and told her to pay the check for me and keep the change. She looked more suspicious than ever, probably afraid I was going to take back the first two dollars. If it'd been Floyd or Gilly Fats saying take-care-of-this-for-me, she'd have just thought what a generous fellow he was. Me, she thought I was up to no-good. Which was, in a way, on target.

Floyd once told me, in a moment of *camaraderie* caused by his imbibing more scotch than any man ought to on an empty stomach, that what made a good news photog was not the ability to take great photographs, but the knack of coming back with an appropriate picture for the story, however ordinary. "And it's a hell of a lot harder than what Scavullo does, ace. It puts hair on your chest." I told him that was just what I needed, and he'd laughed evilly and said even hair on my chest wouldn't make me a good newsman. And what I ought to do was to get married and take pictures of the kiddies growing up if playing with cameras was what turned me on.

I smiled to myself wondering why I'd thought of that as I read the light with my light meter and reloaded my favorite camera, my oldest one, the one with the leather-tooled strap.

Someday I'd pass along my own rules. The lesson for today was: if you want to talk with people who might not want to talk to you, take a picture first and they'll ask questions later.

I draped my camera bag over my left shoulder and hung the Nikon over my right. I approximated the focal distance at about fifteen feet, not because I cared about the picture I was going to take, but just because I keep the discipline. And I don't like the man who develops my film to ever catch me out-of-focus or not properly exposed. Of course it happens, but you try to keep such things to a minimum.

I got out of the booth, swung wide past the table to the far aisle, and was in position, focused and shooting the film before Rachel recognized me and poked at Amy to look too. She did, and I got them both, back-lit and full-face, looking half-huffy, half-amused over their tuna salad plates at Maggie's-at-Mid-Day.

Then I went over and dropped casually into the booth beside Amy, almost sitting on the attaché case. Amy gave a little squeal and passed the case over the table to Rachel who laid it down beside her on the seat.

"Hiya," I said, with more exuberance than I normally show. Anything for a bead on a story.

"Why'd ya take our picture for?" asked Amy with tuna on her chin.

"That's my assignment today," I said. "Suspects."

"Suspects!" yipped Amy, and Rachel kicked at her under the table. A few of the other diners were looking at us, but they weren't really interested.

"Well, you are involved," I said, and then lifted my foot and nudged the attaché case with my toe. "Going into business?"

Rachel snatched up the case and leaned it against the back of the booth, out of my reach.

"How did you know?" asked Amy, talking in her breathy Marilyn Monroe voice.

"Oh, Amy, hush!" said Rachel.

"What's the matter," I said. "Is it a secret?"

"It was," said Rachel in a tone as dry as stale toast.

"What kind of business?" I said.

"We're not ready to tell yet," said Amy.

"That's right," said Rachel, chasing the ice in her Coke with a straw.

"Why? Is it illegal?"

"No." Rachel looked down at her half-eaten tuna plate and pushed it aside. "No, but it's very risky. We don't mean to be rude, but we're very sensitive about it just now."

"It's at a crucial stage," said Amy. Rachel kicked her again.

"Ouch, Ratch. I'm not saying anything I shouldn't. If you run my nylons you'll owe me a pair."

"Let me do the talking, please," said Rachel, just like Terrible Two-Ton Tinnemar.

"Rachel *always* has to do the talking," smirked Amy like a child who'd been corrected for being naughty and resented it. "Rachel always wants to run the show."

"I do not," said Rachel.

Amy filled her mouth with tuna fish and didn't answer.

"Have either of you seen Patty today?" I asked. "I was supposed to meet with her, but she wasn't home."

"I'm mad at her," said Amy, looking happy at the change of subject.

I gave Amy a big smile. "How could anybody get mad at Patty," I said.

"She didn't help clean up after," said Amy matter-of-factly. "And she should of. She sneaked off instead."

"That doesn't sound like Patty," I said. I wondered if they'd question my familiarity with what Patty was like, but they didn't.

"Well, yesterday was a strange day, to put it mildly," breathed out Amy. "And Patty was acting funny the whole day. If you ask me, Patty knows something." Her eyes glowed. "I wish I did," she said. "Waitress."

Rachel was running her fingers down her Coke straw, squeezing it flat, working her way down to the end.

The waitress came over and raised her eyebrows and Amy ordered pecan pie and coffee. Rachel and I shook our heads no. The waitress cleaned off their lunch plates and went away.

Rachel spoke unexpectedly. "What do you do with those little canisters your film comes in? Those little gray things with the black rubber tops?"

I looked at her. "Throw them away."

"If they were in bright colors, they'd be adorable," she said. "So good for makeup pots."

"I *love* them," said Amy. "I kept the one I found on your table last night. I'm going to paint it gold and keep my eyelashes in it. I'm always losing them."

The waitress brought Amy's pie and coffee and Amy sighed with contentment as she forked off the tip. "I'm so lucky. I can eat anything I want and still stay super. It all goes to my bosom."

64 . . .

Rachel looked contemptuously at her. "It does not. It goes to your derrière."

"What *you* eat goes to *your* buttsky, you mean," said Amy agreeably. "That's why you can't eat pie when you want. My bottom was photographed for *Esquire* magazine and almost accepted."

"Oh, Amy, you know your buttocks are *slabs*."

"Perfect pink prominences," said Amy, wiggling in her seat as though that proved it. "Or is that my chesties?"

"Isn't she disgusting?" asked Rachel conversationally.

I didn't say anything. I've never been able to talk girl talk.

I was thinking about my film canisters. I have two pouches on either end of my camera bag. On one is a big plus sign inked with a red indelible marker, and on the other a minus. I work clean. Before I go out on assignment, I remove every roll of film I might use from its box. I mark the canister what kind and speed of film and fill up the plus pouch. That way I don't leave a trail of yellow boxes behind me. The empty canisters go in the minus pouch until I get home or to the *Graphic* or find a trash receptacle. Then I unload the accumulated empty canisters all at one time. Floyd does much the same thing. We both pride ourselves on working litterless. We don't leave film canisters on restaurant tables. And neither Floyd nor I shot off any film in the Colossus restaurant last night.

"Where did you find the canister?" I asked.

"On your table," said Amy. "Do you have any others?"

"Oh, if you do—" began Rachel.

"I asked first," said Amy. "If she has two you can have one."

"Gee, you two are funny together," I said.

"Ratch has the class, but I have the sass," said Amy.

"You mean the gas," smiled Rachel.

"Well, do you?" said Amy.

I checked my minus pouch. I had three. I lined them up in the middle of the table, and Amy snatched one and Rachel got the other two. Both the girls were laughing.

"Was Patty supposed to clean up?" I asked abruptly. I was worried about getting to the post office on time.

Amy shrugged. "The catered help was *supposed* to. But Mrs. S. had to send them away. Police orders. After Lou was killed, you know, the police just took over. So we girls were asked to do it. Twenty dollars each, Ratch's dad said."

... 65

"But then Wanda pulled her I'm-in-mourning act," put in Rachel.

"And Babs did the new-bride-we-have-to-go-home-and-do-kissy-face," said Amy.

"And Patty was just gone, *pouf*," said Rachel.

"So *we* got stuck with it," Amy said. "But we didn't really mind, did we Ratch?"

"Well, we each got fifty dollars for maybe an hour and a half's work. And both of us can use it."

"Uh-huh. For our *business*," cooed Amy. Both girls laughed.

"I wonder if you'd know," I said.

"Know what?" piped up Amy right away. Rachel just looked at me with smoky eyes.

"What happened to the hot dog that Floyd was eating when he got sick," I said.

"*I* know," said Amy. "Dr. Joe took it. He wrapped it in a linen napkin and put it in his pocket. I saw him."

"For God's sake, Amy," snapped Rachel. "He was taking it to be analyzed. You sound as though he were slipping it in his pocket surreptitiously, into hiding."

Amy gave an exaggerated sigh. "She's so sensitive about Joey. Her *fiancé*."

Rachel slapped both her manicured hands against the formica table top. "Now you've done it," she said.

Amy ducked her head down and covered her mouth with both palms. "Oh, gosh, I'm sorry."

"Is that supposed to be a secret?" I said. "I hit this town last Wednesday afternoon and knew about you and Dr. Joe before dinnertime. The way I heard it, only your daddy doesn't know."

Rachel stared at me. "I guess that really is the truth," she said slowly. "But if you found it out so easily, how could Papa not know?"

"I didn't 'find it out.' It just got mentioned."

"Who told you?" She asked as if she knew I wouldn't tell her.

I thought back. "You did yourself. When I took that group picture of The Scenic View. You wanted an extra copy made up for him and you told me to bill you separately, not the Climbers team."

Rachel smiled weakly at Amy.

"Ratch is a goon," said Amy cheerfully. "I'm *so* glad *I* didn't tell the press first!" She really did sound like Marilyn Monroe.

Rachel reached across the table and took both of Amy's hands in hers. She looked deep into Amy's green eyes. "But Amy, dear, dear Amy, please be more careful of what you say. You could get us both in trouble."

Amy nodded her golden head and stared down. "Yes, Ratch," she said very quietly. "Okay, I will."

I didn't know what it was about and right then I didn't care. It was time for me to go. "Thanks for talking with me," I said. I got up. "Are you both coming tonight? Cheerleader practice?"

They nodded. "Six o'clock," said Amy. "*You* coming?"

"Going to try," I said. "See you then."

I left the coffee shop thinking how ridiculously easy, safe, and undetectable it would be to carry poison around with you in a film canister. They're hard rubber so they don't break. They're untraceable. They're airtight and light proof. No spillage, spoilage, or smell. No fear of touching the poison, no fear of leakage. And if anyone saw it, especially if you carried the canister around, like a lot of amateurs do, in its film box, no one would question it. They'd just think you were carrying a roll of film. And what you'd really have would be a portable, anonymous, dose of death.

I mailed the envelope special delivery to Barkley and identified myself to the postal clerk. I asked for Lou LaMont's address.

The post office is not supposed to give out addresses. But like most things it can be arranged. Some guys use a twenty dollar bill right off. Me, I use the personal touch first. I told the postal clerk this was a murder case and I was the press. He was a nice old bird. He told me there'd never been a murder like this in High Mountain before. Personally, he said, he didn't think it was murder this time either. Dr. DeBianco was wrong. He gave me the address and directions: 19 Ewing Avenue, apartment 1-A. Four blocks west, turn left at the corner.

Lovable Lou LaMont lived, or had until yesterday, on the first floor of a wood frame duplex, one in a row of semiattached apartment houses. I anticipated trouble getting inside. I can open some doors with my plastic working press card. The guy who taught me that trick said a half slat of a venetian blind worked best, but any piece of stiff plastic will do. I carry a little screwdriver in my camera bag as a handy little lever. It works on a lot of windows if they're not properly latched. I have a key I bought in a pawn shop in Washington, D.C. that fits most Yale locks. I figured I'd get in one way or the other. There might even be somebody there.

There was. Skyhook Reesenbach, coach of the High Mountain Climbers. The front door was open and I heard sounds in the bedroom. I discovered him piling girlie magazines into cardboard boxes. Ho-ho.

"If you try to take my picture I'll put you on the floor," he greeted me when I walked in on him.

I didn't believe that. Just shows how wrong you can be. To tease him, I swung my camera up in front of my left eye. All I saw in the viewfinder was a blank white wall.

He hit me low, straight on, right at the knees. As I went down I instinctively doubled over to protect my camera. I landed on my side, Nikon safe, the air knocked out of me, but not hurt.

"You're pretty good at a blind-side blitz," I said as soon as I could. He was down too, sprawled on the puce colored carpet, my ankles caught in the bends of his elbows.

"Not for publication, this here," he said. "No reputable photographer takes pictures like this." He glared at me the way, I guess, he cows his troops on the practice field. I smiled wondering if that he-man stuff really psyched out his ball players.

"Don't you laugh at me, missy," he hissed, standing up and rubbing his upper arms. My boots must have bruised him on the tackle.

I stayed where I was and pretended to be checking over my Nikon to see if it was okay. I knew it was, but he didn't.

He smoothed his wispy hair back to cover the bald place. I could tell he was nervous because he started snapping his fingers right away, both hands going in unison.

"Get on out of here," he said. "You got no permission to be in here. Trespassin', that's what it is. Want me to call the cops on you?" He had his hands on his hips, his legs spread, standing over me like a Nazi stormtrooper.

"Mrs. Snowfield gave me permission," I lied. "I stayed at her place last night." I gestured toward the bedside telephone, one of those fancy French Directoire jobs. "Check it out, Coach."

He snapped away with his fingers. He wasn't about to check it out. I'd stopped him because he believed me. Like most liars, I thought. He thinks he's the only one that does it.

"What are *you* doing here?" I asked, getting up as nonchalantly as I could.

He leered at me. "You ever pose for any of these?" He gestured with his index finger at the pile of dirty magazines. "I hear they pay real good." Snap, snap, snap, softly went the fingers.

"They pay lousy," I said. "And no, Pops, I never did." I snapped my fingers back at him.

That made him mad. He doubled both his hands into fists and shook them under my chin. "I'd like to punch you so bad," he said.

"It's just the generation gap, Pops," I said, needling him. "Oldtime chauvinism. You'll get used to things. And you can't go around taking swipes at me. I'm going to be taking pictures of you all season."

"I hate your kind," he said.

"You told me," I said. "Now, listen, Coach, you're the one who's not supposed to be here. You're removing evidence. That's a federal rap." I lit myself a cigarette and sat down on the bed.

"No reason to smear a boy's name," he said.

"Who's smearing Lou's name?"

"The goddamn papers will," he said. "If they get ahold of Louie's personal proclivities." He smiled. He seemed to like that word. "So the boy liked a nekkid girl. So who don't? So he smoked a little mary-wanna to relax from time to time. The public don't understand these things. Does no good for them to know." He looked down at a little plastic baggie with a few rolled joints in it lying at the foot of the bed.

"I'm not after a story like that," I said, and I wasn't. "All I want is a pix or two of the victim's digs. Tell you what. I didn't see you here. I'll go out and get a few snaps of the kitchen and the livingroom. That'll give you time to get finished in here. Then I'll get a shot of the bed, and I'm through. No smutty magazines. No dopesticks. Word of honor. How's that?"

He snapped away with his fingers. "Give me half an hour."

"Done," I said. I started to get off the bed, but he stepped around and stood over me, his body curved like a question mark after a four-letter invitation.

"If you wore dresses like a girlie should, you might be a pretty thing," he said. "Or even if you—undressed." He was looking at me the way a lizard eyes a fruit fly.

Hoo, boy. "I'll get some pictures of the kitchen," I said.

"S'matter, sweetheart? Don't you go for a real man? You do it with those two bozos you run around with." He stood there rubbing his hands over the front of his trousers to let me see he was on-the-mark, ready, set, go.

I got off the bed and he let me pass. I didn't look back.

I went into the kitchen, found the bathroom, used it, and then made myself a cup of coffee with some instant I found there. I wondered if Coach Reesenbach was only clearing out Lovable Lou's pornography collection and his dope stash. He might be using that as a cover, and hiding or disposing of something else more important. I'll give him the benefit of the doubt, I thought. If he was up to more than he said he was, he was a whole lot smarter than I gave him credit for.

About twenty minutes later I heard the front door slam. Skyhook had left without saying goodbye.

I took the pictures I wanted in about five minutes, called Barkley and told him what I had, and then skedaddled myself.

..... VIII

I headed straight north out to the highway, all the windows of the Chevie rolled down to get rid of the smell of Gilly Fats' cigars. I had two hours before I got myself to the Colossus at five, and I wanted to be alone. I had no place to call my own in High Mountain, so I drove randomly, looking for a park to sit in. Or a graveyard. That ought to be a good place to hide.

It was a nice nippy day, October coming in with a soft sun and fresh winds blowing down from Canada. But I didn't feel fresh and nippy inside. I felt confused and oddly hemmed in. The active part of me was eager and driving toward the scoop: the news potential in the murder of Lou LaMont. But the passive part was recoiling at prying into the lives of strangers.

Sports photography has one real advantage over hard-news coverage. In sports, you photograph what everyone sees, the public event, the public person. Private photo sessions are always planned between the personality and the photographer and sometimes your picture editor and the talent's manager. The sessions are orchestrated toward *image*. Sports photographers don't flash bulbs in widow's faces or hide outside of offices to grab off shots of who's sneaking up the back stairs to see the Congressman. Thank god.

And now murder had come to my sports assignment. And the lid was on it, or at least temporarily, so the hard-nose guys from the city desk weren't onto this story yet. I was sitting in the old catbird's seat for a great big scooper. Even my friendly enemy, Floyd, was stalled. I had an open highway, I could go full throttle unimpeded up the straight, and here I was looking for a place to park. You go figure.

I'll find a quaint little graveyard, I thought, and quiet my mind taking some pictures with my new soft-focus filter. I'd been looking for an excuse to use it. The sun's rays were good now, long and slanty out of the west. Lots of gradations in the shadows. Lovely for catching the mica in the tombstones, the bend in the long grass, and the gnarls in humpy old treeroots.

I found my graveyard, but it wasn't little and it wasn't quaint.

. . . 71

They'd built it right into the side of the mountain and let it overflow into a rolling meadow that must once have been a pine forest because there were almost as many fir trees as graves. Down the mountain bubbled a natural waterfall, and a stream, probably manmade, curved through the meadow and wound away to somewhere. White wrought iron benches sat solitary beside the stream and under the trees. The cemetery was bordered by a high brick wall almost smothered with large-leaved ivy. The ivy looked a thousand years old, but I bet it had been planted in less than twenty, and manured and watered a lot.

The double iron gates were swung back inviting me, so I wheeled in and parked where a sign told me to. I took my camera and went strolling.

I spent my two hours happily, walking and sitting in the sweet piney air. I took fragmented pictures. Micro shots of granite curls on carved cherubs. Foreshortened arty shots of patches of ground worn bare by shoes or knees in the lush clover grass. I shot expensive memorials and cheap flat grave plates. I shot the shadow caressing one grave at one minute intervals for five minutes to see how fast a shadow grows.

I found the Snowfield mausoleum. I guess I was looking. It was made of red marble like a miniature Greek temple, and it had two stained glass windows set east and west so that the sun beamed in as the day dawned and died. There were fresh autumn flowers in two big granite urns in niches. Perpetual care, I think they call it. His name was Lemuel Harrison Snowfield, and the brass plate said he'd been born in 1910 and died in '74. There was room there for his wife.

I wondered what would happen if Mrs. Snowfield married Abe Hirshaw, and then died before Abe did. Would she still be buried beside her first husband or buried somewhere else to await her second husband's passing? And then he married another woman who outlived him. . . . There'd be all those double deathbeds with only one body in place, lonely, waiting for its partner who wasn't coming but was waiting forever in its own double space for a body which wasn't coming. . . .

I left the burial grounds feeling peaceful again. I was ready to rev engine, race on, and finish the course.

Cheerleader practice was at six, but I got to the Colossus early, the way I do, to see what there is to see before I look at what I'm told to.

I went in through the players' gate, which is back toward the rear of the players' wing. That way I avoided the front offices and the ticket windows and the long walk through the building, up and down ramps, to get to the field.

The long hall of the players' wing was lit up, and through the open door of the snack bar at the end of the hall I could see lights too. All the other doors in the wing were shut.

Nobody seemed to be around. Stanley Farmer, the maintenance man, was probably somewhere in this wing. And upstairs in the front offices there ought to be people.

Monday is the team's day off. All week they practice, examine the game film of their last game, look at film of their upcoming opponents' play, and prepare for the Sunday mix-'em-up. On Monday they rest their bruised bodies or play at private pleasures, like deer hunting in season or charter fishing or getting measured for new Tripler suits. Some of them probably spend the day in bed.

I poked my head into the beauty salon. It was dark. Then I tried to open the Climbers' locker room but it was locked. Then I opened the door to the cheerleaders' dressing room.

I flipped on the light switch. This room was very different from the teams' locker room next door. It had obviously been designed and decorated for The Scenic View. I gave another mental tip of the hat to Mrs. Snowfield for the careful planning it must have taken to make each room of the Colossus so definitely what it was. And for spending the money too.

Two imitation Tiffany lamps hung from the ceiling. They threw a mellow glow over the room. It was small but charming. On the right hand wall the six lockers were enameled a glossy light blue with white puffy clouds painted on. Across the six lockers a giant graphic of a rainbow arced, purple and red and yellow and blue. The opposite wall had a built-in bookcase stained a warm wood color. It ran the length of the wall and half way up. The shelves were filled with cheerleader props, toy bugles, chocolate brown pom-poms, little pennant flags. Over the bookcase the wall was mirrored, with rows of tiny light bulbs on either side and over the top. In the center of the room a long library table stood on a machine-made but good-looking oriental carpet. Tall backed, armless chairs were set around the table, and on the table were a big blue vase with no flowers in it, two heavy glass ashtrays in a star pattern, a little wicker basket filled with hair curlers, and a bloody towel. The towel was all blotches and streaks, as though someone had sopped

. . . 73

the blood up and then wiped off his or her hands.

When I came in I'd dropped my camera bag on the nearest chair and just looked around admiring the room. Now I began to shake, literally to shake. I looked back over my shoulder at the door, but it hadn't moved. I looked at my Timex: 5:15. I sat down. The prickly dancy feeling was becoming St. Vitus' Dance. Just looking at the towel I knew where Patty was. Knew it as surely as though I'd put her there myself.

I scanned the row of locker doors. There were six of them, and all of them had padlocks through the handles except the first one. I got up, told myself I had a job to do, went over, and lifted the handle. It moved easily. I opened the locker.

David Livingston's astrologer outfits twinkled back at me, all half-moons and stars. There were three of them, one with a purple background, one in red, and one in turquoise blue. His conical hat sat on the bottom covered in silver sequins and little sleigh bells. I stared at the outfits, shocked somehow. It was like finding a clown where you don't expect one.

It took me a minute to figure it out.

He probably wasn't issued a locker, I thought. Just used this one for his costumes because it was available. Six lockers, five cheerleaders. He must keep that box of Fourth-of-July-type sparklers somewhere else, maybe up in his office.

I tried the next locker. The padlock was closed. I pulled at it, but it held. Then I tried the third one. Locked tight.

I tried locker four. The padlock stopped the handle from lifting, but the handle moved and I saw that the padlock's tongue hadn't been shot home all the way. It had been pushed in but it hadn't clicked. Someone must have been in too much of a hurry to pull and make sure the tongue had found the groove.

I realized I'd just muffed the fingerprints, if there'd been any. I frowned, but pulled the padlock off the handle of the locker. I took a deep breath and opened the door.

A pink hair net, the kind you wrap around your head once you've rolled your hair in bouffant curlers, was wrapped around her neck and tied her head to the hook inside the locker. The net tails were knotted and tied in a bow. The body hung straight down from the hook.

Her feet were still in the mountain climbing boots and they were planted on the locker floor. The body was a little taller than the height of the locker inside, so the knees were bent up and pushed against the opposite wall, forming a kind of lap.

I saw the scuffed-up knee where she'd fallen yesterday while hurrying for the second-half kick off. A scab had already started to form.

Dumped over her was a bouquet of long-stemmed roses, most of them caught in her lap, the petals curled and black along the edges. One rose, its head broken too, drooped over her knees, its long stalk hanging in the space between her thighs. There was a white Climbers towel draped over her head. It hid her face. I didn't touch it.

I knew she was dead, but I had to make sure. I couldn't smell anything except the glorious scent of the dried out roses. So I touched her arm very lightly with the back of my hand. Her skin felt like linoleum.

I couldn't not do what I was about to do. If Barkley didn't want to use these pictures, I wouldn't blame him. But if I had the chance and didn't take some, he'd probably always blame me.

So I took seven pictures of the body. I had to use my flash gun, something I rarely do because I hate the flatted-out look you get. But I had to because the light was low on this side of the room and the inside of the locker was dark.

Then I closed the locker door, set back the open padlock, left the dressing room, and went to tell the authorities.

The first door I came to was Coach Reesenbach's office. No light shone from under the door. It was locked, and no one answered when I knocked.

So I went down the hall to the snack bar where I knew there was a telephone. It was brightly lit and empty except for Stanley Farmer. He was standing behind the counter drinking from a coffee cup and staring intently at the bull's-eye in the dart board. In front of him on the counter were two needle-nosed darts with yellow feathers. In the dart board, close to the center but no cigar, stuck the third one.

"How-do, Miss," said Stanley as I walked in. He bobbed his head in friendly fashion and then went back to squinching up his eyes and measuring trajectory.

"You're about twice as far away as you're supposed to be, aren't you, Stanley?" I said.

"That's so, Miss. But ya see, I'm too good that close. So I stand back here for the challenge. Watch this." He picked up a dart, rolled it a little in his fingers, balanced it, raised his hand to his ear and let the dart fly. Thunk. Bull's-eye. He whooped. "See it? Didja see that?"

"Wow," I said.

He giggled, a high nasal sound. "Wanna see it again?"

"Have to make a call first, Stanley. Then okay." I went to the telephone behind the counter and picked up the receiver. The operator on the switchboard upstairs said hello, and I asked for the police. She said "One minute, please," like poor-Johnny-one-note. Beside me I felt Stanley stiffen and saw him drain his cup. He didn't say anything but I knew he was listening.

Lieutenant Weatherwax and Detective Xavier were in their car out cruising, the desk sergeant said. I told him I'd found a body in the cheerleaders' dressing room of the Colossus Sports Complex, and he said to wait, someone would be there shortly.

Then I called Barkley collect and described to him what I'd found. No details other than that, I said. I was waiting for the police now and Gilly Fats was probably with them. Then I asked him to ask me a question, because I didn't want to let Stanley hear I'd taken pictures but I wanted Barkley to know. The switchboard girl might be listening in, but I decided to risk it. Barkley asked, I said yes, and he rang off saying to stay with it. No thanks for the scoop-of-the-century.

Stanley didn't ask me a thing. He said he'd teach me darts. I stood up by the line painted on the floor and threw green-feathered darts in the direction of the board. Stanley showed me how to hold the darts and release them so they didn't spin. I was surprised that most of my throws stuck somewhere on the board. Stanley himself could have hustled money he was so good. He'd tell me just where he was going to place it, and then sink it right in there with a little flick of his wrist and a nasal chortle. He was a funny little man, all wrinkled and gnomelike. All I really knew about him was that he ran a clean locker room and kept the Climbers' equipment shipshape. And now I knew he played a mean game of darts.

They must have been close by because they walked in about five minutes later, Weatherwax and Xavier and Gilly Fats and about six other guys, some in plain clothes and some in uniform. One of them carried an old Speed Graphic camera; the official photographer, I guess he was. I'd have liked to look his camera over but I didn't get a chance to ask.

Dr. Jose DeBianco arrived about a minute later, in tennis shorts and a Climbers sweater. He was wearing new Converse sneakers, the kind Julius Erving endorses, with the little blue star on the instep. Dr. Joe was looking vague again, looking like he'd never been in the Colossus before and didn't know his way.

Gilly Fats went with them down the hall to The Scenic View's dressing room. Lieutenant Weatherwax told me to stay put.

The thought occurred to me they might try to confiscate my film. Thinking that made me nervous so I told Stanley I was going to the ladies room. I went down the hall past where the action was to the toilets. I went into a stall, unloaded my film and hid it in the loose folds of my camera bag. Then I reloaded the camera and went back to wait.

I could hear noises out in the hall, a stretcher rolling, men bumping in to each other, apologizing. But I stayed in the snack bar at a little table, sipping a coffee Stanley poured out for me. Stanley was drinking from his coffee cup again but I got the impression he didn't have coffee in it. We didn't talk to each other.

Lieutenant Weatherwax and Detective Xavier came in with Gilly Fats just behind. I told Weatherwax as succinctly as I could what had happened. Detective Xavier wrote it all down in his neat shorthand with a long pencil. When the point got dull, he sharpened it with a little pocket sharpener he took out of one of the loops in his cartridge belt. He emptied the shavings in an ash tray.

When I told Lieutenant Weatherwax I'd touched the padlock and smudged any prints it might have had, Weatherwax smiled at me as though I'd just told him he was dying of Legionnaire's disease and murmured "bright."

Detective John Xavier asked if I'd indulged my journalistic instincts and taken a picture or two but I shook my head no. Gilly Fats surprised me. He asked why not. He should have known better. I just shrugged my shoulders and mumbled something about the locker being too dark. When people don't know about pushing film and stuff like that you can tell them anything.

"You couldn't find a way?" Xavier winked at me with his log-cabin-fire eyes.

"If I'd had a flash," I said.

. . . 77

Xavier nodded. That made sense to him.

Gilly Fats looked disgusted. "You should always carry your flashgun, T.T., even if you don't like to use it." It was the first time Gilly Fats had ever scolded me. And in public too. Well, I'd tell him later.

Then they started on Stanley Farmer. Detective Xavier opened the questioning. "How come you didn't find this thing, Farmer? Aren't you supposed to check out this place, keep it cleaned up?"

Stanley stood behind his snack counter, both hands grasping his coffee cup. He stolidly shook his head no. "Not them girls' room, I don't. Miz Snowfield tole me to leave the cheerleaders right alone. They're sposed to clean up after themselves. That room is taboo."

Lieutenant Weatherwax bestowed one of his sad smiles on Stanley. "Tell us about your day, Mr. Farmer." He pushed his chair back on its two hind legs and eased the cap on his head. "You got here when?"

Stanley looked belligerent. "Sposed to be my day off, same as everybody else's," he said. "But I come down here anyways, just to check up like I do. Got here about 3:30." His head bobbed on his neck. "Got nowheres else to go. Keeps me out of trouble bein' here. Got no woman at home, ya see."

Detective Xavier said aloud as he wrote, "Never married."

Stanley lifted a hand with a finger tentatively half-raised. "No, no now, I din say that. I says I got no wife now. *Now*, officer."

"Girlfriend?" queried Detective Xavier, pencil point quivering over his notepad.

Stanley almost blushed. He jerked his head and smirked. "No sir, not right now, sir."

"Must get lonely, eh Stanley?" Detective Xavier's voice was suddenly insinuating.

Stanley looked scared but he swallowed some of whatever was in his coffee cup and said, "Yes, it do, officer. I can't deny that one. Been thinkin' lately 'bout gettin' me a dawg to take care of, or a bird that'll talk to me. Ifen I had me a house with a little yard to it, I might buy me an ole mutt-horse and take up ridin' agin. Used to ride a bit, ya know. . . ." His voice trailed off.

"Horses, Mr. Farmer?" Lieutenant Weatherwax asked.

"Horses," said Stanley shortly and stared down at the counter top. "Racehorses, Loo-ten-ant." Stanley drew himself up as tall as his 5'5" could. "Used to be a right fair jock in my time. People forget that. Ever dog has his day, they say, and I sure had mine. Only people forget. . . ." His voice faded out again, but he was looking Lieutenant Weatherwax in the eye.

"I'm sorry, Mr. Farmer," said Lieutenant Weatherwax gently, smiling his death smile. "I never knew."

"Miz Snowfield ought to remind people from time to time. I was an athlete too. How come she hired me. Wasn't always just the broom-pusher, towel-counter I am now. These big fellers round here, them lard-asses, think them's the only ones is athletic. Why, some of them bruisers kill a horse if they was to just set on it. Most of 'em more fat than muscle anyhow." Stanley snorted through his nose.

Everybody's got a story, I thought. If you just hang around long enough, you'll hear it. Some of the stories can break your heart.

Detective Xavier's heart wasn't bothered. He must have been waiting for a chance to turn mean. He started bullying. "Think you're a friggin' hero, don't you? Any of the boys here you particularly resent? Or resented? Like Lou LaMont, maybe?" The pencil point was rushing across the lined paper, making its odd curves and loopy lines.

Stanley shifted his eyes to Lieutenant Weatherwax. Weatherwax was taking off his hat, smoothing his gray hair, examining his police badge.

"Write what you want." Stanley sighed and drained his cup.

"What happened to your wife, Stanley?" Detective Xavier was doodling now, drawing fishes. I could see but Stanley couldn't.

"Me Mollie," said Stanley. Just saying it you knew he loved her. "Me Mollie," he said, "she died. She waited, but then she died."

"Waited?" The pencil point quivered, eager.

"Thaz what I said."

"Waited for what?"

"Waitin' for me, o' course, and then she died. Noo-monia, the doc said. Double noo-monia. Mebbe that room she had weren't warm enough." Under the counter top, with something we couldn't see, Stanley was refilling his coffee cup.

"Why was she waiting, Mr. Farmer? Were you away? In the service, maybe?" It was Lieutenant Weatherwax this time, coaxing him. First one bullied, then the other coaxed. It seemed to be working.

. . . 79

Stanley's head was hanging now. He mumbled something.

"I'm sorry, Mr. Farmer." The Lieutenant's voice was soft, polite, unhurried. "I didn't hear that last statement."

"I says what's me Mollie got to do with now?"

The two detectives looked at each other. Lieutenant Weatherwax tried it. "Come on now, just tell us about it."

Stanley sniffled, and wiped his nose with his fingers. "Got a cold, Mack. 'Scuse me."

"Where were you all that time away from Mollie, Mr. Farmer?"

Stanley wiped his nose again. "Doin' five year," he said.

Lieutenant Weatherwax nodded. Detective Xavier butted in. "What rap they hang you for?"

Stanley was looking very self-composed, almost dignified. "Killin' my neighbor," he said, "who deserved it." Said like that it sounded strange; Stanley's voice, nasal and flat, hitting himself dead center the way his darts hit bull's-eye.

Detective John Xavier didn't seem impressed. "Murder one?" he asked, licking his pencil tip.

Stanley sniffed. "Murder two they says. Manslaughter."

"You cop the plea?"

"Pleaded self-defense all the way." Stanley shrugged. "Jury thought different. All ole history now. You gonna rake it all up? Get Miz Snowfield to can me?"

Lieutenant Weatherwax seemed to be considering it. "Does she know about your record?"

Stanley nodded emphatically. "She's the one hired me on the work-release program. Her groundskeeper, I was to be. Ole man Snowfield weren't too hot for the idea, but Miz S., she give me the chance on account of my jockeying. Miz S., she likes athletes."

I smiled to myself. I guess she did, if Wanda was right.

Stanley went on talking. "Mollie was gonna do inside the house, see, and me do the outside. Mollie, she died before it came time." He paused, took a big breath, and started up again. "Miz S. got that other woman instead, and I got me this here maint'nance job. First round the Colossus, helpin' out to build it, and now lookin' after the Climbers' team. Miz S. been good to me. She buried me Mollie and said ifen I did good, nobody would worry me 'bout what went before. Been here three year now, since we broke ground on the place. I'm proud to of been a part."

Lieutenant Weatherwax sighed and put his hat firmly back on his head. "Nobody's going to bother you, Mr. Farmer. You have my word on that. Now tell me about today. You say you had no knowledge of that body in there until Miss Baldwin here alerted the police?"

"Thaz right. I come in here, checked the rooms I'm responsible for, counted up my towels, called Duke at the laundry, and swabbed down the hall. Then I come in here to rest awhile until the practice time tonight. I like to watch the girls. Usually sit up in the seats somewheres and watch 'em kick. Don't hurt nothin' and they don mind." He blinked his eyes and drank out of his cup.

"Where'd you do your time, Stanley?" It just jumped out of me.

Stanley gave me a funny look, almost a look of satisfaction, like I'd just said the magic word on the old Groucho Marx Show. "Altoona, PA., Miss," he said. "Went in January four, sixty-nine, walked out September fifteen, nineteen hundred and seventy-three. Won't ever forget them dates."

I looked over at Gilly Fats to see if he had picked that up. He blew a smoke ring at me.

"Bet we're gonna check all this out and it better be right," said Detective Xavier.

Stanley sniffed. "Go at it."

Sssssss . . . sssssss . . . "Hello," he said from the doorway, in his voice that squeaked on the *l*'s. "C-c-can I come in?"

Lil Harv was sitting in his wheelchair all sweated up, his hair damp on his forehead, his thin face shiny. He was dressed in a white warm-up suit with red stripes, and it reminded me right away of that bloody towel in Patty's dressing room, white with red blotches and streaks fading away as though someone had mopped up and wiped his hands.

What was it about Lil Harv that spooked me, I wondered. His arms were a little misshapen but not so bad. And he kept his crippled legs covered most of the time so you didn't have to pretend to ignore them. And everybody seemed to like him fine, to respect the way he battled back at his disease and kept up a cheerful disposition. But there it was: I cringed whenever I saw him.

Lieutenant Weatherwax wasn't fazed. "Sure, Harv, come on in," he said, smiling like Earnie Shavers after he lost the decision to Ali. "What are you doing here?"

"Oh, I'm always here. I come every day after school to work out. In the training room."

. . . 81

Lil Harv wheeled himself into the room, backed his UFO against the wall, put on the brake and eased himself out of the chair and stood up.

Grinning, showing off I thought, he crossed the width of the room just using a cane. It took him awhile. He went over to a stool in front of the counter and lifted himself onto it. Then he looked around at us like he was expecting applause.

"C-c-could I have my special, please?" he said to Stanley, squeaking.

Stanley poured out some bottled orange juice. "What's up?" said Lil Harv. "Another investigation?" His legs swung back and forth under the stool. His upper lip had orange pulp on it.

"Have a good work-out?" Stanley asked him.

He nodded, counting his accomplishments off on his fingers. "Walked three miles on the exerciser. Did fifty push-ups. Lifted the thirty-pound leg weights 100 times each. And I got the time down this time, Stanley. By two minutes. Today I did it in two hours and forty-two minutes. Friday it took me two hours and forty-four."

"You'll be down to nuthin' flat in no time, kid," said Stanley, patting Lil Harv affectionately on the back.

Lieutenant Weatherwax looked impressed. "You work out in that room every day?"

"Yep," said Lil Harv. "After school. Only not weekends. I'm not allowed then." Funny how his stutter went away once he got talking.

"What time you get here today, young fella?" Detective Xavier was sharpening his pencil, getting ready to take it down.

Lil Harv seemed happy to tell him. "Mom usually drives me but she couldn't today. So Dad came. He drives faster. I got here about 3:30. Before Stanley anyway." He sat there, swinging his legs, looking like everybody's favorite kid. Detective John Xavier wrote it down.

Out in the hall I heard Amy's breathy voice complaining about not being allowed to enter. Then I heard Wanda too, saying what the hell. I looked at Lieutenant Weatherwax. "No cheerleader practice tonight?"

He looked gloomily at me. "Nobody gets in here tonight. Maybe tomorrow."

I stood up.

82 . . .

"Where are you going?" snapped Detective Xavier.

"To talk to the girls," I said.

Detective Xavier shook his head no. "Stay close here by me," he said, trying to look like Rudolph Valentino. A real quick-change artist. I sat back down.

"What's the matter with everybody?" asked Lil Harv, licking orange juice off his lips. "Why can't The Scenic View practice?"

"When was the last time you saw Patty Cambron?" asked Lieutenant Weatherwax.

"Uh-oh," said Lil Harv. "She's mad at me. Did she tell you something bad?"

"What bad is there to tell?" Lieutenant Weatherwax looked like he expected the worst.

Lil Harv gave a little-boy grin. "Nothing. But she thinks there is. She thinks I stole something."

"What?" said Lieutenant Weatherwax.

Lil Harv looked exasperated. "Something really dumb. The hairspray. She was really mad about it too." He laughed, a gay, innocent laugh. "Can I have another, Stanley?"

Stanley silently poured out another orange juice. The kid went to work on it, breathing deep between sips. "I feel sweaty," he said. "Hope Mom gets here soon."

"Hairspray?" repeated Detective Xavier.

"Yeah. Patty's crazy sometimes. She said I stole the hairspray out of the filigree holder. In the shampoo room, you know?" He shrugged. "But I didn't. What do I want their old hairspray for? I don't use hairspray."

Hairspray. What would hairspray have to do with a needle in the back of Lovable Lou's neck? Or the stealing of it? It didn't seem to connect. But it had to. It connected so well Patty Cambron was dead because of it.

"Why did she accuse you, Harv?" Lieutenant Weatherwax sounded as though some great calamity had been visited on the boy.

Lil Harv picked up on the tone of voice too. "Oh, don't take it so seriously, Lieutenant Weatherwax. That's the way girls are. Goofy sometimes. Patty said she saw it in my gym bag after we did our Vitamin E commercial, Lou and me. It was unzipped and she saw inside, she said. Later, after the commercial, when she was rolling up Lou's hair again for the game. Patty did Lou's hair, you know."

... 83

"No," said Lieutenant Weatherwax. "I didn't know."

Lil Harv smiled his pretty-boy smile. "Anybody could of told you."

Lieutenant Weatherwax nodded. "If I'd been smart enough to ask," he said.

"Well, it's not important, I don't think, Lieutenant Weatherwax."

Lieutenant Weatherwax regarded the boy with affection. "It might be very important, Harv. It just might be the most important thing I've learned so far about this case."

Lil Harv opened his bluer-than-blue eyes wide. "R-r-really? And I told you? I broke the case open?"

Lieutenant Weatherwax laughed, actually laughed. He got off his chair, stood tall, and stretched. "Where's Doc Joe?"

"He went with the body," said Detective Xavier.

Again we heard noises out in the hall. High heels ticking toward us, a low male voice. They stopped outside and a bushy redheaded patrolman stuck his face around the door frame. "Got Mrs. Potter out here, sir. Says she's come to pick up her boy."

Lieutenant Weatherwax nodded, and Mrs. Caroline Potter came in wearing her mink. She paused, looking us over, then acted surprised at seeing Weatherwax and Xavier. She held out her hand to Lieutenant Weatherwax. "So soon again, Jason?" She smiled and twitched her hips just a little. Behind her back Lil Harv made a face.

Lieutenant Weatherwax took her hand and held it. He opened his hand to release hers but she left her hand inside his and said, "I've come for my baby." Lieutenant Weatherwax withdrew his hand slowly. He looked sad.

"I'm not a baby, Mother." Lil Harv's voice didn't squeak at all.

Caroline Potter turned toward her son and beamed at him. Too brightly, I thought. "No, of course not, darling. Are you ready?" She didn't cross the room to touch him, to kiss him. She stood looking at him, beaming brightly, her hands in their mink pockets. Her feet were close together, stiff-kneed. She was wearing the same boots she'd had on last night when I'd photographed her *in flagrante delicto*.

"I'm ready," Lil Harv said, sounding as though he preferred to stay. "Now don't help me. I can do it myself." His mother hadn't been close to helping him. He picked up his cane, swung his body free from the stool, and walked across the room the best he could

84 . . .

to his wheelchair. We all watched him, silent. He maneuvered himself around, got into the chair, and covered his legs with his laprobe, the one with the needle-pointed figure of Overcoat, the Climbers' mascot.

"Get my books and clothes, Mom," he said. "They're in the shampoo room."

"Yes, of course, dear." She smiled dutifully, and left the room. The patrolman walked with her down the hall to the beauty salon.

"She spoils me," Lil Harv said to no one in particular. "Dad says it's not good for me. I disagree. I say it's good for me but bad for Mother." We all laughed. He grinned mischievously.

Caroline Potter came back. Lil Harv's school clothes must have been in the Pan-Am flight bag and his books in the briefcase.

"Thanks, Stanley," she said, "for keeping an eye on him." She had a bill in her hand and pushed it into Stanley's trouser pocket.

"Yes, ma'am. Thankee," said Stanley.

She went over to her son. "Is the brake off?" she asked.

"Yes, Mother. Can't you see?" Lil Harv looked very tired now.

She didn't say goodbye. She wheeled her son out the door. We heard Lil Harv's voice going away down the hall. "Stanley doesn't keep an eye on me, Mother. . . ." The men smiled and chuckled.

"Gutsy little man," said Lieutenant Weatherwax.

"Good attitude," said Detective Xavier.

"Gonna be a han'some divvil too," said Stanley.

Gilly Fats smiled paternally. Lil Harv had captured every heart but mine.

"Well, let's wrap it," yawned Lieutenant Weatherwax. "Stay available, Mr. Farmer."

Stanley nodded. "I ain't goin' nowheres."

Lieutenant Weatherwax nodded. "I want you to lock every room in this wing. I'll leave my man stationed here. Give him a set of keys."

"Yessir."

"You two bunking at Snowfield's tonight?"

"Probably all week," said Gilly Fats. "Don't worry about us. We'll be close by."

"How close?" said Detective Xavier, putting his arm around my waist.

"Close as your sideburns," said Gilly Fats. The men laughed together.

The two detectives and I waited in the hall for Gilly while he ran

. . . 85

upstairs to the main wing to call Barkley. I don't know why he didn't use the telephone in the snack bar. Maybe he was afraid of the operator listening in.

Then we all went outside. It was cold and dark. Gilly Fats and I headed for the *Graphic* Chevie. The two cops went off in their police cruiser.

"Okay, T.T. Let's get some din-din," said Gilly Fats. "I want to fill you in on the Floyd situation. It's a lu-lu."

"Okay," I said. I was quiet as I drove. I was mourning for Patty. I didn't even know how she'd died. Hands around her neck? One of those star-pointed ashtrays? After dinner, I said to myself, why not drive around to the morgue? If Dr. Joe isn't there, I could pump Huey, the male nurse. But Dr. Joe ought to be. Autopsies take a long time.

I found a cheap drive-in joint and pulled in. I didn't feel very hungry. I ordered a chocolate milkshake and coffee. Gilly Fats got four burgers, a side of fries, and two coffees, double sugar.

We ate in the Chevie and he told about Floyd.

"Vapo," said Gilly Fats around the fresh cigar in his mouth. "Ever hear of that?"

"Sounds like flu medicine," I said.

He reached in his jacket pocket and pulled out his notebook. He flipped over a few pages and consulted his notes.

"Dichlorovinyl dimethyl phosphate." He rolled the words out like he'd practiced.

"Oh, sure," I said.

He blew out some smoke. I reached back and rolled down the rear window. "It's a parasympathetic nerve stimulator. Tough stuff. It knocks out your cholinesterase enzyme."

"Gotcha," I said.

Gilly Fats frowned. "Well, T.T., you need your cholinesterase enzyme. It's what keeps your nerve messages working right, like your reflexes, your motor controls, even your heart rhythm. If you lose your cholinesterase, your arms and legs don't operate so good, your heart forgets to beat, you stop breathing."

I looked at Gilly, remembering Floyd flopping on the floor like a gaffed tuna.

"Vapo," said Gilly Fats. "It's a professional pesticide. Sold only to professional exterminators and institutions." He looked at me.

"Like the Colossus?" I said.

Gilly Fats sucked on the end of his cigar. "In the storage closet which is in that big schoolroom there's enough of it to annihilate the county."

"I see," I said.

"Thought you would," he said. "Door is supposed to be kept locked, but Stanley Farmer seems to neglect to do that very often. Easier to just reach in when he wants something. And what's in there anybody wants, Stanley said."

"Plainly visible inside?" I asked.

"If you know what it is. Now Farmer is supposed to fumigate on the last Sunday of every month. After everybody's cleared out of the building. Last thing he's supposed to do before he goes home that day. Spray, then clear out." Three tiny smoke rings.

I lit a cigarette in self defense. "Go on," I said.

"Think I'm ready for a bit of dessert now," he said. "How 'bout you?"

I shook my head.

Gilly Fats punched the button on the speaker and ordered strawberry pie and another coffee.

"Make it two coffees," I said.

"Two coffees," he told the sound box. The voice repeated the order and the box went dead.

"Now yesterday was Sunday, right? September twenty-nine. Last Sunday of the month. Also official opening day. Got that?"

"Got it," I said.

"So Stanley was supposed to spray."

I nodded, encouraging him.

"And Stanley did spray," said Gilly Fats.

"So?" I said.

"Ah," said Gilly Fats. "*So* Stanley took advantage of the fact that everybody was going upstairs to the restaurant after the game, not hanging around in the players' wing. *So* instead of waiting until we all got out of the entire building, which was late, granted, as soon as everybody was out of the players' wing, Stanley sprayed down here. And then—" Gilly Fats paused dramatically.

I waited him out.

"And then he left the storage door open, and access to the liquid Vapo to whoever tried to frost Floyd. Stanley sprayed at 4:30 P.M. We all gathered in the restaurant at five."

"You'd have to know the Vapo was in there," I said.

"That might narrow the field by one," he said.

Gilly's dessert came and our coffees. "Got all that out of the cops today, and Dr. Joe. Now listen to this interesting fact."

I listened.

"Trouble with this Vapo stuff is it takes away your cholinesterase, and you don't get that stuff back right away. You're 'enzyme-depleted,' Dr. Joe called it. And your body has to go to work and build you up a new supply, which takes time. Cholinesterase regeneration, it's called. Takes about six weeks, two months. So for about a month after, you're gonna be moving a little more slowly because your nerve connections aren't tops. And you're very vulnerable to a second dose of the stuff. That's the beauty part of this damn poison. How professional pest-controllers keep your abode bug-free, why they come around every month. It ain't necessarily the first squirt that flattens the buggers, but the second taste, or the third. Get it?"

I got it.

Gilly Fats laughed his low laugh. "So now our Floydie is just like one of them insects. Flat on his back, plumb out of cholinesterase, and a sittin' cock-a-roach for a second splat of the juice."

"Hoo, boy," I said.

Gilly's mug face smiled at me. "Hoo, boy, is right, T.T. But we worked out a system. Well, it was Doc Joe's idea really."

"A system for what?" I said blowing on my coffee to cool it.

"A system to protect Floyd," said Gilly Fats. He still had some cigar to finish before he started on his strawberry pie. He examined the length of his ash. "Kinda clever of Dr. Joe, I thought."

"What's the system?" I asked.

"Okay. Unbeknownst to the world, Floyd has been spirited away from High Mountain General. He's at Mrs. Snowfield's place now, under guard. To keep his whereabouts known to as few people as possible, a No Visitors sign has been posted on his hospital room door, and a policeman stationed outside. Like he was still there. And the nurses when they do rounds will go into his room just like it was occupied, and come out again and go on their way. That's the first part." He stubbed out his cigar in the blob of ketchup in his french fries carton.

"The second part is this," he went on. "In each of our bedrooms, they've moved in a cot, yours and mine."

"Oh no," I said. "Listen, he may be safe enough with us, but are we going to be safe with him? That guy can get mean, you know."

Gilly Fats rumbled a laugh. "I can handle him, T.T. You think you can't?" He started on his pie, still snickering.

"I don't turn my back on him as a rule," I said. "And sleeping in the same room sounds dangerous to me."

"Aw, come on, T.T., be a sport. It's for Floyd's own good."

"Why can't he just sleep with you?" I said.

"That's the clever part," said Gilly Fats. He used a napkin to wipe his shirtfront. It didn't do too much good. "During the day Floyd convalesces it on the chaise. Come beddy-bye time, he don't tell nobody where he's going to sleep. We all go to our rooms. Then Floydie decides where to bed down and goes to one of the two cots. And the guard stays midway between our two doors. Even the guard's not supposed to know for sure where Floyd is. And if nobody knows for certain where he's going to be, and he has a friend with him at all times, Dr. Joe thinks Floyd will come out none the worse for wear."

I smoked my cigarette. "Why not just send him back to New York?" I said.

"Well," said Gilly Fats. "We discussed that. But he don't want to go. And the dicks think that if somebody tried once, that somebody might try again. Try something different, maybe, and get caught the next time. And also, it's possible the murderer don't know about the peculiarities of this here poison. I mean, it ain't general knowledge like Rod Carew's batting stats. And also, Floyd might know something, or have photographed something that fingers Lou LaMont's killer. Maybe Floyd don't even know he knows what he knows, but the killer knows, if you get what I mean. So in that way Floyd can help the investigation. Might even be vital, Weatherwax said. Remember Floyd's film got lifted somehow? Wasn't in Toby's sack when Toby got to the *Graphic?* Well, Weatherwax figures there was a reason for that. That's why they're leaving you alone."

"What do you mean, leaving me alone?" I said.

Gilly Fats slurped off the last of his coffee. "Well, at first, T.T., they bought the idea the poisoned mustard was meant for you. Oh yeah, in case you're interested, it was the mustard that was doctored, not the sauerkraut like Floydie thought. Lab confirmation came in just after you dropped me off at police h.q. But now Sherlock Holmes and his buddy think it was meant for poor Floyd after all on account of Floyd's film getting lost.''

"Gee," I said.

Gilly Fats flopped his notepad shut. "And that about explains my day. How was yours? Productive?"

"Oh, I got a few pictures of the people around here. Mrs. Snowfield, the cheerleaders. Sent some of it out today and I've got some more film to send in now."

"Well, do up the envelope and we'll drop it in the mail chute at the post office on our way home," said Gilly Fats.

"Okay," I said.

He got out of the Chevie to shake his lap free of bun and burger crumbs. I made up the *Graphic* envelope, identified the film on tag sheets as the interior views of Lovable Lou LaMont's bachelor pad, two cheerleaders lunching after the tragedy, and the seven body shots of Patty Cambron, another cheerleader, the latest victim of the sports freak.

Gilly Fats didn't watch me. He turned the radio on to Frank Sinatra singing "I Did It My Way" and sang along in a nice enough voice.

I didn't tell him about the body shots I'd taken of Patty Cambron. I didn't understand why he'd criticized me in front of the police, and I didn't want to bring the subject up. I figured I'd let him get the news in the *Graphic* if Barkley used one. So I just didn't tell him. Maybe I should have.

"Want to ride down to the morgue after?" I said. I got the Chevie going and burned a little rubber turning onto the highway just for fun. I headed for the post office.

"What, you crazy?" said Gilly Fats.

"You mean laying down the rubber," I said, "or going to the morgue?"

"These tires are too bald to leave rubber, T.T. No, I meant the morgue. Not my favorite place."

"Don't you want to get the p.m. report?"

"The post mortem can wait until tomorrow. I'm off duty now, thanks."

"Well, I think I'm going to," I said.

Gilly shrugged. "So be my leg man. Okay by me. Just drop me off at the mansion."

We went by the post office and I dropped the mailing envelope through the opening in the door. Then we stopped at an all-night donut shop and I waited in the Chevie while Gilly Fats went in to get a box of beautifuls, as he called them, for his midnight snack. "Got some cinnamon coconuts and some blueberry creams," he said when he came back, piling himself into the car. Then I drove him out to Snowfield's.

"Sure you want to go all the way back in, T.T.?" said Gilly Fats when we got there.

I smiled. "Give my love to Floyd," I said. "I'll be back soon."

Gilly Fats got out of the car. "See ya later then," he said and waved. I jumped the clutch out and jack-rabbited down the drive.

When I got to the morgue everything was in a flap.

"Not you again!" hollered Detective John Xavier when I came through the door into the white-on-white ante room. It's sure nice being wanted.

Huey, the male nurse, looked as white as the room. He was sitting with his swivel desk chair in the recline position and with his head propped against the white wall. He was sobbing into a large white handkerchief, looking red-ringed-and-red-eyed up at Lieutenant Jason Weatherwax. Weatherwax was standing over him. One hand braced himself against the wall, the other stuck in his belt near the gun holster. He was talking to Huey. Every three or four words, Lieutenant Weatherwax stood away from the wall, made a fist, banged at the wall like it was Huey's head, and then went back to bracing himself. Every time Lieutenant Weatherwax pounded, Huey sobbed anew.

On the waiting bench sat Dr. Joe with his head in his hands. He had on a white lab coat, and he was still wearing his tennis shorts and his Julius Erving sneaks.

Detective Xavier waved his arm in my face so Lieutenant Weatherwax would see me and then went back to pacing back and forth like the Islander's goalie only wthout the skates.

I stood against the near wall and didn't say a word. My camera bag was feeling heavy on my shoulder, but I didn't set it down. I just stood there, waiting to get kicked out.

"All right, Huey," Lieutenant Weatherwax said, "now one more time. Did it happen or didn't it happen? Were you lying then or are you lying now?"

Huey sobbed and didn't answer.

"Kick him, Jason. Beat the bastard," said Detective Xavier, not breaking stride.

"Jesus, Joseph, and Mary," mumbled Dr. Joe. "Jesus, Jos—"

"Oh, shut up, Doc, stop blaspheming," snarled Detective Xavier, walking up to the wall and wheeling round. "You slime."

"Jesus, Joseph, and Mary," mumbled Dr. Joe.

I just stood there and breathed in and out.

Lieutenant Weatherwax banged the wall. "This means your job, boy. You know that, don't you?" Weatherwax hit the wall again. "Before this night's over I'm going to have a paper with what you saw on it and your signature signed in great big capitals." He looked over at me. "You hang around, toots. No violence. You're a witness."

Huey started to sob again, but he stopped, noticing me. He sniffled instead and swallowed. "Publicity, Lieutenant? Please, sir, no publicity."

Weatherwax smiled like Dracula. "We'll have you smeared on the front page of every newspaper in this country if you don't start cooperating, Huey. If you do, maybe we can talk to the lady."

Talk, smalk, I thought. A scooper is a scooper. I kept my thoughts to myself.

"He's my friend," said Huey, and blew his nose hard.

"He's nuthin'," said Detective Xavier. He walked back and forth.

Lieutenant Weatherwax gave a big sigh. "Why'd you call 441-2000, Huey? You just playing games with us? Something like that?"

Huey looked over at Dr. Joe. Dr. Joe still had his head in his hands staring down at the white tile floor. "I'm sorry, Joe," Huey said.

Dr. Joe nodded into his hands. "Jesus, Mary, and Joseph," he whispered.

Lieutenant Weatherwax stepped back from the wall and slapped his palms against his thighs. "Okay, let's hear it for the record. John X., get your notebook."

Detective Xavier stopped pacing and plopped down on the top of Huey's desk. He picked up his notebook which was lying there. He took his pencil off his ear where he'd stuck it for safekeeping, ran a hand through his sandy blunt-cut hair, and licked the tip of the pencil point. "Ready, sir," he said.

No one was paying any attention to me, so I sat my camera bag down and sat on the floor beside it, crosslegged.

Dr. Joe glanced over at me. "Tell Rachel I'm sorry," he said.

Lieutenant Weatherwax banged the wall. "She tells nobody nothing, Joe. You're the one who'll do the telling. All in good time, Doc. For now, you just relax over there and keep on praying. I like to hear you do that."

Dr. Joe closed his eyes in a look of martyrdom.

"Go," said Lieutenant Weatherwax to Huey.

"Do I have to, sir? I'd really rather not. I've thought it all over, and I'd much prefer to forget the entire incident."

Detective Xavier laughed. "He wants to forget the entire incident," he said. Weatherwax gave his basset-hound smile. "Don't that beat all," he said. Then, back at Huey. "At 7:35 I rang the High Mountain Police."

Huey repeated dutifully after him. "At 7:35 I rang the High Mountain Police." He stopped. He looked over at Dr. Joe. "Goddamn, Joe, why'd you have to do it for? Don't you get plenty?" Huey rubbed his hands together and stuck them between his thighs. "I called to report what I saw happen. I was shocked. I reacted without thinking."

Dr. Joe sat staring at the floor. His glossy black head and his patrician nose made a perfect profile shot sculpted against the white wall. Unfortunately, I couldn't shoot it.

"What did you see, Huey?" prodded Lieutenant Weatherwax.

Huey looked at me trying to stay as invisible as possible hunched up on the floor. "Does she have to hear?"

"The public has a right to know, Huey," said Lieutenant Weatherwax. I couldn't believe it. He was using me to pressure Huey somehow. But how was he going to keep me quiet? Maybe he intended to throw me out as a reward to Huey if Huey spilled the beans. But from the look of it, Weatherwax had Huey talking anyway.

Huey looked appealingly at Lieutenant Weatherwax. He was still sniffling into his handkerchief, but his eyes had finally dried up.

Lieutenant Weatherwax patted Huey's head. "It's all right, Huey, I'll decide what the public knows and when they know it. I know what I'm doing. Just forget about that girl over there and concentrate on me. Just tell me what happened. That's a good boy."

"But you already know, Jason. I told you over the phone."

Lieutenant Weatherwax said in a patient voice, "We need it for

... 93

the record, Huey. Now come on and quit stalling."

"Yeah, I want to get out of here, Huey," said Detective Xavier. "I got me a date with one of them cheerleaders."

Huey looked at Detective Xavier appreciatively. "Aw, go on. No kiddin', John X.?"

"Yeah," said Detective Xavier. "That dark-headed one. That Rachel." Xavier laughed and looked at Dr. Joe.

"Don't you wish," said Dr. Joe not looking up.

"Okay, boys. Let's cut the comedy," said Lieutenant Weatherwax. "Come on, Huey, get it over with."

Huey seemed to have made up his mind. He took a deep breath. "Well, how it happened was this. I'd sent out for some sandwiches. Grilled ham and cheeses. And some coffees. Thought I'd surprise Doc Joe. Give him a break. This case ain't been easy on him. Any fool could see that."

Lieutenant Weatherwax nodded. Detective Xavier wrote.

"So when the sandwiches come, I go in the back, to the cut-up room. That's what we call it." He looked sheepishly at Weatherwax, but the Lieutenant didn't react. So Huey went on. "I was goin' to ask the Doc if he wanted a grilled ham and cheese. You know, being a buddy, like."

Lieutenant Weatherwax nodded again.

"Well, those doors swing in. Those green doors back there, Jason. You've seen them. And there's a pane of glass in each one, right?"

"Right," said Lieutenant Weatherwax.

"Well, I never liked that place back there much. Can't blame me for that, can you? Only person I know who does like it is Doc Joe. He always seems happy in there. But okay, he's a doc. They're like that." Huey stopped again and snuck a peek at Dr. Joe.

Dr. Joe hadn't moved. He still sat like a supplicant, staring focusless at a white floor tile, his arms on his knees, his hands folded. He wasn't fretting now, wasn't mumbling to himself.

"So like I say," Huey started up again, "I got this habit of kinda sidlin' up to those swinging green doors, you see, like they might catch me and suck me in there if I ain't careful. What I mean is I don't hit those doors like Richard Widmark in a western, no sir. Call it a superstition if you want."

Both policemen nodded. I caught myself nodding too. We could all understand the feeling.

"So okay," said Huey, getting warmed up. "I creep up, the way I do, and peek in through one of the little glass windows. Just to get the lay of the land, so to speak. And Jason," Huey stopped and blew again, hard, into the handkerchief. The color had come back in his face. He was even getting florid. He shook his head back and forth. "And Jason, what I saw through that window don't bear repeating."

"Repeat it anyway," said Lieutenant Weatherwax, deadpan.

"I saw Doctor DeBianco there, my friend Doc Joe—" Huey's voice got higher and higher and he extended his right arm full length pointing a finger at Dr. Joe's bent back. "I saw that man pokin' it into that dead girl's body." Huey dropped his arm deadweight into his lap. "How could a man do that?" he said.

We all stared at Dr. Joe. Dr. Joe looked at the floor.

Lieutenant Weatherwax cleared his throat. Detective Xavier sharpened his pencil, *sker-uff*. The pencil point slid around the razor edge. *Sker-uff*. Detective Xavier knocked the wood shavings into an ash tray.

"You certain, Huey? You certain that's what you saw, that's what he was doing?"

Committed now, Huey couldn't talk fast enough. "I seen it, Jason, I seen it. I watched him doin' it. Had his tennis shorts down around his socks. His lab coat hiked up. Leanin' over that metal grid with the tray underneath for the slop, pushin' back and forth, holdin' her knees. Smilin' like Dr. Strangelove." Huey shivered the length of his body. "Thought I'd puke," he said.

"So then what?" pushed Lieutenant Weatherwax.

Huey was calmer now. "I high-tailed it out of there, Jason. Called you on the phone. Then I ate them two ham-and-cheeses myself. Drank the coffees too. Be damned if I'd share with him."

"Okay, Huey," said Lieutenant Weatherwax, "that's fine. You just relax now. John X. here is going to use your typewriter and write up the statement. Then once you get it signed, you can go home. If what you say is right, you'll keep your job. Might even be a promotion in it for you. If what you said is wrong—"

"Oh, it ain't wrong, Jason. Just ask him." Huey was all self-righteousness now, the thought of a promotion swelling his chest.

"We'll ask him, Huey. We'll ask him. All in good time."

Detective Xavier hopped off the desk top and came around to the sliding extension of the desk where the typewriter sat.

. . . 95

"You stay sittin' right there, Huey," Detective Xavier said, pulling over a spare chair. "I'll just turn this typewriter around and type from this side."

"Okay, John X. Whatever you say." Huey swiveled his chair up to the desk and leaned over it. "Boy, am I glad that's over."

"So are we," said Lieutenant Weatherwax. He walked over to me, stuck out a hand to help me off the floor, and said, "I'll walk you out to your car."

I shouldered my camera bag and followed him outside. It was really cold now. I wished I'd brought a coat last week, last Wednesday, when I'd first come to High Mountain, a hundred years ago.

"I let you listen in on that for one reason," said Lieutenant Weatherwax.

I didn't ask the reason. I waited for him to tell me.

"We've got a real freak on the loose," he said. "And this freak is somebody we all know, not some anonymous crazy. Maybe it's Dr. Joe. Maybe it's you. Maybe it's somebody else."

"Maybe it's you," I said, being smart.

"No," he said. "It isn't me."

"Well, sorry Charlie, it's not me either."

"My name is Jason," he said.

"Just an expression," I said.

"Okay," he said, "so it isn't you. I never thought it was. Now listen to what I'm telling you."

"I'm listening," I said.

We reached the Chevie. I set my camera bag on the hood and leaned against the fender. Lieutenant Weatherwax put a foot on the front bumper.

"Your colleague, Mr. Ott—"

"You can call him Gilly Fats, Lieutenant. Only not to his face. Nobody calls him Mr. Ott. Call him Gill if you want to be polite."

He smiled like Walt Frazier when they traded him to Cleveland. "All right. Your colleague, Gilly, has probably told you about the arrangements we made about your other partner, Beesom. Has he?"

"Yes," I said.

"Well, we may be wrong," he said. "It still may be you who were the intended victim."

"I don't see how," I said.

"If we saw how, Miss Baldwin, there wouldn't be any danger."

"Yes, sir," I said.

"If you do know something, the sooner you realize you do, the better for yourself, the better for all of us. We don't want any more murders in High Mountain."

"No," I said.

"I let you listen in tonight because I think it is in our best interests that you be kept informed and up-to-date on all developments. You and your friend Floyd Beesom too. I'm convinced one of you has the key to this case. It's just a matter of discovering what that clue is, what it means to this monster running around loose. You're not to tell anyone what you heard tonight. Except Floyd Beesom. And then swear him to secrecy. Not Gilly. Not your boss at the *Graphic*. Not Mrs. Snowfield. None of the cheerleaders. Nobody. I'm putting you on your honor. You heard what you heard because it may help you, and may help you help us. I wasn't feeding you exclusives, Miss Baldwin. Do you understand?"

I sighed. "What a rotten break," I said.

"Murder isn't a game, Miss Baldwin. Don't make the fatal mistake of thinking that it is. Do I have your cooperation?"

I thought about it. "If I do keep my mouth shut, and I do prove of some help in the investigation, when this mess is all over, do I get the exclusive for my paper?"

Lieutenant Weatherwax chuckled. "You're okay, Miss Baldwin. I admire your drive. I used to be like you, when I was younger."

"I stay on the beat," I said, self-conscious.

"You sure do," he said.

"Well, you work hard too," I said to be kind, knowing zip about his working habits. "So is it a deal?"

He held out his hand. We shook on it.

"I'll say goodnight now," he said.

"No," I said, "there's something I want to know."

"What is it?"

"How did Patty Cambron die?"

He took his foot down from the fender, stretched his back, and put his hands in his pockets.

"Not very well, I'm afraid. As far as pain was concerned, Lou LaMont had it easier, quicker. Patty was strangled. With a long, wrap-around hair net. It was pulled so tight it burst the skin around the throat. Then after the knots, the murderer made a neat little bow out of the ends. Then he, or she, Miss Baldwin, stuffed Patty's body in the locker, took another hair net, and hung her head from the hook. Tied that hair net in a little bow too. Her face wasn't very pretty when we found her. Did you see her face?"

"No," I said. "There was a towel over her face and I let it be. I didn't want to see it."

"Her face was as bad as anything I've seen," said Lieutenant Weatherwax. "Strange the murderer would make her face look like that and then be sensitive enough to cover it up, even before the swelling started, don't you think?"

"I don't know," I said. "Are you driving at something?"

He looked down at me from his six feet, and the look on his face reminded me of my father looking at me when I was seven, the first thing I saw when I came out of the anesthetic when I had my tonsils out.

"I thought maybe you had covered her face," he said.

"No," I said.

"The killer did something else," he said.

I waited.

"He stuck one of those needles, like was used on Lou, in the back of her neck too, through the hair net. Doc Joe said the needle hadn't hurt her; she was already dead by then. Doc Joe thinks it was meant as a signature."

"Or she," I said.

"Or she," he repeated. "If a woman could pull a hair net that tight."

"Could she?"

"Doc Joe says yes. The flesh probably swelled after the hyoid bone in the throat was broken, and that made the hair net even tighter." He paused. "Is that all now?"

"One more thing," I said. "Did you find a note, a scrunched-up note, in Patty's shorts pockets, along with my business card?"

He pursed his lips. "We did," he said.

"What did it say."

He threw his head back and looked at the sky. The night was dark, the air too dense for many stars to shine through. The moon was a weak little sliver, hardly worthy of the name.

"I'm trying to remember," he said.

"You remember," I said.

He looked from the sky back to me. "Yes," he said, "I do. It went like this. I'm quoting now. 'I found a can of Novocain in the hairspray holder. The Novocain can sprays too. Dr. Joe has—' That

98 . . .

was all. No more, no less."

"I didn't figure Dr. Joe," I said.

"Who did you figure?" he asked, using my slang.

"I guess I didn't figure anybody yet, Lieutenant. It's all happened so fast."

"You figure Dr. Joe now?" he said.

I thought about it. "Not really. He may be a necrophiliac, but that doesn't make him a murderer. Maybe he just needs to get married."

Lieutenant Weatherwax didn't change expression. He opened the Chevie door for me. "Well," he said, "Dr. Joe can tell it to the judge. Goodnight, Miss Baldwin. And please pay attention to what I've said to you."

"I'll pay attenion. I'll follow your rules. After all, we have a deal."

"Good," he said. "Thank you." He shut my door.

I checked the back seat to see if anyone were crouching on the floorboards but of course there wasn't. I started the Chevie like a little old lady and drove away as nice as you please.

All the way to Snowfield's I didn't think a lick. I just listened to the news from the rest of the world on the radio. From the sound of it, not too much was happening out there. High Mountain had most of the action.

..... IX

Snowfield's wasn't as big as you might think, but it was the biggest house I'd ever been in. An architect probably has a better name, but if I call it southern Plantation style you'll know what it looked like. At night it's kept lit up with floodlights that have a bluish tinge to them because the lights shoot through the furze bushes they're installed under. The lights are supposed to keep uninvited guests from rallying round. The estate probably has a security system too, but I wouldn't know about that.

I was almost asleep at the wheel as I pulled up Lemuel's Lane and parked the Chevie in the circular driveway. I parked it on the side, just right of the big entrance porch. I hoped I could find my bedroom without bothering anybody. If Floyd had his guard in tow, like Gilly said he had, maybe the guard would know where my room was.

In the wash of the night lights I could see down the long east lawn, past the weeping willow tree and the wrought iron breakfast table. Way in the back a macrame hammock swung between the trunks of two white beech trees. Under one of the beeches I spotted a white blur. I watched it until I recognized what it was. Overcoat, the team mascot, snoozing the night away.

If it wasn't so cold, I'd have been tempted to sleep in that hammock and leave Floyd to fend for himself tonight. I didn't feel like putting up with him. But I didn't know where the blankets were, and maybe Mrs. Snowfield wouldn't appreciate me fixing up my own bed roll.

So I stumbled up the wide white steps and went in to find my four-poster.

I found it. I said hello to the guard in the hallway. He was sitting on a wooden chair you wouldn't think Mrs. Snowfield would allow in the place. He was a stocky guy in a wrinkled uniform with a friendly face surrounding an untrimmed black moustache. He was reading an *Amazing Spiderman* comic book and lipping a Lowenbrau. In his lap he had a whole stack of *Spiderman*'s and an open can of Planter's cocktail peanuts.

"Name's Alphonse. French-Canadian," he whispered. "But you can call me Al."

"Name's T.T.," I whispered back.

"I know," he said. "Sweet dreams."

I went into the bedroom. I saw the cot in the shadows. It was pushed against the wall opposite the fireplace, between a walnut chiffoniere and one of those wooden things that are supposed to hold your bedspread while you sleep so it won't get dirty.

The cot was empty. Good, I thought, Floyd's sleeping with Gilly Fats tonight. Then I heard him snore. *Auwww-uhhhh. Auwww-uhhhh.* Floyd was sleeping like a Grizzly in January under the rosebuds and the ruffles.

"Nerve," I said, but I was too tired to care. I undressed in the dark, hung my clothes on the wooden bedspread thing, and got into my yellow silk monogrammed p.j.'s. I don't know why I even bought them. They cost as much as a 15 mm. wide-angle I could use and don't have. But wherever I travel I take them along. They make me feel good somehow. I crawled into the cot and fell asleep in the quiet between two of Floyd's snores, which means in about a second and a half.

I woke up ravenous. It was nine A.M. on the nose. I was alone in the room. Alphonse must have taken Floyd out, set him on the chaise and put him, like a philodendron, out on the sun porch.

I looked out through the gauzy windows. It looked cold, the clouds low, scudding and bumping into each other, heading south like the birds. I looked for the hammock, for the little goat. I saw him still under the beech tree, still curled up with his head turned backward the way animals do it, resting it on his shoulder. Lazy little critter, I thought. He should be up and about by now, chowing down on some steamed oats and molasses, or at least keeping the grass cropped close.

Today I meant to tackle David Livingston and find out what I could about those briefcases. But before I set off I'd take a few snaps of Overcoat and Mrs. Snowfield if I could get them together. The pictures would add a nice warm note after the sensationalism of Patty Cambron's murder.

I put on a fresh pair of jeans, my favorite pink sweater—100% cashmere and a little too big, the way I like it—and my black boots. Then I went out to bag my breakfast.

I found Mrs. Marcella Snowfield in the morning room. She was sitting on a chintz sofa staring at the front page of the Tuesday *Graphic*.

"Oh, good morning, Miss Baldwin," she said, starting to rise.

"Please don't get up," I said, embarrassed. "And call me T.T. I'm not used to being called Miss Baldwin."

She was wearing lavender watersilk and a coral David Webb necklace. She looked as good as anybody could who's sixty-three years old. Which is very good. She'd kept her weight where it ought to be without being sexy about it, had her face lifted good and tight, and had a magnificent silver head of hair. Her eyes were just eyes. I guess even with a trillion dollars you can't have everything. This is just a suspicion, but I think she also thought the world revolved more or less around her, but would never say so.

She settled back in the corner of her sofa. "Breakfast is in the arboretum," she said. "It's too chilly out there under the willow."

The arboretum. So that's what she called the sun porch. Just because she had a gloxinia plant or two, or sixteen.

"The roses," she was saying. "The roses were mine. Did you know that?"

"Roses, Mrs. Snowfield?"

She tapped the *Graphic* with a silver Cross pen. "I've just been reading about poor Patty. The roses. I sent the girls the bouquet that morning, opening day. They put them in the blue vase. The roses looked so lovely I thought. So red against the blue. The girls were delighted with them. I went in and admired them after the commercial was over, before I went up to my box. They were perfect."

"Maybe that's what the policemen meant," I said.

"Meant about what, Miss Baldwin?"

"About you being seen down in the players' wing before the game. Remember, you got upset when they questioned you about it."

Okay, it may not have been polite. But you've got to push for the info whenever you get the opening.

"Oh, yes," she said, smoothly. "I'd forgotten that. You were in the bar then, weren't you? Yes, maybe that is what Lieutenant Weatherwax meant. I'd forgotten about that when he questioned me."

"I've heard rumors about you and Lou LaMont," I said.

She didn't bat an eye. "People can be cruel, Miss Baldwin," she said. "I loved Lou like the son I never had. Some people don't

102 . . .

understand that kind of exalted love. My position isn't an easy one."

"That's just what Coach Reesenbach said to me," I said. "The son thing. Lovable Lou must have really been lovable. I wish I'd known him better."

Her eyes dropped down to the *Graphic*.

I was itching to take a look myself at the front page picture. Even from where I was, I could tell it was one of my shots of Wanda. Two front page scoopers in a row! I wanted to shout and dance around a little. But I didn't. I stood there like a bum of a newspaper person browbeating Mrs. Snowfield.

She raised her eyes back to me. "She's very beautiful, isn't she?"

"You're beautiful too, Mrs. Snowfield," I said.

"Which one of us do you think he preferred?"

"She said he preferred you," I said.

Mrs. Snowfield smiled ever so faintly. "I dare say she was right," she said. "Shall I tell you something, girl-to-girl—off the record, as you people say?"

"Yes," I said. "Off-the-record if you like."

"Just because a woman passes sixty and loses her husband, she doesn't necessarily lose her passion. Did you realize that?"

"I never thought about it," I said.

"When I lost Lemuel, I cried for a year. A very unsatisfactory existence, Miss Baldwin. Oh, I know, you'll say I cried on satin pillows. But I've always found that qualification irrelevant. What was important is that I was crying, my dear, day and night, night and day."

"I'm glad you found some happiness, Mrs. Snowfield. I just think you ought to come clean and tell it to Weatherwax. If they find out from someone else, the way I did, they might distrust you."

She gave me a beautiful smile. "I have 'come clean' as you say so eloquently, Miss Baldwin. Lieutenant Weatherwax knows of my, let me say, avid interest in Lovable Lou LaMont. He just doesn't know how avid. What Jason Weatherwax doesn't know, and what I see no reason to tell him, but I would like little Wanda to know, is that Lou and I were satisfying our avid interest a half-hour before kick-off. On the examining table off Dr. Joe's office. And let me say, it was thrilling. Quite thrilling. Now what do you think of that, young lady?"

"I think High Mountain's a hotbed of iniquity," I said, grinning.

She grinned right back at me. "I think you're right, Miss Baldwin. And furthermore, it wasn't just for my money that Lou preferred me to the beauteous Wanda Pettigo. Oh no. Sexually I was also superior. He told me so. What's she? Twenty-three? And me, forty years older. I'm much more than a rich widow, Miss T.T. Baldwin. I'm a boudoir superstar."

That's what she said. Boudoir superstar.

"A real freak about it, huh?" I said. I was getting a lot more than I'd bargained for out of Mrs. Marcella Snowfield.

She leaned back contentedly into her couch cushions. "If you'd like to put it that way," she said. She tapped Wanda's picture again with her silver pen. "It's such good copy isn't it? The dear girl's eyes full of tears, mourning her betrothed. Better her in the *Graphic* than me, Miss Baldwin. That's all I have to say about it."

"Are you going to marry Abe Hirshaw?" I asked, going for broke now, nothing to lose.

"Perhaps," she said, looking like Mehitabel with another dance or two left in her. "But don't let me keep you from your breakfast." She looked down again at Wanda's picture, caressed it with her palm. I had been dismissed.

I had one more parting shot to make. "You didn't kill him, did you, Mrs. Snowfield?"

She didn't even look up. "Only with kindness," she said.

Hoo, boy. That lady was a double handful.

I headed for the arboretum. It was just off the kitchen. No servants in sight.

Floyd was stretched out on the chaise looking pale and old without the man-tan on his face. He had the *Graphic* in his lap.

"How much this picture cost you, ace?" he said as I came in and told him hi.

"Let me see it," I said.

He handed it over. "Keep it. I got no more use for it."

I looked at the picture. It was good. It was even bigger than yesterday's front-pager of Lou LaMont falling at Billy Badman's sack. I looked for the credit line. There it was: "*Graphic* photo by T.T. Baldwin" in small black type.

"It's great," I said.

"How much it cost you, ace? Besides poisonin' your partner and putting him out of commish?"

Reaction as expected, I thought. I sighed. Out loud I said, "Oh, two lies, a cup of coffee, and half an hour. Not too bad, eh? I'm hungry. What's to eat?"

"Some of Gilly's donuts on the table. Oatmeal on the stove. Coffee."

I bet Mrs. Snowfield had champagne and peach crepes. Well, beggars can't be choosers. I settled on the oatmeal, put raisins in it and milk, and got myself a big mug of coffee. The coffee was A-one.

"Where's Gilly Fats?" I asked the grump.

"Out workin'," Floyd said. "Like you ought to be."

"I was out late last night," I said. "Fireworks."

"I heard. Been up since six-thirty."

"You're supposed to be sleeping a lot," I said. "How do you feel?"

"No worse. Still weak in the pins. Frustrated. I don't like the little second-stringer coppin' all my by-lines."

"You'll be back in harness soon enough, Floyd. Don't go grudging me a picture or two."

"See it don't go to your head," he said.

"You're such a delight to work with," I said.

"Bet on it, scoop," he said with satisfaction.

"I thought I'd get some pix of the team mascot and Mrs. Snowfield today," I said. "You know, human interest stuff. She keeps him here during the week. Lets him run around and play. He's outside now under the hammock last I looked. Would you like to help? Maybe do it yourself?" I was trying to be nice. I should have known better.

Floyd snorted. "I can still find my own shots, Baldwin."

Well, I tried.

"Okay," I said, wondering if he'd ever call me T.T. Gilly Fats always did. Floyd never.

I finished my breakfast, staring all the time at my front page pix. Floyd was quiet. I took my dishes to the sink, washed them, said see-ya, and got out of there.

The little goat didn't move as I approached it. It was a pretty little thing, not grown yet. He had long strawberry-blond hair that faded to silver on the ends and on his underbelly. The hair was thick and wavy like an Irish setter dog's. His dainty cloven hooves were kept shiny with polish. His horns had just started to grow, two little flesh-covered nubs sprouting up proud beside his too-big ears. He didn't have his beard yet. That ought to come in the spring in his second year, to make him attractive to female Tibetan goats.

Overcoat's eyes were almost closed by blond lids and long white eyelashes. Oh dear, I thought as I came up, the little fella's sick.

I knelt down beside him and smoothed his coat. He didn't move. I touched his funny little muzzle to see if it was hot, the way they tell you to do with dogs. He nipped gently at my fingers but that was all. I went back into the house to tell Mrs. Snowfield.

She was on the phone but she hung up when I stopped in front of her. I told her Overcoat was sick. She didn't ask me any details. She called Stanley Farmer and told him to come over right away. She told him to bring Dr. Joe.

"I don't think Dr. Joe can come," I said.

She looked at me as if she didn't care what I thought. "Dr. Joe was released on $900 bail this morning," she said.

Some people know everything.

She went over to a wooden cabinet with small-paned glass doors that had liquor bottles and glasses in it. She poured herself some Johnny Walker neat. "Like one?" she said with her back to me, belting hers. I told her I'd stay with Overcoat and went out to wait. She was pouring out another.

I found some fresh water in a pail hung on a hook to keep it upright outside the stable that had been built for him. The stable door was open so he could come and go as he pleased. It was clean with fresh straw laid down for his bedding. In the food trough was a big helping of oats with some quartered apples in it and some sliced carrots and some green stuff that looked like cabbage. Overcoat hadn't eaten his supper last night. There was no manure in the straw and it wasn't tamped down so he hadn't slept inside either. Overcoat had been sick for a long time.

I hauled the bucket of water over to him but he wasn't interested. He still hadn't moved. Still had his head tucked down on his shoulder, his muzzle twitching. He was panting just a little now and there seemed to be a whistle in the breathing if you listened close.

I waited for Stanley Farmer and Dr. Joe. They got there very quickly. They must have both been in the same place, probably at the Colossus. I asked if I could help but they didn't pay much attention to me. They worked together well, with very little talk. Stanley knew how to assist Dr. Joe.

So I got out of their way, composed the scene, and started taking pictures. I didn't like myself for it, but when you're a photographer and there's a picture there, you've got to get it if you can.

Stanley held Overcoat's head up and Dr. Joe forced down some fluid that looked like mineral oil. Then Dr. Joe stuck some gray pills deep inside the goat's mouth and massaged its throat until they got swallowed. Then Stanley lifted Overcoat onto his feet and held him up while Dr. Joe rubbed Overcoat's sides. Then Dr. Joe inserted a slender red tube which he'd greased into the goat's rectum. Overcoat was bleating now, pitiful little *baaahs* of protest.

I didn't watch anymore. I went back to the house. Overcoat had got to me.

From the look of it, Floyd and Mrs. Snowfield were going to be good friends. Mrs. Snowfield already had a snootful by now. Floyd had joined her in the morning room and he was catching up fast. It was no place for me to be. I went to my bedroom and called the Colossus to try to catch David Livingston but somebody said he was out. I got his home number and called there.

Babs Livingston said she was in the middle of chopping eggplant pulp for *aubergines Imam Baaldi*, and couldn't talk very long. Then she talked forever.

She spelled the name out for me and said I had been deprived when I told her I'd never eaten any. She said a priest had fainted once from the pleasure. She said if I ever did eat some to try a Riesling wine with it, only to be sure it came from Germany and not from the Napa Valley. She said she thought her David was at the hospital now on business. She knew he would be back at the Colossus after lunch, and I could get him then. She didn't know what his business was at the hospital, but it wasn't picking up male orderlies in case I'd heard it was, the way some nasty people said because David swished. He's all male, she said. He only swished for show. After all, she said, she should know. She said she'd never looked in David's briefcase and wondered what interest I could have with that.

She wanted to know if I'd heard the news about Dr. Joe and did I believe it. She said she certainly didn't and neither did Rachel. And that even if it were true, Abe Hirshaw was really to blame for it all because he had instilled such a high moral sense in Rachel, Ratch couldn't bring herself to go all the way with Dr. Joe even though she wanted to and they'd come awfully close and it made Dr. Joe just crazy.

. . . 107

She said she'd invite me over for dinner sometimes if I was going to be around for awhile. Finally she said she really couldn't talk any more, the sausage was spitting in the skillet and goodbye, so sorry she couldn't chat.

Whew.

I went back to check on Overcoat. He wasn't under the beech tree anymore. Stanley met me halfway to the stable.

"You don't want to go in that stable now, Miss," he said.

"No," I said.

"Doc Joe's cuttin' the little thing's stomach open. By orders of Lieutenant Weatherwax. He thinks what got your photographer friend got Overcoat too."

"I think it's the film," I said. "Floyd's missing film. I think somebody fed Floyd's film to the goat. I think it was the chemicals in the film. The silver. The potassium bromide."

"I dint know about that," said Stanley.

We went back into the house and sat together in the arboretum. I smoked. Stanley looked out the window. In the kitchen a buxom woman who looked Germanic, the first houseperson I'd seen, was cooking something for lunch that smelled odd. Mrs. Snowfield came up and asked Stanley and Dr. Joe to stay for luncheon and of course me too, she said. Stanley went out to relay the invitation to Dr. Joe. I smoked my cigarette.

Abe Hirshaw came over and sat in the morning room with Floyd and Mrs. Snowfield. Mrs. Snowfield shut the doors. Even out on the sun porch I could hear him yelling. One time he said something about "a corpse-cuddler," and then he hollered something about "a taint on my daughter."

After awhile Dr. Joe came in with Stanley and said to me, "Yes, young lady, film. About two rolls of the stuff." Then he went away to wash up and call Lieutenant Weatherwax. If he was embarrassed about last night it didn't show except that he wasn't looking vague anymore. He had his jaw set and steel in his spine.

Lunch was poached bass and cauliflower creamed somehow. There was a white wine but I just drank the water. Mrs. Snowfield sat at the head of the table and Floyd got the guest-of-honor spot at the other end. He was loving it. Abe Hirshaw looked spiffy in gray Irish wool with bone buttons and a Jacques Bellini bone-colored silk tie. He sat on Mrs. Snowfield's right. I sat between him and Floyd. Dr. Joe sat on Mrs. Snowfield's left and Stanley, in his khaki trousers and work shirt sat beside the doctor, quite at ease. Stanley was unmoved by the grandeur of the smaller of Mrs. Snowfield's dining rooms.

I guess Al the guard had gone off duty because I didn't see him anywhere about. If there was another guard on the job, he was hiding pretty well.

Mrs. Snowfield and Abe Hirshaw did most of the talking. They talked about the impossibilities of picking up a decent quarterback this late, and Mrs. Snowfield kept assuring Abe Hirshaw that Black Jack Flowers would be wonderful and that the whole idea of the Climbers' introducing a premier black quarterback into the NFL overjoyed her. She thought it would be thrilling, quite thrilling, if Black Jack took them to the Super Bowl.

Mrs. Snowfield knew her football. She said the best thing she'd liked about Sunday's game was the way Hi-Rent Florring, the Climbers' center, had neutralized the Johnny Reb's three-four defense, taking out the Johnny Rebs' nose tackle, Wreckin' Sam Crews, all by himself.

Abe Hirshaw, like Mrs. Snowfield, picked at the bass. He sniffed his wine before each sip, shot his cuffs every other forkful, and smiled and agreed with Mrs. Snowfield a lot. He avoided conversation with Dr. Joe.

The rest of us ate like Secretariat after winning the Belmont. I was quiet. So were Dr. Joe and Stanley except for an occasional nod and compliments on the food. Floyd was charming and inoffensive, so you know he was oiled.

Over the spiced-pear sherbet and the coffee, Abe Hirshaw mentioned that a double burial for Lovable Lou LaMont and Patty Cambron would be held Wednesday morning at 10 A.M. out at the cemetery. There would be no publicity, he said, looking at me and leaving Floyd alone, but we were all invited.

After lunch Stanley said he thought he'd bury Overcoat on the playing field, behind the end zone, and what did Mrs. Snowfield think of that.

Mrs. Snowfield thought that was just the thing to do. Then she asked Abe Hirshaw what were the chances of having an Overcoat II in time for Sunday's game. That seemed a little cold-blooded but I didn't say anything.

Sunday the Climbers played the Coastville Johnny Rebs again because of a snafu in the scheduling when the two new teams came

... 109

into the National Football League. And because the Johnny Rebs didn't have a stadium of their own yet, they were playing again at the Colossus.

Abe Hirshaw said he'd try.

I said I'd go with Stanley. That way I could see David Livingston in person and get some pictures for Barkley, some fish eye panoramas of the playing field with Stanley small down behind the goal posts shoveling dirt into a shallow wide-mouthed hole.

I told Stanley we'd take the *Graphic* Chevie if he wanted. Stanley said to wait. He'd wrap the body in burlap and get it into the car and let me know when he was ready.

Dr. Joe shook hands with everybody, even Abe Hirshaw. Mrs. Snowfield kissed Dr. Joe on the cheek. Being supportive, I guess. He left in one of the Climbers' brown Caddies.

Floyd yawned without covering his mouth and said he'd take a cat nap. He bundled up on the chaise, put the phone on his lap, and called Barkley.

Abe Hirshaw and Mrs. Snowfield went into the morning room and closed the doors.

The Germanic lady began to clear the table and I helped her while I waited for Stanley. I complimented her on the lunch and she smiled broadly and said "danka."

Stanley came and got me. He'd made a neat package. He'd folded the burlap ends down and tied the body up with that hairy white rope they use on hay bales sometimes. The package didn't look anything like the cuddly billy goat that had pranced for the crowd on Sunday. Death hurts to look at, wherever you see it. Stanley put the package in the trunk.

We roared off, as much as the old *Graphic* Chevie could roar, and I played Nicki Lauda at the wheel, switching lanes around the proper drivers in High Mountain like we were all running the Indy 500. Stanley seemed to enjoy it.

"You know your friend Floyd back there?" he said. "He knows who the killer be."

"He does not," I said.

"Yes, he do," said Stanley. "He tol' me so."

"Who?" I asked. Bedridden Floyd must be undergoing a personality change. He didn't normally brag without cause.

"I don' know who," said Stanley. "He dint tell me who. Just said he knew who. Said he needed my help to prove it."

"When did he do that?" I asked.

"Called me on the phone," said Stanley, scratching his neck. "Early this A.M."

"Gee, he didn't say a thing to me," I said. I thought about it for awhile, but I didn't come up with much.

We got to the Colossus in jig time. There were several cars in the lot. I pulled over as close to the players gate as I could get, so Stanley wouldn't have to carry the body any further than he had to. There was a policeman on the gate and he said we couldn't go in, Lieutenant Weatherwax' orders.

Stanley consulted his big wristwatch. "It's nigh on to two," he told the guard. "Practice ought to be over by now."

The guard grinned. "Yeah," he said, "practice's over. They almost didn't get to practice today. Ole Skyhook had a conniption. So the Lieutenant said they could practice okay, but they couldn't use the players' wing. Couldn't suit up or wash up after or nothing. I watched 'em. Sure looked funny in their street clothes. They ran wind sprints more'n anything else. Threw a football or two. Skyhook couldn't even run his game film from Sunday. I think he's still hollerin' up in the front office. He's really ticked."

"All we want to do is go on the field," said Stanley. "I got to bury the team mascot here. Overcoat's done died." He pointed down at the package sitting on the gravel. "Can't leave it unburied."

"That little goat dead too? Damn Sam. Gonna have to check it out," said the guard.

Stanley nodded good-naturedly. "You call up the big man. We'll wait."

The policeman used his radio car. He came back in a few minutes. "The Lieutenant said to go on and do it, but to let you know I'm watchin'. Also he said you ask Luther if you need anything inside. Luther's guarding the entrance into the wing from the field side. He'll fetch you tools if you need them. Under no circumstances, said the Lieutenant, is the lady or you to go inside the players wing."

"Gotcha," Stanley said. I shifted my camera bag to my left shoulder.

The policeman let us in. We walked the length of the football field because Stanley wanted to bury Overcoat on the far end, by the southside goalposts. "More sun falls that way," he explained.

I stood and looked around at the vast stadium watching the way the shadows fell until Stanley came back from Luther with the tools. Two spades, two shovels, and some white lime powder.

"You don't have to help, Miss," Stanley said. "Luther wouldn't."

"I'll help," I said. "I'll help you dig the hole. That's the toughest. But I want to take pictures of you from way up in the stands while you shovel the dirt back. That way I'll get a whole view of the field and the seats and the goal posts and you filling in the grave. Is that okay with you?"

"Whatever you say, ma'am." He handed me a spade and a shovel. "Know how to do?"

"I'm afraid so," I said.

Stanley sprinkled out a white powder line for us to follow, a circle about two and a half feet in circumference. That may not sound like much, but you try digging it, down three feet, in solid rock-hard earth.

I'd like to say I pulled my share, but I didn't. The spade was rounded to a point, and I was jumping up with both feet on the spade and still not breaking much ground. Stanley was skinny but he must have worked the rock quarry when he was doing time, because he made the earth give way. The rate we were going it looked like an all day job and no light when it came time to photograph.

Stanley had dug about a quarter way round the powder line and I'd managed about a tenth when Coach Reesenbach came jogging over, flopping his hands and yelling something that didn't sound nice. Probably excited because we were tearing up his field, but since we were behind the end line, I didn't see why he'd care. "Saints deliver us," he said as he came up. He wasn't puffing. "You want to take over the whole world, don't you?" He was shouting at me, naturally.

I didn't say anything.

He took the spade away from me. "There's some things your kind still can't do, girlie."

"We can do it," I said. "It just takes us longer."

"Got an answer for everything, doncha," he grunted, and made the dirt fly.

I didn't protest. I'm stubborn but I'm no dummy. My pink sweater needed a good dry cleaning, and I needed a good rest. If there'd been Miller Lite around I might even have drunk that, I was so thirsty.

"Thanks," I said.

112 . . .

Skyhook ignored me. "First we can't practice," he muttered to Stanley. "I can't run my film. Can't use my office. Can't do any damn thing. Stuck with a black quarterback and no mascot and a crazy killer on the loose. Men dyin' on the field, cheerleaders stuffed in lockers and a smart-ass girl who thinks she's a photog. Life ain't been good, Stan. Life ain't been good."

"I'll bring you something to drink," I said.

"Thankee kindly," said Stanley. He was sweating.

I went to bother Luther, who turned out to be the bushy redheaded cop I'd seen yesterday. He brought me three warm Diet Pepsis and said that was the best he could do.

Stanley drank his. Skyhook rinsed his mouth with the stuff and then spit it out. I left them, took mine up into the stands at the opposite end, and set up my shots.

I only have one fisheye lens, but it's a good one. I don't use it much because how often do you want a 180° curve in newspaper pix? Mostly Barkley wants close, close. It was my single most expensive lens and it belongs to me, not to the *Graphic*. This lens gives you the whole picture in a perfect convex bubble. It's used a lot in water shots, yacht-racing, deep-sea fishing, surf-boarding, to showoff wave arcs and curved horizon lines.

My fisheye gave me just what I wanted: the whole round curve of the stadium's rows of empty seats, the field, the distorted-to-infinity goal posts and the two men shoveling the ground. Since it was after three, I even got the goalpost shadow stretching over the field like a giant two-fingered claw.

Coach Skyhook and Stanley did the job in a little over an hour. With me or without me, it probably would have taken Stanley more like four.

When the job was done, I went in search of David Livingston. I had to go back through the players' gate and walk around to the front entrance to the front offices. Livingston wasn't there. He hadn't come back after lunch, and they didn't expect him now. Nobody knew where he was. They really run the place tight.

Lil Harv was there, though, smelling like a whole river of fish. He must bathe in the stuff. "T-t-they won't let me in," he said, three-quarter tenor, one-quarter squeak.

"They aren't letting anybody in," I said. "Lieutenant Weatherwax has the whole wing sealed off. I guess they're still investigating."

"I'm stuck," he said, looking helpless.

. . . 113

"What do you mean, you're stuck?" I said.

"Well, what am I going to do?" he said. "Mom dropped me off and she's gone somewhere. To play tennis, I think, with Mary Ann Matthews? She won't be back to get me 'til six."

"Call your pop," I said.

"I did," he whined. "He's not home. He's never home in the afternoons. He goes to people's houses and measures for things. Shows them wood chips. I called and he's not home." He looked like he was going to cry.

"Well, gee," I said. "I'll drive you home." I had nothing better to do.

"You will?" he said, sounding like I'd promised him an autographed picture of the Four Horsemen of Notre Dame. "Hot dog, thanks a lot."

"Let's go," I said, feeling the kid had manipulated me again.

He whipped his chair around like it was a real live pinto pony with spurs put to its flanks. "Oh boy," he said, "I'll watch television."

In the car Lil Harv did isometrics. "Can't lose a day not stretching my muscles," he said. "They shorten up on me. It's called progressive deterioration. That's what I slow up by exercising. My progressive deterioration, you know."

I didn't know, but all I did was ask directions.

He chattered about the murders while we drove. A very outgoing kid.

"It's topic A around school," he said, between four-counts and holds.

"Sure," I said.

"Yeah. I'm doing an essay on it for English lit. Miss Flitterhaus, she's my homeroom teacher, said I was in an advantaged position. And *hooold*."

"I guess," I mumbled.

"Yeah. Miss Flitterhaus said if it was good she'd send it to the High Mountain *Courier* for me. Then I'll be a newspaper person too, just like you."

"I take pictures, I don't write," I said.

"Same thing," he said. "One, two, three, four."

It sure well wasn't but I wasn't going to go into it.

"When you come to the vee, stay right," he said.

I stayed right.

"And three and four. Patty was my best friend there, you know. She was the nicest to me. She was in love with Walt-the-Talk, I think. She should have known I wouldn't take the hair spray. Shouldn't she? And *hooold*. Do you think Patty thought I was the murderer? Was she accusing me? I mean, in a roundabout way?"

"Why would she think that?" I said.

"Because I was there, you know. Just me and her and Lou. And four. I was in one of the dryer chairs with the bonnet down but not turned on, you know, playing lunar cosmonaut. We were the only ones there."

"When was this?" I asked.

"After the commercial was over. While Patty was rolling up Lou's hair again. For the game. And three and—"

"Nobody else at all?" I said.

"Nope. Four. Well, your two friends were there but Patty kicked them out. And Wanda came in once to talk to Patty but she didn't speak to me or Lou. She was mad at Lou because he wouldn't marry her and she wanted to. She just stayed a minute. And then when his head was all rolled up, Marcella came and got him and took him away somewhere."

"Marcella? You call Mrs. Snowfield Marcella?"

"Yeah. I get to call her Marcella because I don't work for her, *hooold*, and because I'm crippled, I think. When you're crippled you can get away with anything almost. See that green Buick? Turn left just past it."

"Get away with murder?" I said and turned left.

He spoke right up. "Probably. If I cried a lot afterwards. How could you punish me? I've got maybe nine years to live if I'm lucky. Medically, I'm already considered a dead man."

That was the first speech he'd made since I'd known him when his voice hadn't cracked at least once. He'd sounded grown up. Older than me, even.

"Now, on the left, third house in," he said. He was back to his adolescent-kid voice, really murdering the *l* in left. "I'd appreciate it if you'd pull all the way up the driveway."

"Okay," I said. Lil Harv was home. All I had to do now was get him in the house.

While he was getting out of the front seat, I went around to his side and took out the UFO.

"Don't set it up," he said. "I walk with the cane from here.

... 115

Just carry it for me if you would. Want to see my house?"

"Sure," I said. What was I supposed to say, no dice?

I carried the wheelchair up onto the porch. I had to wait awhile until Lil Harv got there. While I waited I tried the front door knob. The door opened.

"Hey, your door's not locked," I said.

"Maybe Pop's back after all," he said. "Working down in his studio. His studio's really neat. I'll show it to you. Ever smell fresh sawdust?"

"Yes," I said. "I love it."

"Me too," he said.

We went in. It was a very nice house, good furniture unimaginatively placed. No Potter Sr in sight. He must sell all his own stuff, I thought, and then buy machine-made. Didn't make sense to me, but I wasn't there to start arguments.

"Mom? Pop?" Lil Harv sang out. Nobody answered.

"Guess Mom forgot to lock up," said Lil Harv with a shrug. His Tintex-blue eyes shone as he looked around. "Gee," he said, "it feels strange being here on a Tuesday all by myself. Come on, I'll show you my room, and Mom's room, and Pop's studio downstairs. Pop works there, sleeps down there. Sometimes he lets me sleep with him, only not too often. Too much trouble, he says, carting me up and down the steps. Pop doesn't sleep with Mom, you know. They quit when they found out about my disease."

Lil Harv seemed to maneuver better in his own house. He knew how to bounce off pieces of furniture to keep himself swinging forward at a good clip.

"You get around pretty good," I said.

"Thanks," he said and blushed.

From the living room he took me to the kitchen. Very modern. Everything in order. "Nice," I said.

"Now I'll show you my room." We headed down the hall, Lil Harv leading the way, using the hall wall for support, doing fine.

His room was light and airy, painted in the Climbers colors, dark brown with light brown trim. A bunk bed. The top bunk was used like a shelf with strange looking pieces of equipment piled on it. Guaranteed muscle-builders. He had a desk under a window with lacy curtains, a small television, and a bar across the doorway to his bathroom so he could chin himself whenever he got the urge. A poster of Arnold Schwarzenegger with his muscles flexed on the wall. A cheap three-shelf bookcase.

Sitting beside an authentic Potter Sr chest of drawers, which Barkley would drool over if he saw, was an apparatus that looked like the electric chair Alcatraz got rid of when they turned it into a public park. Only it was upholstered in red vinyl. It had two pulleys on top, steel weights suspended by cable in the back, and two vertical iron bars with pads hanging down in front that connected to the pulleys and weights, only don't ask me how.

"Hoo, boy," I said, "what's that? They tie you there when you're bad?"

Lil Harv laughed and bounced himself down into the seat. "I'll show you," he said. "It's my Pec Deck."

"Oh sure," I said.

He laughed again. He was enjoying himself. It was nice to see, even if he did still spook me.

He demonstrated. He leaned his arms against the pads and pushed and the weight behind the chair lifted a little. "See?" he said. "It develops my pectorals, and my shoulders and back."

"I see," I said.

"You like my room?" he asked shyly.

"I think it's super," I said.

"Thanks," he breathed, like it was a life and death matter to him.

He popped back up. "Come on. I'll show you Mom's room."

I followed him out.

About all I remember of Caroline Potter's bedroom was the big rumpled bed with orange satin sheets hanging off the sides like a slice of night life in a Goya painting.

The door that led to her bathroom was open, and we heard water running and Caroline's laughter and a deep baritone yelling at her to punt it.

Lil Harv's face went through a few indecisions, and then settled on chalk-white. He'd recognized his hero, Walt-the-Talk's voice, and so had I. After all, it was almost famous.

Lil Harv lurched across the room through the bathroom entrance. I let him go.

I didn't have my camera equipment with me. I put my hands in my jeans pockets and waited. The thought crossed my mind that fun in High Mountain didn't have too much variation. Everybody seemed to go for the same old ballgame. With the pitchers in rotation, of course, the way they do it in the bigs.

It seemed I waited a long time under the circumstances. Walt-the-Talk was congratulating Mrs. Potter on "hanging it high and deep," and she was wanting to know if she'd got the extra point. All very chummy.

The water was running like background music in the movies when something exciting is about to happen. I was enjoying myself. Up to now it had been a disappointing day.

Nobody screamed. The water stopped like the music couldn't bear the tension any more, and Caroline Potter shot into her bedroom all wet and sleek and bewildered like a seal at the aquarium who'd just jumped through the hoop but hadn't got a fish and didn't know why.

She looked at me wild-eyed like I'd set her up, and started picking frilly things off the floor and then throwing them down again. She had a nice white body, nothing to be ashamed of.

Lil Harv jerked himself into the room, his face pinched, his eyes glowing like blue neon on a foggy night in the slums. He was trying to say something to his mother, but he was stuttering too much to get passed the "I-I-I—"

He didn't stop. He pulled the right side of his body forward, then the other side, swinging half-steps, out the bedroom door. He used the door knob to swing himself into the hall, and bumped down it, saying something like "saw-saw" over and over.

Walt-the-Talk appeared hesitantly around the bathroom door frame. He looked like he'd just lost his license to talk. His mouth was opening and shutting, saying "who is it" like a parrot in a pet shop who only knew that one thing. He couldn't see because his hair was all sudzed up in pink lather and the soap was running into his eyes and he'd squeezed them shut. He was dropping water all over the Karastan carpet. He had a towel askew around his middle. The towel was one big red poppy, like the kind Georgia O'Keeffe paints. He was having trouble with the towel. His body was nothing to be ashamed of either.

"Who is it? Who is it, Caroline?" he cawed.

"Please get dressed, Walt," she said so softly it almost sounded coy.

I went out into the hall and started for the front of the house, figuring I'd just leave. When I got to the kitchen I heard a bumping sound, somewhere under the floor. The door to the lower level was open so I poked my head in for a look.

Lil Harv was on the stairs, trying to get up. Going up stairs must be hard for him. He was sitting backward on a step, using his arms to lift his body up one stair, then bringing each leg, one at a time, onto the step beneath. On his lap he had a portable chainsaw, the kind that runs on gasoline. Great scott.

"Hey, Harv," I said, trying to be light about it. "What're you doing? You can't go sawing up your mother."

He was crying hysterically. "Y-y-yes, I-I-I will. You just watch," he said. He stomped on the stairs. He had to lift a leg with both hands and then drop it to stomp.

I came down the stairs and sat beside him on the step. "Push over," I said.

"N-n-no," he said, and gave me a shove that sent me down three steps. The kid was as strong as Bruno Sammartino.

I stayed the three steps down. "You're really strong," I said, still trying to be friendly.

He was sobbing and flailing his hands. "S-s-she blames it on me," he said, all squeaky. "She blames it all on me."

"Well, she doesn't want to blame herself," I said, going along with him, not too sure what he was talking about.

"But it's her fault," he gasped out. "S-s-she's the carrier."

He lifted his body up a step and started working on lifting the legs. I stayed where I was.

"The carrier of what," I said.

He stopped crying for a minute to look down at me. "My disease," he screamed. "My *disease*." He was bawling again. "It's Duchennes."

I didn't know what he was talking about.

He had his legs up on the next step. He lifted his body and the chainsaw on his lap up another. I was five steps down now.

"Well, she can't help that," I said.

"Yes she could of," he shouted down at me. "The doctor said she could of. She s-s-shouldn't of had me at all, don't you see? She should have adopted." He was blubbering like his heart was broken, tears running into his mouth. He took big gasps of air like he was choking.

"Can I come up and sit beside you?" I asked.

He wiped his nose on his shirt. Then he nodded.

I scampered up the steps and sat down. He shifted over a little to make room. I put my arm around his thin shoulders. He sure didn't feel muscle-bound.

... 119

"You're going to make me cry too," I said. He leaned his tow-blond head against my shoulder, brought his arms up around my neck, and slobbered on my best pink sweater.

"Nobody likes me," he said. "I'm a freak, you see. She hates me and Pop and herself because I'm a freak. She hates me most." He coughed and sputtered. "She's ashamed of me."

I held him. I smoothed his hair. "You're not a freak," I said.

I could smell the cod-liver oil he took too much of to try and get healthy. I ran my hand over his back and felt the muscles he'd built up trying to slow his progressive deterioration as he called it.

"Your back feels good," I said.

"Thanks," he said, sounding like the sixteen-year-old boy he was. He wasn't crying so hard now, but he was still going good.

"It's her that's the real f-f-freak, you know," he said. "It's her genes that made it happen. It's he-he-hereditary, like hemophilia in the Tudors."

He beat against the handle of the chainsaw. "I hate her, I hate her, I hate her. And so does Daddy."

"I like you," I said.

He shook his head still buried in my neck. "N-n-no, you don't. I can tell. Nobody likes me 'cept Pop. And Patty used to. Only she's dead now. Like I'm going to be soon."

"I do too like you," I said. "Blow your nose."

"Don't have a tissue," he said.

"Where are they?"

"There's some paper towels in the kitchen," he said. "On a roll over the sink." He was still holding onto my neck for dear life.

"Well, let me go and I'll get some."

He let me go with a little sigh. "What's she doing now?" he asked.

"I don't know," I said. "Want me to find out?"

"Yes," he whimpered.

I left him hunched up over his chainsaw.

I went up the stairs and into the kitchen. I found the paper towels and took a handful. It was quiet up there. I took the towels down to him. "Stay here and I'll check out your mother," I said.

He nodded. "Kill her while you're at it," he said.

"Oh sure," I said. He giggled at that.

If Mrs. Potter and Walt-the-Talk were in the house, I couldn't find them. It looked to me like they'd skipped. The bed had been made up and her bathroom looked like it hadn't been used all day. Dry. Fresh towels in place. Very good.

When I got back to Lil Harv, his father was standing at the foot of the steps, inside the studio, wanting to know what Lil Harv was doing sitting on the stairs with the chainsaw. There must be an outside door that led directly into his workshop, and he'd come in that way. Potter Sr was wearing his usual baggy jeans and an open-throated white shirt with a cardigan sweater buttoned up over it. He had his clorox-stained beret hanging on his ears.

He looked surprised to see me at the top of the flight of steps. "What's going on here?" he asked me.

"I brought Lil Harv home," I said.

"I couldn't work out, Pop. Lieutenant Weatherwax. He sealed the whole wing off. She brought me home."

"The saw?" said Potter Sr with his eyes quiet. He came up the steps and took it away from his son. "You know you're not allowed to touch the tools."

"I was going to murder Mom," said Lil Harv, not stuttering at all now. "She's a whore, Pop. I saw her."

His father disappeared around the curve of steps. Putting the saw back, I guess. Then he came up the stairs, picked up his son with no trouble and carried him into the kitchen and set him down in a kitchen chair. "There you go, my man. Want your special?"

Lil Harv smiled his pretty-boy smile. "Yes," he said.

"You? Miss Baldwin, is it?" Potter Sr said to me. "Get you a scotch and soda, maybe?"

"T.T.," I said. I scratched my head. "Got a ginger ale?"

"Can or glass?" he said, opening the refrigerator.

"Can is good," I said, standing there, feeling self-conscious.

Potter Sr got a bottle of beer for himself, orange juice for the kid, and the soda for me. "Sit down," he invited, but I felt better leaning against the wall, so I stayed where I was.

Potter Sr sat down at the kitchen table opposite his son. He took off his beret and sailed it over onto the counter top. He patted his bald head. "Think it's gonna grow?" he asked Lil Harv.

"Nope," said Lil Harv, orange pulp on his upper lip. They both laughed. Probably an old routine they had.

"Okay," said Potter Sr after a swig or two of his beer. "Let's have it."

I didn't think Lil Harv would tell it straight but he did.

His father's expression never changed. His eyes stayed quiet. He drank his beer. When Lil Harv finished, Potter Sr said he thought Lil Harv should spend the night at Mrs. Snowfield's and would Lil Harv like that.

It didn't suit me too well but my opinion wasn't asked. Lil Harv said he'd like it fine.

Potter Sr called Mrs. Snowfield from the telephone in the living room. "You're staying at Snowfield's, aren't you?" he said when he came back.

I said I was. I said I'd drive Lil Harv over there if he'd like. Lil Harv looked ready for a nap. He was slumped over the table with his head in his arms, his eyes closed, his face still pale.

"I think I'll get his things together and feed him first," said Potter Sr. "I'll bring him over myself. Later tonight."

"All right," I said. "I'll be getting back then."

Potter Sr walked me to the door. "It's nothing new," he said to me. "She started tramping around a long time ago when Lil Harv was first diagnosed. He was five years old then."

"I'm sorry," I said.

"She blames herself," he said in a calm voice. "It seems the Duchennes strain of muscular dystrophy is carried on through the female. Usually only shows up in the male children. Latent in the female. Caroline hadn't known. Her grandmother had had a bad baby, but it died very early. In those days they hushed up such things. Caroline was an only child. She hadn't known."

"I'm sorry," I said again, wanting to get away.

"I've tried to be patient with her," he said quietly. "Just let her be. I love my son. I don't think he knew about his mother before today. Well, I'll have to do something now."

"Goodnight," I said.

"Goodnight," he said. He shut the door.

I drove to the post office and mailed out my film.

The fuel gauge was low so I pulled into a gas station. When we use the *Graphic* Chevie and have to buy gas, we fill out a chit with the gallons bought and the price paid, and the manager of the station signs it so we can get the money back. We keep the chits in the glove compartment.

That's how I found the note. It was just a slip of white paper like you'd find anywhere. It was printed in pencil in a childish scrawl, like someone who was right-handed had written with the left or the other way around.

Your neck is as easy to squeeze as hers was. That's what it said.

While the man filled out my *Graphic* chit, I tried to remember when I'd last looked in the glove compartment. Last night. Last night when Gilly Fats and I were eating in the drive-in, he'd used the glove compartment door to sit his pie and coffee on. I'd closed it when I was writing out my tag sheets. Nothing but chit slips then. So the note had been put in sometime today. By someone who knew I was driving the Chevie.

Lil Harv could have done it, taking his time getting out the passenger side. Caroline Potter or Walt-the-Talk could have done it while I was inside on the stairs. The Chevie hadn't been locked. Potter Sr could have done it before he came in. Someone could have done it at Snowfields today before I left. Stanley. Dr. Joe. Mrs. Snowfield. Abe Hirshaw.

The whole day had been full of depression, but I wasn't depressed any more. And I wasn't scared. I was angry.

Whoever wrote that note didn't know me very well. I had news. Bad news. My throat was harder to squeeze than Patty's was. I was a hell of a whole lot meaner.

I drove back to Snowfield's in a rage, not doing the Chevie's gear box any good. Let the sucker come.

..... X

I was still hopping mad when I got to Snowfield's, but I was smart enough not to let it show. I left the note in the glove compartment, like I hadn't found it yet. If I didn't mention it, let's see who went nosing around to see if it was still there.

Floyd was looking almost his old self, rosy and kewpie-doll cute, sitting in the main room snuggled up by the fire with a glass of hootch in his hand. Gilly Fats was with him, puffing away, laying out papers on a coffee table and talking earnestly. I told them I was very tired from digging all day and that I was going to bed.

"Got lots to tell you, T.T.," said Gilly Fats.

"I'm beat," I said, trying to look it.

"No din-din?" asked Gilly Fats.

"I'll sneak something from the fridge," I said.

"Can't take the haul," said Floyd.

"Goodnight," I said.

They looked at each other, puzzled.

"Told you she'd never last," said Floyd to Gilly Fats.

"The kid's tuckered," said Gilly. "See you tomorrow, T.T. Remember, it's the funeral."

I nodded, waved, and went off to my bedroom. Tonight, at least, I'd get to sleep in the canopy bed. Maybe Floyd would bunk in with Gilly this time.

After I started a hot bath with bath oil sprinkled in I found tubside, I went off to the kitchen to see what I could rustle up to take back to the bedroom.

The German-looking lady was carving a turkey that smelled like heaven and flirting with Alphonse, the guard.

I asked her for a bedside tray, and she said to run along, she'd fix something up and send Al with it.

"Thanks so much," I said.

"No problem," said Alphonse.

I soaked in the hot tub and thought it all over for a long time. I made notes on a pad. I washed my hair, washed my sweater. I toweled down and put on my p.j.'s. I got into bed with my note pad, two pencils, and an Aggie Christie mystery. I'd see how Hercule Poirot handled pickles like this.

Al the guard knocked and came in. He had a bedtray loaded with turkey and yams under a silver top and a whole pot of coffee just for me.

"Not too bad, eh?" he said, taking off the plate cover. His moustache lifted when he smiled, like it was smiling too.

"I could get used to this," I said, grinning.

"Enjoy," he said, and left me.

I was alone. Good. Now I wouldn't have to put up with Lil Harv or Floyd or the person who wanted to strangle me. I ate my dinner, read how M. Poirot solved everything with ease, and then lay in the dark with my pad and pencils under my pillow in case any great thoughts came by. What came by later was Floyd but I pretended to be asleep, and then I was.

I woke up being attacked. At least I thought I was being attacked. I was being swatted over the head by a rolled-up *Graphic*, swung with good follow-through by Floyd Beesom. I came up swinging.

Floyd was sitting on the bed. "You're getting to be too much, Baldwin," he said.

"Too much what?" I snapped. "What a way to wake a person up."

"Gettin' tough with the old lensies," he said, dropping the *Graphic* so it fell face up on the bed.

The picture of Patty Cambron hanging in the locker took up the whole front page of the Wednesday *Graphic* except for the *Graphic*'s banner. It was very contrasty, black blacks, white whites, the way flash makes your shots, but in this picture the high contrast added drama. There she was hanging from the hook with the towel so white it almost looked in color. It was one hell of a photograph, if I do say so myself.

To cover being impressed with my own work, I pointed to the white towel's whiteness. "Bounce," I said, referring to the quality flash has of picking up its own light when it hits something bright enough. That bright something will increase the light out of proportion.

"Halfway great," said Floyd.

I stared at him. Floyd was definitely having personality changes. "Say that again, Floyd," I said. "Slow. I want to hear you say it again."

... 125

He exhaled, like it cost him. "Great, Baldwin. Your picture's great. That's the last time I'm gonna say it. Now get up."

I flopped back on the pillows. "You complimented me on a picture, Floyd. That's the first time."

"Yeah, well, probably be the only time. Don't get dazzled."

At that moment I loved him. "Thanks, Floyd. It means a lot to me."

"Jeez," he said. "You got a dress for graveside?"

"No," I said. I was looking for my credit line. There it was: "*Graphic* photo by T.T. Baldwin" in beautiful black type. I bet the printer had my own slug made up by now, and he just dropped it in place under the photo tagged for page one.

Floyd got off the bed "You got half an hour," he said, and waddled off. Still wasn't walking right.

I dressed in what I had. Jeans, a shirt and sweater. Gilly Fats was chowing down in the arboretum and I joined him. Donuts for Gilly. Oatmeal again for me, only no raisins this time. Coffee.

"You're getting just like Floydie, T.T.," said Gilly Fats, yellow custard oozing out of his cream donut. "Runnin' with a beat and not letting your partners in on it. Super shot, kiddo. Scares me to death. How come you didn't come clean with old Gilly?"

I didn't know how to tell Gilly that he'd carped at me in front of the detectives and that was why. So I just shrugged and said thanks, but I didn't want to say anything until I knew how it came out since I don't use the flash gun much.

"Ah, artistic temperament," said Gilly Fats, a donut in each hand.

I laughed and the awkward moment passed.

Floyd was going with us to the cemetery. He said he was getting cabin-fever being inside so much, and he intended to take today's burial pictures, and I was to keep my hands in my pockets and my camera in my bag if I knew what was good for me. I said okay and felt magnanimous. Floyd's escort today was a bulbous policeman, hanging stomach, hanging jowels, bulging biceps. His name was Ozark. He kept a toothpick in his mouth. When I asked him why, he said it beat smokin'.

The four of us trooped out to the *Graphic* Chevie. Already in it, in the front seat with the UFO neatly folded in the back, sat Lil Harv. He was suited-up in black velvet, his blond hair floating away from his head like he'd just washed it.

"I want to go with T.T.," he said.

"Okay," I said. Oh nuts, I thought.

Gilly drove. Lil Harv sat in the middle between us. Floyd and Ozark lolled comfortably in the back.

They were burying Lou LaMont and Patty Cambron around the curve of the mountain, out of sight from the highway. There was a big green tent strung up over the burial site.

Gilly Fats pushed Lil Harv in his wheelchair. Floyd made Ozark carry his gear. I walked ahead.

Amy Bland, standing in a group, saw me and came over. She pulled me off under the outstretched arms of a statue of the Blessed Virgin that decorated the grave of one Constance Grace Riley. Constant she was and bore her burdens gracefully the monument told us. Not your usual life of Riley, I thought disrespectfully.

"Listen," Amy hissed in my ear. "Have I got news! Dr. Joe and Ratch have run away. Eloped! What do you think of that?"

"Oh wow," I said inadequately.

"Wow is so right!" said Amy in her breathy voice. "I think it's divine! So romantic. Ratch was terrific. As soon as she heard about his trouble, she bailed him out with her own money, and took right off with him. I was sworn to secrecy until this morning to give them time to get away. But I was in on the plan from the beginning. I made the reservations. Las Vegas they went to. In Nevada. Don't you love it?"

I said I loved it but I didn't think Weatherwax and Xavier would.

"Oh, pooh on Weatherwax and Xavier! What do they matter? I'm so proud of Ratch. She didn't get disgusted with Dr. Joe which would have been very easy to do, right? She stood right up and was counted. She blamed it all on herself and her infernal chastity she said, and they flew away yesterday at 2:05. I gave her white satin slippers for something new, and she borrowed Bab's red negligee with the malibou trim for something borrowed, and she took her Aunt Tiddy's violin bow for something old, and bought herself a pair of undies for the something blue. All in a whirl we did it. Dr. Joe was so happy he cried, the teddy bear." Amy jumped around from foot to foot, excited. We could have been in a singles' bar instead of at a cemetery. "Can you stand it?"

I told her I could hardly stand it.

"You're invited to the wedding dinner," breathed Amy. "Tomorrow night at Babs'. Seven o'clock. They're going to face the charges together. Ratch right alongside him. And she doesn't care what Abe thinks about it. Even if he disinherits her, she said. Isn't Ratch wonderful?''

I said it sounded like it.

"Yeah. And listen, it's okay to bring a present."

She ran back, and I took my place quietly on the fringes of the crowd.

Graveside, Abe and Mrs. Snowfield stood together. Wanda had one arm of Walt-the-Talk Amos, and Amy, hurrying over, took the other one. He didn't look as despondent as he should have considering Patty used to be his girl. They stood in a clump with Babs and David Livingston.

Stanley Farmer, in a black suit that looked worn and ages old, shuffled uncomfortably beside Coach Reesenbach. Mrs. Potter, swathed in her mink coat and hat and probably sweating in the sunny 60° day, stood hangdog beside her husband. Every time she tried to get closer to him and touch his elbow, he moved away and shook his head slightly as though what she was doing wasn't in keeping with the occasion.

The entire Climbers team, all in gray trousers and Climber blazers, stood in rows behind the official speaker, who looked like a maitre d' but was probably a nondenominational minister.

Lieutenant Weatherwax and Detective Xavier were there in their uniforms, relaxed, respectful.

While the service went on, Floyd took pictures. He was full of smiles at being back in harness. I'd always known he was a good photographer—okay, a great photographer—but I'd never realized he loved his work the same way I did mine. With Floyd you never knew.

I didn't listen to the ceremony. I watched the people gathered there. One of them was the cause of this. One of them had made this day happen as surely as Bruce Jenner had planned his win in the Olympics decathlon. But which one? And why, for god's sakes?

Who profited? Coach Clifford Skyhook Reesenbach, for sure. Lovable Lou's death made him a millionaire. He could start his own smutty magazine if he wanted now. Looking at him, the Coach didn't seem particularly happy or sad. He looked like he was planning his defensive counter to a reverse strong-side sweep.

Who else? Black Jack Flowers. He was a tall, muscular Negro with a bearded face that hadn't been manhandled by the pack. He was standing solemn with his hands crossed in front of him. Before Lou's death, a bench-warming quarterback, number two to the star. Last week, before it all happened, he'd told Gilly Fats he didn't mind "sittin' on the pines," as he called it. Said it beat gettin' beat up and made for a healthy old age. That could have been jive. Inside he could have been seething for the chance to play as a starter. But looking at him now he didn't look like someone who'd lusted for the crown and grabbed hold of it. He looked slightly humble, as though God had said your turn now, not him. So scratch Black Jack Flowers.

Who else. Not Billy Badman O'Leary. As far as I knew, Badman was still hiding out, terrified. All he'd gained was a bad rap. And he was going to lose his job if he didn't get back to camp.

Mrs. Marcella Snowfield lost a lover. All she'd got out of this was scandal and team problems. And maybe lost her shot to be a first-time-out Super Bowl champ.

Abe Hirshaw, clever, ambitious, patient. Mrs. Snowfield's lawyer, financial counsel, suitor. He was her number one now. But any day some flat-bellied boy with a laughing face could unseat Abe of the starched collar and prissy fingers. He'd better marry her quick or he'd lose his temporary advantage. What Abe gained was tenuous, I decided. If Mrs. Snowfield wanted to marry him, I think she already would have. Abe would have to do a lot more than murder Lou LaMont to marry Marcella Snowfield.

Amy Bland? Her hand was drooping inattentively on the arm of Walt-the-Talk. She and Ratch and David Livingston were involved in something. And until I knew what, I wouldn't know where she fit in. She was still excited, her eyes shining. She kept trying to catch Potter Sr's eye. Once or twice she did, and smiled at him like he was a Barricini candy store. Amazingly, he smiled back, but his eyes still looked lobotomized.

Walt-the-Talk was a guy who made it his business to profit whatever happened. An opportunist of easy virtue. Not necessarily a schemer, the way the murderer was. Just a guy on the make, trying to do it all. I didn't see what he gained. Unless it was Wanda Pettigo, glowing like a sunrise in spite of herself. She, of us all, looked shocked. Her perfect face was blank, like expensive writing paper. From time to time Walt-the-Talk stroked her hair, the color of falling forest leaves. She didn't notice.

David Livingston. Babs Livingston. Funny, but I couldn't lump them together. They seemed so separate. He, sneaking where he shouldn't be. For what? Strutting his stuff, overtly fey. She, long wasp face, middle-class manners, fussing over her dinners for two, ordinary in the best sense of the word. She didn't know what her David was up to half the time. Or so she said. I believed her. Scratch Babs. But him—I'd check out the briefcase first.

Then the Potters. They didn't go together either. If he loved his wife, it didn't show. I had no motive for Potter Sr. Just that brooding quietness in his eyes and his blacksmith forearms. If it came to it, I could see myself being strangled by his hands. No problem, as Alphonse the guard would say. I wasn't as mean as all that. But the death of Lou LaMont hadn't brought his wife back to him nor freed him of her, whichever way he wanted it.

And Caroline? Had she bedded down with Lovable Lou? I hadn't heard any rumors so. And what if she had? She didn't look like a woman to lose her head over any man. I saw no gain for Mrs. Potter, only bad times ahead for her.

Lil Harv. He'd been there all that Sunday morning. He and Patty Cambron and Lovable Lou. Only he was left alive, sitting safe in his wheelchair watching the other two get buried. What if he'd seen Lou and Mama, got mad the way he did yesterday, and stuck a needle into Lou's neck in spontaneous anger? Possible. Lil Harv said it. He had nothing to lose. If you asked me, little doll-face was capable of anything.

That left Stanley Farmer, a man with a checkered history. A one-time professional jockey, a convicted killer, a veteran of the big house where they teach you dirty tricks. A lonely little man who took pride in his work and wanted respect. Tops at darts. And he'd done time in the prison where Lou LaMont's father had been a prison guard. After the service, I'd talk with Stanley.

Dr. Joe? He ought to know how, but I had no reason why. And Rachel Hirshaw, same thing. No reason. Theirs was a private drama. And I had a feeling they were going to come out all right.

I looked around as the service drew to a close. Had I missed anybody? Missed the killer staring bald-faced at me? Watching with me while the minister sifted the turned earth through his fingers like health-store flour and let it drift reverently down on the mahogany lids of first Lou LaMont's coffin, then Patty Cambron's. Like they were precious seeds. And so covered, would, god willing, sprout and blossom come spring.

I sighed and looked down at my boots. John Lennon was right. You can't see through the eyes. I didn't know who the killer was. I had the feeling I wasn't even warm.

Everyone was chatting together now. Shaking the hand of the minister, shaking their clothes loose, ready to get back to what they'd been doing.

I'd try to ride back into town with Stanley. Hopefully we'd be alone and I could ask him about Altoona and Lou's father. And I could lose Lil Harv, no small thing. I didn't want a Tonto in on my Lone Ranger act.

Stanley said he'd meet me by the third Climber Caddie. I said okay. I left him talking to David Livingston and Babs, something about David's astrologer outfits.

There were about a dozen brown Cadillacs with faces of Overcoat painted on the hood. They were all parked willy-nilly along the side of the narrow black-paved road that led to this part of High Mountain Cemetery. No way to tell which was the third one.

A football team has forty-five players, not including the taxi-squad, the guys that don't play until everyone else on the team is dead, which never happens so all they get to do is practice. The whole team came pouring down the hillside just after me, and called hello and whistled and stacked themselves like Cheez-its into six of the Cadillacs and drove off, tooting the horns and carrying on like they'd just won a big one. Friendly fellows, not good at mourning.

So since I couldn't figure which Caddie was the third one, I looked into all of them, looking for something that would tell me which one Stanley was using.

I found David Livingston's attaché case sitting on the floor of the back of a four-door Cadillac with the front window on the passenger side rolled three-quarters down. I reached in easily enough and pulled the back door button up to unlock it. Then I glanced up the hill to see what David Livingston was up to. I couldn't distinguish him in the crowd of people, so I opened the door and closed it behind me and sat down on the floor in the back so I couldn't be seen from outside and went to work on the lock. Most briefcase locks are cheap; therefore easy. If you're really in a hurry and don't care about the mess you make, all you have to do is lever the tongue real hard until it pops. Any screwdriver will do. It ruins the lock but it gets the case open.

I used a bobby pin. Took me about twenty seconds and I'm only a journeyman at lock-picking. I knew I didn't have much time and I couldn't risk sticking my head up to see where Livingston was and how much time I had.

I opened up the briefcase. Lots of publicity material on the Climbers first off. But under that, three long yellow sheets, the kind they call legal-size, lined in light blue and written on in pencil. Rows of people's names. Pluses and minuses after the names and numbers. Such as M.A.M. + 20, John X − 50 + 5, Abe + 100, Nancy L. − 10 + 1.

Well, I was glad to see it. I'd been afraid David Livingston was dealing dope out of the hospital, smuggling out the heavy stuff with a little inside help, and using Ratch and Amy as runners, delivery girls, for a percentage cut.

What this made David Livingston was a chinzy little book, an independent branch of off-track betting. From my point of view, nothing to get alarmed at. Of course it was a good story. It could bust Mrs. Snowfield's NFL franchise sure enough. Livingston had to have a contact with a big boy, someone who pushed the actual money back and forth. David probably just kept the vig, the ten percent you pay on your bet when you lose. Handed over the real money. I say probably because you need a bankroll to handle the action yourself, and Livingston didn't look that fat in the wallet to me. But Mrs. Snowfield could.

If Mrs. Snowfield was the big boy, that put the entire Climbers' team in the position of shaving the points on any game the lady stood to bank a bundle on. And if you were going to bribe a player, the best player to bribe would be the quarterback. He's the one who initiates the play. Either runs the ball or lofts it for a pass. And passes are easy to muck up even when you're trying to throw them right. So it's hard to say it's deliberate if the QB gets intercepted or misses his man or throws the ball away.

Of course, if Mrs. Snowfield tried to corrupt Lou LaMont and failed, that did give her a motive for murder. She was the one who, according to Lil Harv, came and got Lovable Lou before the game. And lied to the police about it. She told me they'd had a sexual interlude. Come to think of it that was an odd thing for Lou to be doing. After all, he was about to start the first game of his professional career. You'd think he'd want all his energy for playing football, wouldn't you?

Someone opened the Caddie's back door. I almost fell out. I'd

132 . . .

been leaning against it. The someone was David Livingston. The papers floated out of my hands. The briefcase spilled its papers over the backseat.

"You bitch!" yelled David. He grabbed the handle of the flopped-open briefcase and swung the case at me. A brass-reinforced corner caught me right over the left ear and sent me sprawling out onto the grassy side of the road. I sat on the grass, a little stunned, and looked to see what he was going to do next. He was scrambling around in the car retrieving his papers and putting them back any-which-way into the attaché case.

Under the Cadillac I saw one of the yellow sheets. It had slipped back by the left rear wheel. I made a dive for it, head first, stretching my arms out as I went. I got my head and shoulders under the car and my fingers on the paper.

I could feel blood running down my cheek, but except for a hum in my head, I didn't feel any pain.

Inside the car I heard David hollering for me to give him back his "loan-sheets." Ho-ho. Then I felt my ankles being grabbed. He was dragging me out from under the car by my feet. And that hurt. The tarred road looks smooth when you're driving on it, but it's hard and scratchy on your belly.

Before the back of my head cleared the Caddie's underside, I stuffed the yellow sheet down my sweater. But in doing so, I forgot and lifted my head and conked myself good on the automobile's chassis. My head felt like it was on fire. The blood from the cut over my ear was splashing down on the sleeves of my sweater. David Livingston was pulling my legs out of their sockets and snarling unkind words. From far away I could hear someone feminine yelling for someone to stop something or other. I kept my head up tight against the steel underpinning of the car. I was getting nauseous from the oil smell. But let's see him get me out.

Abruptly the hold on my ankles relaxed. I fell for it. I dropped my head onto my stretched arms to rest a second and got yanked about two feet. Clear of the car and onto the grass.

I had a sense of people around but all I could see was blades of grass out-of-focus like in a Clairol commercial. One of my cheeks felt like it had been ripped off and I was afraid to reach up and touch it and make sure. Better not to know. David Livingston was twisting an ankle now, chanting *give-it-to-me-give-it-to-me* like a disciple of Charles Manson.

Then for some reason Livingston dropped my ankle in mid-twist.

I turned over on my back just in time to see Gilly Fats cold-cock him right on the chin. Livingston went down like the Dow-Jones average has been doing. Without a peep.

Now it was Babs' turn to holler. She started to scream like Renata Tebaldi and her famous high *C*. But the roar in my head was louder and shut her out. Screaming, but me not hearing a thing, Babs took a swing at Gilly and popped him one in the gut. He took it like a gentleman. He stood there and told her to go on and take her best shot. Gilly I could hear fine. But Babs sounded like a silent movie. I don't think Babs understood the opportunity she'd been given because she stopped pounding the two hundred-plus pounds of Gilly and bent over her David, asking him if he was all right. I could hear her now she dropped down in decibels. I lay on the grass and listened to the roar in my head. It wasn't so bad once you got used to it. In fact, it was kinda nice.

Now everybody was standing around in a semicircle. Lil Harv all wide-blue-eyed in his wheelchair, Floyd with his lens almost down my throat, the jerk. Mrs. Snowfield and Abe Hirshaw looking from me to David Livingston to each other and nodding as though I'd just confirmed something they'd known all along.

Ozark took charge. He stooped over me and asked how I was. Right as rain, I think I said. David Livingston came to and went back into action. He rolled toward me, grabbed my sweater and tried to get his hand down my front. I clutched my chest to keep the paper safe and Ozark pulled him off.

"What *is* this?" wailed Babs. I felt sorry for her. She was such a nice person.

"She's got a paper of mine," said David. He had a bright red spot all over his chin. He'd be black and blue tomorrow. Gilly had got him right on the button.

I started to nod but that wasn't a good idea. "No paper," I said.

"Ridiculous," someone said. I think it was Mrs. Snowfield.

Ozark lifted me up by my armpits and stood me on my feet.

Floyd was grinning happily. "Your face is a mess, Baldwin," he said.

"Give the paper back this minute," said David Livingston.

"Please give him back his paper," wailed Babs.

"What kind of paper?" asked Lil Harv, the only one who was showing any sense.

"No paper," I said. My stomach was starting to hurt. I was

bleeding there too. I knew I'd never have a face again.

"What kind of paper?" repeated Lil Harv. Dear little buddy.

"It's in her shirt," said David Livingston. I said nothing.

Ozark asked me if I had a paper. I was ready to confess it. Let the police investigate. Gilly'd still get the story.

"No!" screamed David Livingston.

"No what," said Ozark, his toothpick bobbing on his lower lip.

"She doesn't have a paper," said Livingston sullenly. "I made a mistake."

Everybody looked at David like he was daffy. I looked at him like he was daffy too.

"We'll straighten it out between ourselves," Livingston said, giving me a mean look.

"Sure," I said. "You made a mistake."

"That being the case, you oughtta apologize," said Ozark.

"I apologize," said David Livingston.

"Oh, David," wailed Babs.

"Think nothing of it," I said.

"Want to ride back in?" said David Livingston with a nasty smile.

"I'm going with Stanley," I said. Stanley had already gone, somebody said.

"Catch you later then," said David. He started walking away with Babs. Amy and Walt-the-Talk and Wanda were already in the car waiting for them. Amy called out to me not to forget tomorrow. Seven P.M.

"Let's go, T.T.," said Gilly Fats.

"I think I'll go to the house here and clean up," I said.

Gilly Fats said they'd wait. I told them to go on, I'd catch a ride back somehow. I wanted to be alone.

"She's gettin' odder and odder," said Floyd.

"What's it to you," I said. I walked over to the Chevie, got my camera bag, and walked away up to the cemetery house to wash my face and see what was left of it.

My face was all right, after all. I had a good-sized cut over the left ear that needed a stitch or two. Some road scratches on my right cheek, and a few abrasions on my stomach. But once the blood was washed away, nothing looked too serious. My legs hurt where they connected to my body, but I'd be okay. If this is as bad as it gets, I thought, I can take it.

. . . 135

When I came out of the keeper's house, all mercurochromed and band-aided, everyone was gone. But one lone brown Cadillac was cruising the roads around the graves.

I let it catch up to me. It was Stanley. "Said you needed a ride," he said.

"You're okay, Stanley," I said.

"I'm a good stitch man, Miss," he said. "I'll take you back to the Colossus and fix you good's new."

"Let's talk first," I said.

We drove around the cemetery, very slowly like the signs said to do. I asked him about Altoona, and he told me.

It seems that Lou LaMont's father, one Roger Lee LaMont, was something of a hero at the state pen there. About seventeen years ago there'd been an escape attempt in one of the cell blocks. And Roger Lee, with his hand gun and a piece of pipe, had singlehandedly foiled the escape, got the three escapees back into their cells with only slight injury, and kept the whole section under control while doing it. A nice bit of work with only one hitch. One of the inmates was seriously wounded. A bad'un according to Stanley. One of your paid assassins, he said. But the man was in his cell at the time not trying to escape. Studying somethin' he'd been, Stanley thought. The guy got hit in the groin by a ricocheting bullet from Roger Lee's .38 and had to be removed to the prison hospital for emergency surgery.

To make a long story short, the operation went on for hours, touch and go the whole way, and in the end the man lived but lost his sexual function. He had a long convalescence. The prison authorities decided to commute his sentence. The prisoner hadn't been what they call uncooperative while he'd been confined. The prison had done him an injustice. And the prison board thought that castration had probably gentled him quite a bit. Also, they didn't want a lawsuit. So the man was released and lost track of.

This was around 1960, Stanley thought. Nine years before Stanley himself got there. But he heard about it from Roger Lee himself as well as from the lifers who'd been incarcerated in the cell block at the time.

Of course, Stanley said, the inmate hadn't felt too kindly toward Roger Lee, and no one could blame him for that. Roger Lee had worried about the guy one day laying for him. But Stanley said he'd asked Lou about it when Lou arrived in High Mountain, and Lou said Roger Lee was never bothered and died of a natural heart attack watching Lou win for Penn State one Saturday in Lou's sophomore year.

Stanley didn't know for certain, he said, but he had the feeling that man was around High Mountain today. And Floyd Beesom thought so too. He and Floyd both thought it was the former inmate who'd murdered Lovable Lou because Lou had recognized him somehow. And the ex-con hadn't liked that kind of recognition.

Stanley said Floyd Beesom was trying to identify who the prisoner was. Stanley remembered Roger Lee referred to the guy as William. But Stanley expected William had changed his name by now.

Stanley said Floyd was working hand-in-glove with Weatherwax and Xavier. Only it was on the quiet so I was to keep the news to myself. Floyd had given him permission to tell me. If I asked, Stanley said, which Floyd had bet I wouldn't. I could understand that. That was the Floyd I knew. Old Floyd hadn't had as much of a personality change as I'd thought.

Stanley said a few things more. William had played on the football team at the prison, and been just crazy about any kind of sports. A real sports freak, Roger Lee had called him. Always studying it up. And also, William liked to work with his hands. Build bookcases, cabinets, that kind of thing. The deputy commissioner had been real proud of William's work. Said William had a flair. And that was about all Stanley remembered about William from his talks with Roger Lee LaMont.

I told Stanley he'd remembered quite a bit. Stanley was pleased.

He drove me to the Colossus. Everything there was back to normal. The police guards were gone. Coach Reesenbach was running a game film in the schoolroom and the players were taking notes. The team had practiced. The snack bar in the recreation room had coffee for us. The laundry had been delivered. In the training room, Lil Harv was working out, walking his mile on the treadmill.

"Only thing wrong now," said Stanley, "is Doc ain't in his office."

Stanley took me into Dr. Joe's examining room to stitch my scalp. He cleaned the side of my head, and then sprayed it with a can of Novocain he got out of Dr. Joe's office which wasn't locked. "Got the key to the cabinet right here," said Stanley, patting his fat key chain. The spray felt cold on my skin, moist, no smell to it. "Freezes ya right up," explained Stanley. "You won't feel a thing."

I shivered, thinking about Lovable Lou and the needle in the back

. . . 137

of his neck. How could you do it, so he wouldn't be aware?

"Spray it on my hair, Stanley," I said, "and on the back of my neck."

"What you want it there for?" Stanley asked. "This stuff costs."

"Trying something," I said.

Stanley shrugged, but he did it. He sprayed the back of my hair, then lifted my hair and gave me a squirt or two on the back of my neck. The can hissed a little. The spray felt like nothing on my hair, but I could feel the moisture when it hit my neck.

"How long does it take to freeze the nerves, Stanley?"

Stanley pushed out his lower lip. "Maybe count to ten," he said.

I counted to ten. "Stick me a little in the back of the neck, Stanley, please."

I think he'd got the idea by now. He shook his head like he didn't approve, but he took a needle and touched the back of my neck. "Feel anything?"

"No," I said. "Did you pierce the skin?"

"Not yet," he said. "Just pricked ya a bit."

"Well, go on, do it," I said, all of a sudden impatient. Like a picture, I could see in my mind Patty Cambron spraying Lou's dark curls with what she thought was a can of hairspray. Spraying the back of his head with the big rollers in that would make his hair bounce with those big black curls Lou liked so much.

I could see her patting the rollers to make sure the curls were wound tight, see her standing back examining her work and saying, there now, in twenty minutes I'll take it down and brush it out. You'll be beautiful, Lou.

And then, of course! Someone, anyone, could say, hey, Lou, just a minute, let me see, damn, a curler loose back here. Let me fix it. *Let me fix it.* And Lou would say sure, fix it, pal. And the someone would have a long acupuncture needle in his palm or in his vest pocket, or anywhere, for god's sake, and instead of tightening the roller pin, the someone would lift a roller up, just so it'd feel right to Lou, and then sink the acupuncture needle down into the neck, right in the fatal position the way he'd been shown by Dr. Harley Yong Zu, right where the *medulla oblongata* joins the *pons Variolii*, and shove it down through the flesh and the muscles of the neck as far as he could get it, and then say something like, there now, feel better, that roller feel tighter? And Lou, a nice guy, would say sure, thanks pal, feels great. And then he'd go off and wait to

138 . . .

have his hair taken down and brushed out like the star he was going to be after the afternoon was over. Sure. That's how it was done.

"Well, feel anything, Miss?" said Stanley. "I ain't gonna put that needle in any further."

I didn't feel a thing. "How deep is it, Stanley?"

"Deep," said Stanley. "An inch at least. I'm takin' it out right now." I still didn't feel a thing.

He came around and stood in front of me, the needle in his hand. He was sweating. "Well?" he said.

"I didn't feel a thing," I said.

"Sweet Jesus," said Stanley. "I got the shakes."

I had my prickly, dancy feeling. "It's okay now, Stanley. Stitch me up. I know how he got Lovable Lou." While Stanley put seven neat stitches over my ear with bright red thread, I told him.

"Tell it to the dicks," was all Stanley said. "Me, I need somethin' to pull my socks up."

"Me too," I said. We sat in the recreation room. Stanley drank brandy out of a coffee cup. I drank celery tonic in a snifter.

We passed the afternoon throwing darts. Even with a ten-point handicap and standing back twice as far, Stanley beat me cold.

Gilly Fats and Floyd came by around six. They barged into the recreation room looking for me and Lil Harv. Lil Harv was ready. He'd joined Stanley and me about a half hour earlier. He'd changed back into his black velvet suit and left his warm-up togs with Stanley. Stanley put the pants and jacket on a shelf behind the snack bar counter. Lil Harv had wanted a locker with the Climbers, but Stanley said no.

On the way back to Snowfield's, we made a whiskey stop for Floyd, a cigarette and toothpaste stop for me, a donut stop for Gilly, and a health store stop for Lil Harv, who had to replenish his cod-liver oil and Vitamin E, he said. I asked him if he had enough money, and he said all he had to do was charge it. "That's neat," I told him, and Lil Harv agreed.

Gilly helped Lil Harv unload at Paxton's Natural Living. Instead of putting him in the wheelchair, Gilly Fats just carried him in. "Easier this way," rumbled Gilly. Lil Harv thought it was fun. Floyd went along to see what a health food store was like.

While they were all inside, I opened the door of the glove compartment. The note was gone.

During the drive to Snowfield's, I told them how I thought Lovable Lou got the needle in his neck. Floyd and Gilly Fats took the news calmly. Lil Harv got all excited and said he was sure that's how it happened. I asked him how he could be so sure, and he said because it made sense.

Gilly Fats said there were more ways to kill a cat besides choking it to death with butter, but the metaphor was lost on Lil Harv.

"T.T.'s got it right," Lil Harv insisted. "I was there at Dr. Zu's lecture. He drew the back of the neck on the blackboard and showed us right where to stick the needle in. We all learned how that night. Even I could have done it, if I wanted."

"Maybe you did," I said.

Lil Harv giggled like I'd said something funny. "Not me," he said. "Not me."

At Snowfield's I called Lieutenant Weatherwax on one phone, and Gilly Fats and Floyd brought Barkley up to date on another. Lieutenant Weatherwax thanked me for my theory, as he called it, and asked how I was feeling after my scrap. I told him Stanley had sewed me up like I was a six-round club fighter and had done a first-class job. Lieutenant Weatherwax said he was glad to hear it, and in case I was interested, Dr. DeBianco had been arrested again for bail-jumping, but had been rebailed in Rachel Hirshaw De-Bianco's custody. I thanked him for the info and rang off.

Mrs. Snowfield wasn't there for dinner, and the German-looking lady wasn't around. But there was a big pot of turkey stew with dumplings on the stove. On the kitchen table was a huge bowl of salad and two loaves of French bread.

Al the guard had replaced Ozark for the night. We ate in the kitchen, the five of us. We laughed and told stories and forgot about death and killings.

After dinner we played Monopoly with a set Potter Sr had brought over with Lil Harv. Floyd soused it up while he played. Gilly Fats finished a half-gallon of banana fudge ice cream and enthralled Lil Harv with his smoke ring virtuosity. I was the first to go bankrupt. I overextended my cash reserves building hotels on Illinois, Indiana, and Kentucky Avenues. Lil Harv had warned me not to build too fast but I hadn't paid any attention.

Al the guard won. He controlled the cheap Connecticut, Vermont, and Oriental Avenues strip, and the not-so-fat New York and Tennessee Avenues and St. James Place. But we all kept landing where Al was landlord, and he busted us, one by one.

About midnight we went to bed. Floyd followed me into my bedroom. I asked him why he didn't favor Gilly Fats with his company. "If someone sneaks in, Floyd," I said, "Gilly's stronger than I am."

"Not as cute," said Floyd.

I undressed in the bathroom. When I came out Floyd was curled up on the cot.

"Nitey-bye, Baldwin," came out of his covers.

"Floyd," I said.

"Um-m-m," he said.

"Who was in the Chevie today besides you and Gilly Fats? After you left the cemetery. . . ."

"Nobody," he said.

"Think, Floyd. It's important."

Silence. Then, "Nobody I saw, Baldwin. Sorry."

"Nitey-byes, Floyd," I said.

I heard him snoring in the darkness. It was oddly comforting. I went to sleep to the rhythm of it.

..... XI

On Thursday my photo of Overcoat being buried ran on page seven. Floyd's picture was on page one. Of me. I was sitting sprawled in the grass, my shirt and sweater twisted and covered with dirt. I looked mortally wounded with blood dripping all over my face, and I had a bewildered expression like I didn't know which end was up. An unflattering photograph. The tag line read: "*Graphic* photographer roughed up pursuing suspect in High Mountain double murder mystery. Story on page seven."

I went looking for Floyd to thank him for the hatchet job, but he was gone. "With the police gentlemen," the German-looking lady said. Lil Harv had been taken to school. Mrs. Snowfield was out.

Floyd left me a note. Gilly Fats had been called back to New York City for an emergency meeting with Billy Badman O'Leary. The Badman was holed-up somewhere in Manhattan and wouldn't come out of hiding until he'd talked to the only man he trusted, the *Graphic*'s Gilbert Ott. Barkley had set up the secret rendezvous, with an exclusive interview, naturally. And Gilly had left early this morning. Good for Gilly, I thought. He'll talk the Badman into going back to the Johnny Rebs. Gilly could milk the story of his success for a week of newshole space.

Today I figured on tackling David Livingston head-on at Babs' little dinner for Ratch and Dr. Joe. Other than that the day was open, except for buying a wedding present for the DeBiancos. I thought a yogurt-making machine might be nice.

I ate a leisurely breakfast. The German-looking lady made me bacon and eggs, and I put away about three cups of coffee.

After breakfast I went over my photographic equipment. I cleaned my lens' faces and all my filters, chamoised my camera bodies, checked the batteries, got all the dust and lint out of my camera bag, and decided I'd buy some film in town when I bought the yogurt machine.

I wasn't hungry at lunchtime, so I took the Chevie out for a spin. I drove up to the top of High Mountain and looked at the view. I wondered who had murdered Lovable Lou and Patty.

First I considered the women. One of them could possibly be avenging her father's wrong wrought by Lou's father. Some twisted idea of poetic justice.

Mrs. Snowfield I put in a separate category. She could be avenging a brother possibly. Or her late husband Lemuel Snowfield. A long-shot, but possible. Or, if the inmate-from-Pennsylvania-State-Penitentiary-at-Altoona idea was wrong, Mrs. Snowfield could have other motives. If Marcella Snowfield was a queen-pin of organized crime with her own gambling territory, that was a whole different line of thought. So I isolated Mrs. Snowfield for the time being.

Of the women, I could scratch Rachel Hirshaw right away. Her father Abe didn't need avenging. And even if he did, I doubted if Ratch would be the one to do it.

All I knew of Babs Livingston was that she had the air of proper schools and an attitude of respectability. I'd ask her tonight who her father was. But for the time being, I was still scratching Babs. She didn't strike me as the daughter of a hit-man.

Amy Bland obviously came of lower-class stock. But she was so candidly herself, so doorman-during-Christmas-week friendly, that it was difficult to ascribe the murderer's deviousness and violence to her. Whoever killed Patty must have been in a rage. I'd never seen Amy get irritated, much less lose her temper. Amy went through life batting her eyelashes and wiggling her derrière and wanting everyone to like her. There may be a lot of I-want in Amy, but I didn't think there was any I-hate. Eliminate Amy Bland.

Wanda Pettigo was a bit of a witch. Classless, like all real beauties. Wanda could have been a princess or the daughter of a subway conductor. I could maybe buy Wanda murdering Lou in a moment of woman-scorned fury. But I couldn't see Wanda pulling the hairnet so tight it broke the hyoid bone in Patty's throat. Wanda and Patty were roomies, good friends. Nope. Wanda didn't do it.

And I couldn't see Caroline Potter avenging her husband, or anyone else, in any way whatsoever except by screwing a person to death. And that's not how the victims died. So forget about Caroline.

Of all the women, then, I was left with one long-shot possible: Mrs. Marcella Snowfield, for undetermined reasons.

Going quickly over the men again, I could bump Walt-the-Talk Amos out of the race right off. I could testify in court to his sexual

... 143

function being not only unimpaired, but in first class working condition.

Potter Sr sprung to mind, of course, because of William's alleged bent for carpentry. The stickler here was Lil Harv. Lil Harve was sixteen. If seventeen years ago William suffered his malfunction, that put Potter Sr in the clear. *If* Lil Harv was really his offspring. Which, with Caroline as the certified mother, was anybody's guess.

Seventeen years ago David Livingston was about ten years old.

I couldn't imagine Abe Hirshaw as a paid assassin at any time in his life.

Dr. Joe should have been in a Cuban medical school seventeen years ago. Probably not even talking English.

With Coach Reesenbach anything was possible. But once you get to know him, he's more talk than do.

Stanley Farmer had leaked the information about William. Not a clever thing to do, if William was Stanley himself.

Lil Harv could be acting as a surrogate for his father, or his assumed father. Lil Harv was a law onto himself.

Of the men, then, I had a live possibility in the coach who'd been bequeathed a million dollars. Blackmail? And suspicions about a crippled teenager considered medically terminal. Sense would dictate Coach Reesenbach as the one. But of the two, I'd choose Lil Harv as the more lethal.

In town I bought the yogurt-making machine and charged it to the *Graphic*. If Barkley complained, I'd call it a necessary bribe for inside info. I had the wrapping person do the box up fancy in white brocade paper and a big white bow with a wedding bell.

I bought a pack of film: twenty rolls, Tri-X, ASA 400. I didn't spot anybody I knew.

I drove back to Snowfield's to get ready for the party. Floyd was back, clinking glasses in the main room with Mrs. Snowfield. The fire in the room was cuddly. Gilly Fats was still in New York City.

"Going to the party?" I asked them.

"Not I," said Floyd. "Too sick." I made a face at him.

"I'll give you a check to take over for me if you'll be so kind," purred Mrs. Snowfield. "I really don't feel up to socializing tonight."

She was socializing all right. A *pas de deux* with old Floydiekins.

"Anything to report?" I asked Floyd.

"Let you know if and when," he said, dismissing me. Smiling

144 . . .

captivated at Mrs. Snowfield. Always working an angle.

I bathed and put on the same jeans and my clean pink sweater, took along my camera bag just in case, got the card with the check in it from Mrs. S., and scattered gravel scooting the Chevie down Lemuel's Lane to the highway.

The Livingstons lived on Flatland Place. It was easy to find.

I arrived promptly at seven according to my Timex. I was the first one there. Even beat the guests of honor. It was a modest little place. Clean, relatively bare.

David was in the kitchen puttering with the "snitters," as he called them. The snitters were the *hors d'oeuvres*, small triangular pieces of bread smeared with anchovy paste, or shrimp in a green mayonnaise, or a liver-and-onion-paté smothered by a sweet pimento and topped with a mushroom cap. He was wearing scottish kilts in a green tartan plaid, dark green kneesocks and a green sweater. He had a white apron over everything.

Babs was in their one big room counting the flatware as she lined the pieces up on the long table. She was wearing a yellow satin blouse and a long black crepe skirt with a slit up the thigh.

I handed Babs the present I'd brought. I'd signed the card "from the *Graphic* sports staff." I passed over the card from Mrs. Snowfield.

I went into the kitchen and handed David the sheet of yellow paper. "I've copied it over, of course," I said.

"It's perfectly legal, you know," he said, tucking the paper inside his waistband. He went back to stirring the green mayonnaise savagely with a big spoon. "It's not what you think."

"What is it then," I said, ready to listen.

He looked exasperated. "I'm only going to tell you because I promised Babs I would. As far as I'm concerned, it's none of your business."

Babs popped her head in. "I want you two to be friends," she said. "You've got awhile. The party's not 'til eight. I had Amy move you up an hour, T.T." She put a glass of champagne in my hand. "Might as well get started on some bubbly. We have." She flitted out into the other room.

"I don't usually drink," I said, staring dubiously at the fizzy stuff.

"Champagne isn't drink, *dolling*," said David. "It's a partaking of the ambrosia of the gods."

I still stared at the champagne.

. . . 145

David wiggled his fingers at me. "Sip it, sweetheart. You're too stuffy. We're celebrating that rarity, a wedding made in heaven. So fall off the wagon for once. It'll do you good." He emphasized the good.

"You're either a runner for a legitimate book, or a chinzy little independent on his own. Which is it?" I sipped at the champagne. To tell you the truth, it tasted fine. I sipped a little more.

David went back to putting mushroom lids on slices of pimento. "It's my own little sideline," he said. "Nobody else involved. I'd only just started, sweetheart. And there's nothing crooked about it. I only take bets from friends and only on Climbers' games. Last Sunday was the first game. I charge ten percent off the top, twenty percent if you lose. I extend credit. No money's even changed hands yet. That's all there is to it. I take the betting line out of your own newspaper. I wanted to supplement my income a little. Just look around. You can see we could use the extra."

"Amy and Ratch are involved," I said.

David made a sound with his mouth that sounded like *tsk-tsk-tsk*. "Only marginally," he said.

"How's that," I said, lapping up the champagne in my glass. Not bad.

"Well," said David, "since you asked." He sighed. "They were in charge of new accounts. I did intend to broaden my horizons beyond my immediate friends. High Mountain has a population of about a hundred and twenty-five thousand. I didn't see any real reason to restrict myself to the maybe two hundred I personally know."

I refilled my glass from a magnum bottle of Taylor's New York State that sat on the kitchen table next to the bowl of anchovy paste.

"Have a snitter," said David.

I had one. I hadn't eaten lunch and I was getting hungry.

David watched me eat it. "How is it?" he said, a hand to his chest like he was afraid I wouldn't like it.

"Super," I said.

"Marvie! Have another." He poured himself some champagne. I had another snitter.

"Amy and Ratch were going to get ten dollars for each new customer they brought in," David went on. "But I had to make the money first, before I'd pay them. They're ambitious girls. They wanted to do it. They like to buy clothes and things. We aren't

146 . . .

harming anybody. Believe me, duckie, anyone who bets in High Mountain can afford to. It's not like I'm robbing baby of his milk."

"Why didn't you let Babs in. She likes clothes too, I'll bet."

David lifted a warning finger. "Ten percent if you win, twenty if you lose." He forced a laugh. "Seriously, T.T., Bab's a homebody. Sure she likes clothes. So do I, ducks. Look at me tonight. But I'll earn Babs her clothes, thanks very much. Babs works as one of The Scenic View. She gets fifty dollars a game. That's her pin money. I'll make the rest of it. I prefer it that way."

David had three platters of snitters now. "Just the deviled eggs and I'm done," he said, wiping his hands.

Out of the refrigerator he took a plate of halved egg whites, hard boiled, and a bowl of egg yellows crushed into a paste.

"It's very small time, T.T. And nothing crooked. I wasn't corrupting the ball players or cheating the people who bet with me. I wasn't trying to influence the line. I was looking for a way to make a little extra, that's all. If you tell on me, I'll lose my job as public relations for the Climbers. And probably get canned as the official astrologer and baton-twirler to boot. I'd hate that." David began filling the halved egg whites.

"Nobody cares if you don't," he added. "Even John Xavier is a customer."

"I saw," I said.

"I know you did," he said.

"What were you doing sneaking into Floyd's hospital room?" I said.

"Oh that," he said. "That's a serious problem I have."

"How's that," I said.

He stopped spooning the egg yellow into the egg whites. "I've lost one of my astrologer gowns," he said. "The rainbow one."

"What's that got to do with Floyd Beesom?"

David wiped his hands on his apron. "I thought your friend might know what happened to it," he said.

"Why should Floyd know more than anybody else?"

"Well," said David. "I've asked him since. And he says he doesn't know. But it was missing at halftime last Sunday. I had to wear my purple gown the second half. Not nearly as pretty. . . ."

I remembered Patty running away from me in the parking lot. Slipping, like an omen, scraping her knee. I remembered the beckoning figure behind the portal, the rainbow gown visible in the sun.

Beckoning for Patty to hurry. The halftime was over. The second-half kick-off was happening. I remembered hearing the crowd roar. I shivered. I was getting my prickly, dancy feeling.

David was still talking. "Things were so mixed up during the half. Lovable Lou off in the ambulance. Everybody whispering Lou was dead. Dr. Joe saying murdered. I take my gowns off whenever we have a break, so they won't get mussed. Silk, you know. Wrinkles awfully. And if you iron them too much it takes the sheen away. I hung it on the doorhook of The Scenic View's dressing room. That way any of the girls could just hand it out to me. I put it on in the hall if they're dressing inside. So I hung it up and during the half I went to the recreation room. Had a Pepsi. Tried to find out what was what. And then when I went back to get my gown, it was gone. Not on the hook, not in my locker." He shrugged slightly. "Your photographer friend was in the hall for awhile taking a snap or two. I thought he might have seen somebody take it. Or taken it himself. People do steal things they like, you know. And he had a camera bag he could have stuffed it into. I was going to go through his closet at the hospital. His camera bag if it was there. I wanted my rainbow gown back."

I was quiet for a minute, digesting all that. David went back to fixing his deviled eggs.

"Well, did you find it?" I finally asked.

"No," said David, "I haven't. I can't understand it."

From the other room we heard Babs give a yell like a female Tarzan. She burst into the kitchen almost knocking me down.

"What's the matter?" gasped David, holding his heart again.

"The cake," said Babs, her hand over her mouth. "The wedding cake."

"You didn't," said David.

"I did," said Babs.

"Well, I'm not going, poopsie. I've got to finish my eggs. T.T. can drive you over."

Babs still had her hand over her mouth. "Would you?" she whispered. "I left the wedding cake over at the Colossus."

"Sure, let's go get it."

Babs put on a big sweater. "The Colossus chef baked it for us. I was supposed to pick it up at five. I forgot all about it 'til right now. David, I need the key to get in."

David looked cross. He went over to the closet and reached into one of his suit jacket pockets and pulled out a key chain heavy with keys. "They're all labeled," he said. "You may have to go down to the basement. To the walk-in freezers. I bet that's where Cecil put it when you didn't come on time. Little dummy."

"Let's go," I said.

Babs ran out with me and hopped into the *Graphic* Chevie. "Please hurry," she said.

On the way over I asked her what her father did. She said he'd been a real-estate broker in Connecticut, but he was retired now and lived with her mother in Quiet Lakes, Florida. She didn't ask me why I'd asked. All she was worried about was getting the cake back before Ratch and Dr. Joe arrived.

While Babs ran up the steps to open a front door, I paused and looked at the hulking building. In the daylight the white concrete girth of it looked merely massive. Under the moon it glowed. It looked more like a temple, a place of worship, than a sports stadium. It reminded me vaguely of Lemuel Snowfield's mausoleum.

"Come on," hissed Babs. "We've got to hurry."

I was thinking how so many people I know don't see things unless they're looking for them. It's always amazed me. Floyd says it's a matter of the photographic eye. You either have it or you don't. He says that's why people like pictures. To show them what they should have seen but didn't. But you can't believe everything Floyd says.

Inside it was as dark as a cave in Transylvania. Babs didn't know where the main light switch was. We held hands finding our way to the restaurant.

"The cake should be on the table in the kitchen," she said, keeping her voice low, the way people do in the dark.

In the restaurant we found a switch and got one bank of dim overheads on.

The kitchen table was scoured clean. There was no cake on it.

"Oh damn," sighed Babs. "We'll have to go all the way down to the basement."

The elevator wasn't working so we took the back steps down two flights. The first flight down would put you on a level with the players' wing. The second flight brought you to the basement.

The basement was mostly big throbbing machines. We got the lights on. We found the wire cage where the foodstuffs were locked, out of the way of tempted hands. Babs got the cage open with one of David's keys. Through that door, past rows and rows of big cans and bigger bags, we had to open another wire cage. Behind that one were the freezers, the steel refrigerated units for the food kept cold or frozen. There were four of them, fronted by wooden slabs—butcher-blocks—for doors. On each door was an oversized handle and a padlock dangling like a charm.

Babs found the key to door one and got it open. Boxes of fresh vegetables and fruit. Lots of lettuce and lemons. A ton of potatoes. Vats of soup stock or special gravies sitting on the floor. No wedding cake. Babs put a couple of lemons in her sweater pocket.

We relocked the first freezer and opened the second one. Meat. Slabs of pork, stacks of steaks, whole turkeys and chickens already dressed. Miles of sausage links, mounds of eggs.

"I'd like to photograph this," I said, fingering the zipper on my camera bag.

"No time," said Babs and shoo'd me out. We locked door two.

Behind door three we found the cake. It was smaller than most wedding cakes, only two tiers. But it was beautifully iced and decorated with tiny pink roses and green candy leaves. On top was the paper-lace chapel and the bride and groom dolls standing side-by-side.

"I was afraid we wouldn't find it," said Babs with a weak little laugh. "Thank God."

Then we heard the footsteps. Over our heads but back toward the front. Coming our way. We were at the far end of the basement, under the players' wing.

We both stopped breathing for a second. "What's that?" said Babs.

"Maybe Weatherwax left a guard," I said. "Just in case."

"In case of what?" said Babs, looking at me like, all of a sudden, she didn't trust me. "David said the police cleared out yesterday."

I didn't want to tell her about the poison sitting in the storage closet in the schoolroom. "I don't know," I said lamely.

Babs scooped up the cake. It was sitting on a round metal tray with two curved handles. "I'm getting out of here," she said.

"I've got to find out who it is," I said.

Babs looked at me like I was mentally disturbed. "What do you mean, *got* to?" she said.

I didn't know what I meant. I just knew I had the feeling of a scoop on the way. And I meant to track it down.

"You're safer down here," I said, "until we know who it is. Upstairs, you're vulnerable. Same as outside. But here, you can lock yourself in a cold box if you have to. King Kong couldn't get you in there. And the first one's not so cold. You won't freeze. Is there a telephone down here?"

Before I'd started talking, Babs hadn't really been scared. I think I scared her talking about vulnerability. She wasn't mad at me any more. She was listening.

"Yes," she said. "Outside the first cage." She set the cake down on the baker's rack where we'd found it.

The footsteps were almost directly over our heads now. This massive building, I thought. So much concrete. And you still got the echo from underneath of a single pair of heels tapping down the tiled floor in the emptiness.

"Let's lock up this one. It's too cold. And open up the first box." I whispered, as though the walker upstairs could hear if I raised my voice.

Babs looked at me like she couldn't move a muscle if she wanted to.

I ignored the look. "Put the cake down in the first box. Leave the door open. I'm going upstairs. I'll go up the stairs on this side. That'll bring me right up beside the recreation room. You call David. Tell him what's happening and where you are. Get him to call the police and ask them to meet us here. Then you go back and stand by that box. If you see or hear anything down here, don't wait for explanations. Lock yourself in. If everything's okay, I'll come down and bang on the handle of the door with one of those long spoons. Twice, then pause, then bang twice more. Remember two bangs, a pause, then two more. If you hear anybody banging and the pattern's not right, stay quiet and don't open the door. Got it?" I was taking off my boots so I could move quietly in my stocking feet.

Babs didn't argue. She did as I asked her to. She put the wedding cake inside the first cold box, locked the one we'd been in, and went to call David. She was trembling but she did it. She was a lot more scared than I was. Probably had more sense.

I was excited. I like to be on the hunt. I got my good old Nikon ready, the one with the leather strap. I used the normal lens, the 50 mm. I attached the flash gun, and set my film speed at 60 to synchronize with the timing of the light. I left-shouldered the camera and headed for the stairs. I no longer heard the footsteps.

It was black on the stairs but I got up easily enough. In the players' wing it was dark and quiet as a coffin. Standing where the stairs met the hall of the wing, I realized I was holding my breath. I let it out slowly, puff by puff.

I could hear the ticking of a clock, and the motor of something give a jerk and start to hum. Loud sounds in the silence.

Then I saw just a slip of light. Like someone had a penlight and touched it on then snapped the light off. I heard a rustling noise, like the person was wearing too big slippers, the feet moving first and then the slippers sliding along. Which didn't add up with the tappy heels we'd heard down in the basement. The light came from the schoolroom. Where the Vapo was.

Whoever it was, it wasn't acting like a police guard.

I knew that if I could get into the examining room where Stanley had stitched me yesterday, there was an inner door there into Dr. Joe's office. And an inner door from there into the schoolroom. Those doors are probably never locked, just the outer doors that open into the hallway might be.

I prayed Stanley hadn't locked the door to the examining room when he left yesterday. I'd be better off going that way to confront whoever was walking. More options. Staying in the hall there's no way to go but forward or back.

The light glimmered again. Stayed on a moment. I heard a squeak like a door being opened wider than it was used to. I heard a voice muttering but indistinguishable.

I pranced on tiptoe down the hall, holding my breath. I reached the doorknob of the examining room. I turned it and pushed and the door opened. I sidled in, quiet as a crowd when the trapeze artist lets go.

I had to breathe again. I did the little puffs, waiting for my breath to get back to normal. My heart was beating so loud I had to convince myself I wasn't really making a racket.

I waited. I heard liquid being poured out, splashed out into something metal, like a pail. The Vapo. It had to be the Vapo. What I was hearing was a premeditated murder in the making. Someone was getting ready to put the final kaput on Floyd.

Now I could even smell it. It made me want to sniff, to cough. No doubt about it. Roach-food.

I inched around the room, using the examining table to orient myself and guide me to the door on the far wall that led into Dr. Joe's office. I made the door. The Vapo was still gurgling out of its container into the pail.

I slid into Dr. Joe's office. I remembered the lay-out of it. From this door to the door that led into the schoolroom was a clean sweep. I was twelve feet away from being face to face with the murderer.

The room reeked of insecticide fumes. Just beyond me, in the dark, I heard a cough and somebody said, "phhhewww." But the voice was indeterminate, sexless, just a long, drawn-out sigh.

Using the sound of the liquid to cover any squeaks. I crossed Dr. Joe's office in about four hops. I was on the hinge-side of the door and it opened inwards. On the other side where the door latched was the light switch. What I intended to do was switch on the light to Dr. Joe's room, yell "In here, guys!" and start snapping off frames as fast as I could. This is one time I could have used a motor drive, an automatic sequence device, on my camera. But I don't own one, and Floyd uses the *Graphic*'s.

I slithered across to the other side of the door where the knob was. I backed myself flat against the wall and reached out with my left hand, turned the knob, and pulled the door open the length of my arm. About two feet. Enough. But the door creaked. And the liquid stopped flowing.

The schoolroom was the only room in the players' wing with windows. The wall that overlooked the parking lot was more glass than concrete. The moon wasn't in its brightest phase, but it did lighten that side of the room. Made the shadows more gray than black. Illuminated faintly the crescent moons and stars on the rainbow gown that stood, hulking, in front of the supply closet. Breathing hard. I could hear the breathing.

And then I heard Babs Livingston. I couldn't believe it.

"T.T.," I heard her calling me. "It's all right now. The police are here. Come on out. Where are you?"

Goddamn the girl. Whatever could have made her do that? I hit the switch on the wall. No light went on. The rainbow gown was rustling like too-big slippers, moving. Getting away.

I did what I could do. I yelled "In here, guys!" I aimed my camera toward the bulk and starting firing frames as fast as I could. Flash is slower than normal. There's a beat you have to wait while the electronic unit recharges itself. I got a sense of movement, saw the gown disappearing out the schoolroom.

For a moment there was silence. Then I heard Babs say, "Where'd you come—"; then a truncated scream, some kind of plopping sound, and a final kind of splat and a bump. We were still in darkness.

The closest way to the hall was out the office door. I hit it on the run, aiming the camera at random, down the hall, as fast as the flash would let me.

In the light of my flash I could see the huddled lump that was Babs slumped down almost at my feet. The cake was smashed up against the wall, falling in gooey ice-cream-filled pieces down over Babs' arms. The little bride and groom dolls rocked in her lap.

The rainbow gown with the half-moons and stars was running down the hall toward the Climbers' team locker room. I flung the cake tray down the hall after the fleeing figure. It rattled and clattered like a homemade bomb set off.

I was down on the floor of the hall. I didn't know how I got that way. I was shooting up, getting all the depth of field I could to stay in focus. When the tray skittered near him, the figure turned and glanced back. I caught him in the flash. On its head was a football helmet, a Climbers football helmet with the face mask in place. The person looked big, looked male. But I could tell it was wearing shoulder pads to disguise the body build.

The gown opened the door to the Climbers' locker room and light spilled out into the hall. Not a lot, but enough. Enough to tell that Babs needed looking after. A doctor's scalpel was sticking out of her chest.

I stood up shakily and found a hall switch. I turned on the lights. I started down the hall after whoever-it-was, cursing my knees because they were shaking.

Before I got where I was going, I heard someone say *stop* in an authoritative voice. I turned around and saw Detective Xavier with a gun in his hand.

As soon as I saw him, the adrenalin must have stopped pumping. I felt exhausted. It took all my strength to lift an arm and point towards the Climbers' locker room.

I didn't know where he'd come from but I was glad to see him. I went back to Babs. She was alive, conscious. I had to kneel in the squashed cake to get close to her. She was trying to say something.

"Hang on," I whispered. "Help's coming. Just hang on."

"David," she was saying. I bent closer to her.

"David," she said. "Was it David?" Her eyelids rolled up. Her eyes were hard and glassy like a china doll's. "Was it David?" she said again, gripping my hand, hurting it. "Was it David?"

"No," I told her. "No, it wasn't David."

Her lips were moving again. It looked like she was trying to smile. "I knew it couldn't be David," she said, spitting up a little blood, making bubbles of pink spit at the corners of her mouth.

Her hold on my hand relaxed. "I knew he loved me, after all. He isn't queer." She had trouble getting the queer out. "No matter what they say." She smiled like she was dying. "I knew it wasn't David." Then she seemed to sleep. Her hands fell away from my hand, curled gently around the toy bride and groom. I looked up and saw two men in white uniforms standing over me. I backed away. They took her out on a stretcher. She still had the bride and groom in her lap. The blood around the scalpel made perfect circles on her yellow satin blouse. She was all smeary with the wreck of the wedding cake.

Detective Xavier joined me in the hall. He had holstered his gun. He was carrying a picnic thermos in his hand.

"This way," he said.

I followed him and noticed for the first time that I'd cracked my camera lens. Must have hit it on the wall when I'd jumped out into the dark hall. Must have slipped on cake icing. That's how I got on the floor.

I followed Xavier silently down the hall, up the ramp, and down the next hall, past the restaurant, to where the front offices are.

He went into one office and I trailed along behind. Two policemen besides Lieutenant Weatherwax were in there. So was Stanley. Lying on his stomach with a yellow-feathered dart sunk deep into the back of his neck. There was a sea of blood under him. A chalk-line had already been drawn around the body. That meant Stanley was dead.

A green file cabinet stood in one corner of the office. Its top drawer was open. Files and papers were strewn around the room.

"I think we'll find Lou LaMont's personnel file missing," Lieutenant Weatherwax was saying.

A doctor I didn't know turned Stanley's body over. Stanley's mouth was pulled back, fixed in a snarl. Stanley hadn't gone without a fight. Three red-feathered darts, like buttons, were imbedded in a row down his chest. Pinned under the middle one was a bit of paper with a cryptic note. *Sorry. I liked you*, it said. It was written in the same awkward handwriting as the note I'd got.

Lieutenant Weatherwax looked like Humpty-Dumpty once he knew he'd never get put together again. "Take her away from this," he said to Detective Xavier. "Get her statement at home."

We went down to the basement for my boots and camera bag. He escorted me outside.

"I have the Chevie," I said. It was the first thing I'd said to him. "And I'm going to the hospital."

"I'll drive you," he said. "I'll get one of the patrol cars to bring me back."

"What was in the locker room?" I asked.

"An open door to that beauty salon, and the door from the beauty parlor to outside was open too. One of Livingston's dancing gowns, a football helmet. Out on the field I found a picnic thermos full of liquid Vapo. We'll check it all for fingerprints."

"He was wearing gloves," I said. I patted my camera with the cracked lens. "I may have pictures, maybe not." I wound out the film, took it out of the camera, and handed it over. "I'd like it back. For my paper," I said.

"You'll have it back tonight. Negatives and contact sheet."

"Okay," I said.

The rest of the way I told him what had happened. We used a portable tape recorder. He said he'd bring the typed statement for me to sign along with my contacts and negatives.

"I'll be at the hospital," I said, "waiting for her."

Xavier got out at the police station across the street from the hospital.

I parked the car in the lot. I headed for emergency. I felt very tired, very sad. Alone, I admitted it to myself. I'd recognized the man in David's gown.

..... XII

Friday and Saturday went by in a blur of hospital waiting time, and long solitary drives up the back roads of the mountain that gave the town its name.

The pictures Xavier brought back showed no face; just a floating gown of half-moons and stars and a football helmet. No use at all.

I didn't take any pictures. I was incommunicado with Barkley. I avoided Floyd and Gilly and all of the Colossus personnel. At night I slept in the Chevie parked in the hospital lot. I showered at the hospital, ate in the cafeteria there.

I didn't feel guilty about Babs. She shouldn't have come down the dark hall when she did, even if the police had arrived and she thought it was safe. She should have stayed with them. I understood she wanted to get back for the party, and I was sorry it happened, but I didn't blame myself.

I was sitting on my secret like a hen brooding over an egg. And I didn't know whom to trust. I had no physical evidence, just my own personal recognition. If I told and wasn't believed, I had no doubt about it. I'd be another lump on a tray in the morgue with a tag tied to my toe.

Babs' left lung had been punctured by the scalpel. The surgeons operated. She was critical but stable. The doctors said her survival chances were very good. Only her husband was allowed in her room. David spent most of his time in there.

I saw a lot of Lil Harv. Friday after he worked out, Potter Sr dropped him by and we sat together in the waiting room. Me staring at my boots like a doper lost in imagined kingdoms, Lil Harv babbling away talking about whatever came to his mind.

I'd been afraid he'd make me into a mother substitute, but he seemed to have adopted the stance of my parent. He kept me company in the cafeteria. He pretended not to notice when I didn't answer his questions. He endlessly repeated what he'd been saying, without getting impatient every time I looked up, startled, as though I didn't know he was there, hadn't heard what he'd said.

Saturday he brought his schoolbooks with him. He studied out loud, chuckling over things he knew and I didn't. We spent Saturday that way. After dinner in the cafeteria, I told Lil Harv I was taking a drive. Lil Harv said he'd come. I drove him out to Snowfield's.

On the way there, I told him who I'd seen. I don't know why. I just needed to tell somebody. I swore him to secrecy first. After I told him he didn't jump around and get excited like I thought he would. He just patted my thigh like a wise old man and told me everything would be all right.

I didn't stay at Snowfield's. I almost busted the gears getting off the place. I drove around most of the night, in circles. Around and up, around and down, around the mountain roads.

Sunday morning I was myself again. It was a fine Indian summer day, and I felt feisty and ready for a little action.

Lil Harv was scheduled for another Vitamin E commercial, the last in a series of three. He was due at the Colossus at 9:30. I climbed out of the locked back seat of the Chevie at dawn, showered and dressed in the hospital bathroom, and called Barkley at his home.

He was annoyed. "Haven't heard from you in two days, Baldwin. And now you call in at 8 A.M. on Sunday. It better be good." I told him who the killer was and that I didn't know what to do about it.

"What's to do?" he said, like the identity of the killer was no news to him. "Just keep taking pictures, T.T. That's all you do. What you get paid for." He didn't say have a nice day. The phone just went dead.

I got out to Snowfield's by 8:30, in time to give Lil Harv a ride. Floyd and Gilly Fats were coming too. And Ozark. Made quite a carfull.

Gilly Fats asked me where I'd been hiding, and I lied and said I'd been feeling guilty over Babs, but I was okay now.

" 'Bout time too," said Floyd. "Barkley don't like spontaneous sabbaticals."

"I doubt if he missed me," I said back, and Floyd said I had a point there, and things were back to normal with us.

Gilly drove. I sat by the window in front and Lil Harv sat between us, his hand on my thigh. Floyd, the UFO, and Ozark sat in the back.

"Guess who's filling in for Lou today, T.T.," said Lil Harv. "Gilly Fats, that's who!"

"You didn't let me guess," I said.

"You never would of," he said, and giggled happily.

"How'd you cop that gig, Gilly?" I said. "That sounds like fun. An easy hundred greenies."

Gilly Fats beamed. He blew tiny smoke rings. "More like two hundred and fifty, T.T. And I got it because of connections." He rumbled a ho-ho-ho.

"Marcella did it, T.T.," said Lil Harv. "She won't let any of the Climbers do any more commercials on game day. And no more at all without her permission. She said Lou was a special case, but no more. Gilly's the only other guy she knew big enough."

"I'm big enough," said short squat Floyd.

Lil Harv shook his blond head and giggled. "No, you're not," he said. "Not you. And Gilly's really too fat."

Gilly ho-ho'd.

"But Marcella said that with the football helmet over his face, and shoulder pads on, he could get away with it. He's supposed to be Lovable Lou, see. Mr. Rizzulli, who's in charge of things, said he would use old footage of Lou for the close-ups, with the helmet off. See, all Gilly has to do, T.T., is stand downfield and heave the ball to me. Gilly only gets about three seconds on camera. I'm the star."

"We'll see about that," said Gilly.

"I'm going to be upfield on the fifty. In my wheelchair, see. And I have to catch the ball, twirl my chair around, put it on automatic, and roll downfield to the end zone. I'm supposed to lift out of my wheelchair as far as I can and just catch the ball with my fingertips. A real great catch! That's to show how much stronger I'm getting taking Perfect Body Vitamin E. In the first commercial, I'm sitting on the bench. Wishing, you know. In the second one, the one we did last week, Lou was throwing me an underhand easy little lob ball. But in this one, I'm really catching it like Lynn Swann can. Super, huh?" Lil Harv turned his face up to me. His blue eyes were snapping with happiness. "Super, huh?" he repeated.

I laughed, happy for him. "Super is what it is, Lil Harv," I said. I was even getting immune to his cod-liver-oil smell.

He grinned and patted my thigh under his hand.

We pulled up by the players gate at 9 A.M. The big-camera boys had the cable all laid and were already taking test shots.

I watched the film crew set up, envious of their equipment in spite of myself. I'd have loved to peer into those big babies, but

... 159

I didn't want to ask to like a little kid. So I hung around and rubbernecked like a little kid.

Gilly Fats and Lil Harv went off to "make-up" as Lil Harv called it. Gilly Fats pushed Lil Harv's chair importantly. Gilly was enjoying himself, getting a real kick.

Floyd looked disgruntled. He went off, with Ozark toting his gear, and sat in a box seat to watch. Maybe he wanted to look through the big babies too, feel them in his hands the way I did. But Floyd had his dignity to think about.

So what happened was I got to try one of the biggies and Floyd didn't. The guy operating it saw my tongue hanging out and gestured me over. It was a big zoomer. To see what you've got in there, you've got to stand up on your toes and peer into it like it was a periscope in a submarine. You kinda hunch over it like you would a Clydesdale workhorse. To lengthen or shorten the lens you wind a handle on the side. Wind forward to pull in close, backward to pan back. It was like driving an oversize semi. My 35 mm cameras are so flexible, and I'm so used to them, they're like extensions to my fingers. This camera was a machine. I zoomed in and out on the end zone a couple of times, keeping the winding constant the way the man said. I panned up and pulled back on the sky. It was intoxicating. "Thanks," I said to the man after. "That was wonderful."

He snorted. "Just a job," he said. The guy had to be crazy. Kind, but crazy.

I ran over to report to Floyd. "I ain't interested," he snapped. Fooling nobody.

We settled down together to watch the commercial.

Gilly Fats looked pretty good suited-up as a Climber. They'd found him a pair of pants big enough, which was the only real problem. Except his gut. That was gone. They must have girdled him. He looked awesome, massive, wearing the Number One jersey over shoulder pads, and with the helmet on and the face mask down.

He strode up and down for our inspection. "Whatja say, hey?" he said, wanting to be complimented.

We clapped and whistled, Ozark too. He could whistle through his teeth without dropping his toothpick.

"Played a little ball in my time, don't you know," Gilly said, posing for us, strutting his stuff. "Didn't realize how much I missed it."

160 . . .

"You're lookin' good, Gil," I said. "Roger Staubach got nothing on you."

Gilly pantomimed fading back and spiraling a long bomb. "At least!" he said. We whooped and stomped.

Some woman rolled Lil Harv out to the fifty yard line. Lil Harv had been bronzed down and was blonder than ever. He was looking very serious, like he had lines to remember or something. People are funny, I thought. They puff up like toads full of hormones when you aim a camera at them. Well, so what.

Places please, somebody bellowed through a megaphone. Gilly jerked to attention and lumbered out onto the field to take his place on the twenty-five.

They had Gilly take a few practice throws. He did pretty good. He took his three and a half steps back, brought the ball up behind his ear, its nose arced high, took two steps forward and heaved the ball Harv-wards. The first time Gilly overthrew. Then he got his range and got the ball where Lil Harv could catch it.

The director, I guess, consulted with Lil Harv for a minute or two. Then they decided to try take one.

They ran it. It looked just great. Gilly back-peddled; threw. Lil Harv lifted himself up, caught the ball in two hands, jiggled the ball on the fingers of one hand, then tucked the ball in his lap. He released the wheelchair's brake, spun around, and sent the wheelchair humming down the field. The camera went after it, down the sidelines in a flat-bed truck, panning with Lil Harv as he scooted down the hashmarks to the end-zone for the supposed touchdown. Rolling into scoring territory, Lil Harv flipped the ball over his head for a backward spike, and threw up both hands in victorious jubilation.

"Wow!" I exclaimed, impressed. "Wow!"

"Awww-right!" chimed in Ozark.

"WAY TO GO! Way to GO!" hollered Floyd.

The director gestured for us to shut up and they reran the sequence. Take two. That went on through six takes.

Then they changed the angle of the cameras. One covered the opposite side of the field, and one shot from the end zone. They did about five takes that way. Sometimes they stopped, but most of the time they ran the sequence right through, and most of the time it looked well executed. Lil Harv did a fine job. It was heartwarming to see the crippled body in the chair reach up, seem to almost fumble, then heroically recover, spin his wheels, and sprint like a bandit for the TD. They're going to sell a lot of Perfect Body with this, I thought. I just might start taking it myself.

The person with the megaphone called time. The technicians conferred.

Lil Harv started horsing around. "Watch this, Gilly," he called. He tucked the ball in his lap and started his chair gunning toward Gilly Fats like he was going to run him down. Gilly Fats let him come, then jumped awkwardly aside as Lil Harv burned by. The wheelchair almost left the turf as it bounced full-speed down the football field. The tires left little lines in the grass. Coach won't be happy with the condition of his field, I thought.

Lil Harv's laughter floated out over the stadium. "Catch it, Gilly," he sang, and threw the football as far as he could in Gilly's direction. Lil Harv overthrew. Gilly had to turn his back to chase it down.

I guess, after all, Gilly didn't suspect. He turned his back on Lil Harv like he had all the time in the world. He loped toward the ball, lazy-like, and squatted down on his haunches to pick it up.

But as soon as Gilly turned his back, Lil Harv put the juice to his motorized wheelchair and took off after Gilly. Lil Harv aimed the chair for Gilly Fats' backside like press guys head for the free-lunch table. Full speed ahead.

One of the technicians noticed what was happening, and yelled for Gilly to watch out.

Gilly swung his head around, his hands just groping up the ball. He saw Lil Harv bearing down on him like the little choo-choo that could. Gilly lurched his body around, trying to side-step out of the path of collision. The wheelchair hurtled on. Lil Harv was doubled down, elbows tight in his lap, his blond head jutting like a ramrod just above his knees.

Gilly was slow. Just a little too slow. The wheelchair blitzed him and Lil Harv came caroming off his seat like a billiard ball making the first break.

Lil Harv's head slammed into Gilly's adam's apple so deep he butted Gilly Fats, all 250 plus pounds of Gilly Fats, clean into the air.

The wheelchair jammed against Gilly's foot and stalled. Then it began to spin in a circle too tight for its speed. It tipped over and whirred threateningly like a beetle helpless on its back. The tires spun full-tilt, running up the sky, going nowhere.

162 . . .

Lil Harv's body tumbled head over end, hit the ground still bundled in the cocoon of the lap robe, and rolled over and stopped.

Gilly's body jackknifed forward. He was still holding the ball. Then, oddly, his body doubled back. He walked on air for awhile like Evel Knievel's motor bike, and then fell, flat on his back and head. He fell alone, no shadows on his face, and his body had a kind of wrong-way curl to it. Gilly still held the ball, and under his face mask his lips were pulled into a grotesque grin of comprehension.

All of us watched what happened like we were toy soldiers positioned by an armchair general, and had to wait until we were replaced.

Lil Harv didn't seem to be hurt. He sat up tall like a fast-sprouting daisy and looked over where I was. He cupped his hands to his mouth and shouted, "Did I get him, T.T.? Did I get him good?"

The woman who was part of the filming crew ran out to him. So did one of the technicians. The technician went to the wheelchair first. Turned off its motor. Righted it. Then he joined the woman. Lil Harv was standing himself up. Standing crooked but without help. The woman tried to fuss over him but he shook her off. He walked by himself, as close to strutting as his crippled legs would let him, back to the UFO and sat himself down. The woman retrieved the laprobe with the needle-pointed figure of Overcoat. She draped it over his legs.

The director and a camera man were hunched over Gilly. Gilly hadn't moved. Still stared and smiled grotesquely at the sky. The director and the camera man didn't know what to do. The guy with the megaphone called through it for a doctor.

In the first row of seats Floyd and I sat like dummies. Ozark leaped the rail and went out onto the field.

"Good a way to go as any," said Floyd flatly, not looking at me. "Couldn't have planned it better myself."

I didn't know what to say so I kept my mouth shut. I looked at my Timex. 10:50 A.M. The gates opened to the public at 11:00. I unzipped my camera bag and began feeling for my Nikon. Floyd already had his camera in position with its zoom mounted on a monopod. He probably got off fifteen frames before I got my first shot.

The woman was rolling Lil Harv in his wheelchair toward me. His pretty-boy face looked blissful.

Dr. Joe, black-suited, came on the jog out the rampway, running

... 163

toward the body of Gilly. His black bag was bouncing, his crow's-wing hair flashed in the sun. I focused in on Lil Harv's angelic face. The face of a murderer, just after the deed.

The wheelchair stopped just under the row of seats. Lil Harv smiled triumphantly up at me. "I did it for you, T.T." he said. "I did it just for you."

I ran out onto the field for close-ups, the kind of pictures Barkley wanted.

..... XIII

"I think Floyd Beesom here was the first to know," Lieutenant Weatherwax was saying. It was 9 P.M., and we'd just finished a private feed in the Colossus restaurant, compliments of Mrs. Snowfield.

Me and Floyd and Weatherwax and Xavier. And Marcella Snowfield, of course. The chef stayed late at her request, and served us himself. Steak, potatoes, and salad. Now we were on the coffee, the hot cherry cobbler and the brandy. That is, they were. I stuck with the coffee and a cigarette.

They were all smiling deferentially at Floyd.

He would be the first to know, I thought morosely. For all the good it did anybody.

"Want to tell us how you tumbled to it, Mr. Beesom?" Lieutenant Weatherwax tried to smile expansively, but his face fell into its grooved gloominess. I expected Xavier to start taking notes, but he didn't. He was plowing into his cobbler.

Floyd was comfortably juiced. The way he likes to be. He began to expound.

"It was simple once you looked at the overview," he started off. The bore. Going officious on us.

"I started putting it together in the hospital. Going over what happened to my film. I was the only one who knew what was on that film. That's one advantage I had over the rest of you."

Mrs. Snowfield looked positively enchanted. The two policemen looked respectful. I hoped I looked unimpressed.

Floyd went right on. "Other than some pregame shots, more or less the same thing Baldwin here had, and obviously unimportant, since her film wasn't bothered, were some sneak shots I'd taken through that door that goes from the outside into the beauty salon Marcella rigged up for her team."

Marcella now. Wow.

"The wall opposite the door was one long mirror over the counter where you roll your hair up, and the room is lit very bright. So I stood in the doorway there, unobserved, and grabbed off a few shots. The girl, Patty Cambron, was rolling up Lou's hair. I thought a shot of that would be good when we ran a personality profile, one of the *Graphic*'s regular sport items."

Floyd paused and slurped the rest of his scotch and soda. Mrs. Snowfield poured him out another. "Go on," she urged, "go on." She pushed the fresh glass toward him. Floyd covered her hand with his, taking the glass. Weatherwax and Xavier and I waited it out.

"So then," Floyd said, "our Gilly drifts in. She was almost through. Just some back hair left. Lou LaMont was studying the scouting report on the Johnny Rebs. Gilly asked him a few questions, and Lou started trying to demonstrate. Patty couldn't work right. She told Gilly the beauty salon was off-limits to the press. Then Gilly picks up a can of hair spray, the one in the filigree holder, and starts spraying Lou's head real heavy, saying he could fix hair good as she could.

"She tells him to leave, please. So Gilly says okay. Then he leans over Lou's shoulder, sudden-like, and points down to a player listed on the scouting report. Watch out for this guy, Gilly says, he's a cheap-shotter, a late hitter. I get the shot. Then Gilly says how come I can shoot and he can't interview. He's seen me, you see, in the mirror. I hadn't been trying to hide. Just be unobtrusive so I could get good candids. Well, I think that was the first Patty Cambron realized I was there. She pushed Gilly out my door and locked the door on us."

Floyd shrugged. "Thought nothin' about it at the time. Gilly and I laughed it off. Things like that happen to us all the time. Right, Baldwin?"

I nodded. Right.

"So then," Floyd went on, "later in the hospital, I isolate that sequence of events. Also, when Doc Joe told me that Monday afternoon in the hospital about the bug-juice, I remembered smelling insecticide in this restaurant here Sunday night when Gilly and I were at the table. And at the time, the only person next to me was good ole Gilly Fats. Crackin' a beer. What he'd done was fill one of my film canisters with that Vapo poison, flip its lid when he unscrewed the beer cap, and pour it into the mustard. Gave the mustard spoon an absent-minded twirl or two which I didn't pick up, and drowned out the smell. Only smelled the fumes for a second or so.

166 . . .

"I pieced that little vital item together talking things over with the late great Stanley Farmer. A real nice man he was. He told me he'd seen Gilly before we all went upstairs for the police interrogation that night. Said Gilly was writing his news report in the schoolroom. Stanley went in to get the Vapo, so he could spray. Gilly asked him about it, how strong it was. Stanley said he exaggerated, which might have been what saved my life, dose-wise. Stanley left Gilly alone in there. Guy has to write somewhere, Stanley figured.

"And also," said Floyd, "I noticed a film canister sitting on our table. I knew I didn't leave it there. At the time, I thought Baldwin was getting sloppy. I was going to say something to her about it when I got the chance, but I never got that chance. I got zapped instead."

Floyd kewpie-doll-grinned. "Sorry, Baldwin. I should have known it wasn't you. You've always been neat like me."

I let it pass.

Floyd went back to his lecture. "Then there was the matter of who torpedo'd the weiner. Well, the only hand that used the mustard was Gilly Fats'. I remember him stirring up the pot when Coach Reesenbach came by. But he didn't mustard-up the Coach's dog. He mustarded one of Baldwin's. She left two on the plate next to him. Ole Gilly just poisoned one of those dogs and waited for me to want one. Then he handed it over."

I heard pain in Floyd's voice now. Yeah. If it had happened to me, I'd hurt too.

Floyd got his voice unemotional again. "It was Gilly who spilled it first about the Pennsy state pen. Monday afternoon Stanley and I went over that. About Lou's dad and all. Told you guys about it later." Weatherwax and Xavier nodded.

"And so the dicks here got on that angle. Took 'til Friday to come up with the goods. Altoona tried to cover at first. Barkley checked Gilly's personnel records. Gilly'd been with the *Graphic* twelve years. Beat me by a year. But I remember him telling me a long time ago he'd worked once for a Pennsy paper. He must have forgot we went back that far together. All Barkley had were two small Pennsy town papers and a Philly one. Fifteen years back. We needed seventeen. So Barkley tried to contact the two Pennsy papers Gilly listed. Asking for their files. One of them was long defunct. The other had changed hands about four times and had no record of a Gilbert Ott at all. So there we hit the stone wall.

"But we cooked up a plan, Weatherwax, Xavier and myself, to allay any fears Gilly might have we were on to him. And to lay a trap to catch him in.

"Dr. Joe told us about the cholinesterase enzyme problem I had. Very medical. Unknown to sports writers, right? So together we tell Gilly. And tell him to tell nobody but Baldwin, who we all know is harmless." Floyd flashed me a grin. I made an ugly face.

"Then we bring in my guards, Alphonse and Ozark, who were supposed to come off like slightly dim rubes, but who are really two top-notchers out of New York State homicide. I was supposed to bed down with Gilly once I felt strong enough to take the risk. The only thing was, I preferred Baldwin's company once beddybye time came round. Safer. And then, Friday, the report came in conclusive from Altoona. Gilly tried to make his move that night, but was foiled by Baldwin here. Unintentionally, of course."

I let him ramble. After all, he was right.

Floyd drained his glass again and promptly got another refill from Mrs. Snowfield, who hadn't taken her eyes off Floyd's face the whole time.

Charisma, I thought. Right now Floyd's got the charisma.

Floyd wet his whistle and resumed. "Then Billy Badman O'Leary contacted the *Graphic* looking for a way to clear himself. Scared to death Badman was. Barkley thought he'd give us a breather for a day or two, so he called Gilly back, quick-like. Gilly went okay. But he took Badman out to lunch, assured him the dicks up here were on to the killer and Badman was out of the woods entirely. Badman told us Gilly put him on a plane to Coastville. Then Gilly must have hot-footed it back to High Mountain, not checking in with Barkley. What Gilly planned to do, probably, was to use New York as his alibi, say he wasn't even here when I got mine."

Mrs. Snowfield gasped at the treachery of Gilly Fats' thought. Floyd favored her with a sloshy smile. "Yeah," he said. "A friend indeed, eh?" Mrs. Snowfield patted his hand protectively.

"So to wind it up," Floyd said, "that Friday we were all busy. Weatherwax and Xavier went through Lou's stuff looking for something to nail down Lou's connection with the prison. They found it. Lou's scrapbooks, or his father's. The whole business about William Purlwinkle getting busted up by Roger Lee LaMont, and LaMont a hero quelling an escape attempt. There were pictures of

Purlwinkle in the paper. Gilly alright. Younger. Leaner. Meaner-looking. But old Gilly, sure enough."

Floyd shook his head. "I think Gilly would have let dead dogs lie, but Lou LaMont must have recognized him. Gilly went to that Dr. Zu's lecture. Took Lou out after. I'll bet Lou made a bad mistake. Told Gilly he knew who he was. Probably told Gilly not to worry. Long as Lou got the good press, Gilly's secret was safe. That would burn Gilly all right. Always prided himself on his integrity.

"Gilly had just heard about those fatal acupuncture positions. And Gilly was no dope. He knew about the Novocain. Freezon they call it sometimes. Anybody who covers football knows about it. The idea probably came to him that night. I remember he insisted we get to the Colossus extra early that Sunday. Said he wanted to watch Lou's commercial. Get a story angle maybe. He saw his opportunity. Covered the Novocain can with the filigree holder, butted into the hair place, sprayed Lou good and gave him the needle. Then just waited for him to die. Later, he must have heard Patty Cambron suspected something. Got her downstairs and gave her the old chickenhead twist."

I remembered going for a walk down to the players' wing after Floyd had been felled. Remembered standing in the Climbers' locker room. Hearing a door shut.

Gilly and Patty must have followed me down. Waited until I went into one of the rooms, then slipped into The Scenic View's dressing room. Gilly strangled her, hung her up, got back up the hall and was on the phone to Barkley before I got back. Stanley said Purlwinkle had been a paid assassin. I guess when he had to find the cool, Gilly found it. I shivered. I'd been right next door while Patty was being slaughtered.

"Who covered Patty's face with the towel?" I asked.

Lieutenant Weatherwax responded. "Stanley," he said. "He wasn't supposed to, but he often went in and said hello to the girls. The locker door was open when Stanley went in. He was terrified he'd be blamed. Mrs. Snowfield knew about his record. But he said he couldn't leave her looking that way. So he got a towel, covered her best he could, put the padlock on the door, and pretended to know nothing. Floyd wormed it out of him."

"We didn't hold it against him," said Detective Xavier.

"A fine man," said Floyd. "He came on his own time Friday

night to check out Lou's files at the Colossus. Looking for some clue to William's identity. At the same time Weatherwax and Xavier were at Lou LaMont's apartment going through his memorabilia about himself."

"Took us too long," said Weatherwax, his face mournful.

"Yeah," said Detective Xavier. "Lou sure had a lot of clips about Lou.

"The way we figure it," Xavier continued, "Gilly hightailed it back here and went straight to the Colossus. Had a key somehow. Got in, heard Stanley, and went in and killed him. Then set off to collect the liquid Vapo. Only unbeknownst to him, Baldwin and Babs were downstairs in the basement. Heard the goon."

"Almost got us both killed," I said.

"Babs is doing fine," said Lieutenant Weatherwax. "The doctors say she'll recover, no ill effects."

"I'm so glad," said Mrs. Snowfield. "I sent her the most beautiful chrysanthemums."

"Gilly wrote me a threatening note," I said quietly.

"We knew," said Floyd, like he was Hercule Poirot himself. "I knew what you meant that night you asked if anybody had been around the Chevie. I just couldn't tell you then. Afraid you'd scotch the plan."

"Why would he threaten me?" I said. "I didn't know anything."

"I think it was you not telling him about taking pictures of Patty's corpse," said Lieutenant Weatherwax. "He griped that day to Floyd about it. He must have been pretty scared by then. Two murders and planning a third. He didn't know if you'd seen something or not. You scared him, Miss Baldwin."

"Gee," I said. "That's why he snapped at me in front of you when I said I hadn't taken any."

"Reckon," said Detective Xavier. "It didn't make sense to him. He figured you as one who would. He was right, as it turned out."

"Yes," I said. "I am one who would. I'm a news photographer, after all."

"And not half-bad," said Floyd, grinning.

That was nice of him. "Thanks," I said.

The party was breaking up.

"What's going to happen to Lil Harv," I asked.

Lieutenant Weatherwax smiled his sad smile. "Not too much, I'd say. He's undergoing psychiatric tests now. The doctors say e's positively joyous. He'll probably spend the rest of the time he has being looked after. He did it to Gilly just the way Gilly did it to Lou, he says. Lil Harv's especially proud of that. While they were being made-up, Gilly never suspected a thing, to hear Lil Harv tell it. He told Gilly he had to spray his hair. And even though Gilly was going to be wearing a helmet, Gilly said okay. Lil Harv got one of the acupuncture needles out of Dr. Joe's cabinet. God knows why it wasn't locked. Lil Harv knew just how to do it, he said, because you'd explained it to him, Miss Baldwin." Lieutenant Weatherwax gave a long deep sigh. "Lil Harv's probably best off where he is now."

I shook hands with the policemen and Mrs. Snowfield. Floyd kissed Mrs. Snowfield's hand.

Our things were already packed in the *Graphic* Chevie. Mrs. Snowfield said she expected us both back in two weeks for the next November home game. "We'll be three-and-oh by then," she said. "And we'll have Overcoat II. Wasn't Black Jack thrilling today? That second touchdown pass! Skyhook thinks Black Jack's the only one who can take us straight to the Bowl. And I *love* his thighs. What do you think, Miss Baldwin?" She was grinning at me.

I grinned back at her. "Beautiful," I said. She gave me a wink. I got in the Chevie on the passenger side. Floyd drove us away. I turned backwards and watched the glow of the Colossus until I lost it.

Finally we were going home. To the *Graphic*.

"I wonder how Gilly stole David Livingston's gown," I said.

"Easy," said Floyd, full of himself. "The big brown bag he kept Ninth Avenue specials in."

I nodded.

"Car needs a tune-up," said Floyd.

"Yeah," I said. "I've been driving it a lot. You know, Floyd, I've been thinking."

"Yeah, Baldwin."

"Well, the next time there's a murder, Barkley will know who to send to cover it."

"Yeah, Baldwin. And who's that?"

"Me and you, Floyd."

He shook his head. "No, scoop. You got it all wrong. He'll send Beesom and Baldwin. Beesom and Baldwin. In that order."

"Oh yeah," I said. Sure.

. . . 171